THE JOURNEY TO EDEN

David Walking Tall

PublishAmerica
Baltimore

First printing

Hardcover 978-1-4512-8455-3
Softcover 978-1-4512-8456-0
PUBLISHED BY PUBLISHAMERICA, LLLP
www.publishamerica.com
Baltimore

Printed in the United States of America

Teaser

4,000 years ago an elder chief named Walking Tall, who lived in a different galaxy on a large and far away planet sat at a sacred fire with his young grandson and told him an amazing story of love and triumph, that began a long, long time ago.

Join Walking Tall and his grandson Stalking Crow by the sacred fire and listen while the twisting story of a warriors journey to Eden unfolds.

"Captain on the bridge!"

"Commander Report."

"Aye, , Sir, we have two unidentified vessels holding position over our bow."

"Elizabeth, there's been an accident. David's been shot and Big Jim's dead."

"So let me guess you're the biblical devil that I've read about."

"The diary devise was found on Mars wasn't it?"

"People of Earth, a terrible tragedy has fallen upon us."

"Congratulations Elizabeth your having twins."

Bio

David Walking Tall is a 38 year old man. He resides on the planet Toshna in the outer quadrant of the spiral galaxy called T. 67 where he along with his 15 year old son Jordan and his loving wife Christina, live life peacefully.

Thank you list

David Walking Tall would like to thank our Creator, the mighty architect of the universe and his close family and few friends for there support in helping make this book possible. If your reading this and sharing my joy then you know who you are, If your not. Well I'm sorry and I sincerely hope you find your way to the path of true happiness, and to you the reader. I thank you for helping the dreams of a dreamer come true.

David Walking Tall

To Chriss
Thank you
For Everything

This book is dedicated to some of the greatest men and woman that I have had the wonderful privilege of knowing. My soul Fathers and my spirit Mothers.

Joseph H. Swarbrick
Linda A. Swarbrick
Wells L. Hogan
Gordon L. Beck/Wind Walker
Eugene Van Wagner
Beverly J. Beck
June P. Hogan
Elaine Stermer
Robert C. Gamble
Earl W. Beck/Bald Eagle
Charles H. Zimmerman
Dolores R. Applebee
James G. Beck/Grey Wolf
Jordan L. Jarvis/Wares His Hair Long
Douglas Burgesses
Christina M. Jarvis/Light Shines
Frank The Tank Harvath
M. Talon
Dorothy M. Lewis
Esther M. Polzin
Roselyn Polzin

And last but not least the person to whom I owe my very existence to, my mother Rosemary, Joyce, Marie, Swarbrick.

Thank you all for bcing apart of my lifc and may your shiny, sunny, souls shine on for all eternity. I love you.

David Walking Tall

To my hero's

Stephen Hawkins
Jesus Christ
Dr Martin Luther King JR
Peter Steele
Toasunke Witko/Crazy Horse
Nikola Tesla
Kevin Costner
Hypatia of Alexandria
Ace Frehley
Rosa Parks
Johnny Cash
Galileo
Clint East wood
J.S. Buckingham
Jimmy "The Rev" Sullivan
And Ludwig Van Beethoven

Thank you for your contributions to humanity. Planet Earth wouldn't have been the same without you.

David Walking Tall

PART I

The Beginning

4,000 years ago and after a great ceremony for his peaceful people, an elder chief named Walking Tall, who lived in a different galaxy on a large and far away planet, sat down at a sacred fire and called to his young grandson as he passed by.

"Stalking Crow."

"Yes Papa?"

"Come here and sit at the fire, I have a story to tell you."

"What's it about?"

"It's about a journey," The chief replied and said as his grandson walked up and sat at his side. "A journey that began with a warrior named David Leviticus and a woman named Elizabeth Parable, Who on a green and blue planet called Earth, were married in the year of 2030. Their ceremony took place on the first day of the ninth month in the province of Montana. It was a beautiful day, not a cloud in the sky and it was an unseasonable 70*. Planet Earth had been going through a lot of changes back then. The weather was warmer, the polar caps had melted, all of the great costal cites and providences where gone and after World War III ended the planet's governments finally came together and formed as one. So for most people during this time of peace it was business as usual, or so it seemed that way. Now my young warrior stare into the fire and I will take you all the way into the house that Elizabeth inherited from her grandmother, where she with her long blond hair and hazel green eyes, sits in front of a mirror and tearfully daydreams."

"Elizabeth."

"Yes Na Nun? "

"Come here child, the angels are talking to me."

"What are they saying?"

"They're saying its time to go."

"Time to go where Na Nun?"

"They're saying its time for me to go home, but before I go they want me to tell you that everything is going to be alright."

"What's going to be alright, Na Nun?"

"Got to go child, got to go."

"Elizabeth," a voice then called while she startled out of her day dream, "it's time."

"Alright Father I will be right out."

Wiping the tears from her eye's Elizabeth pulled her self together and made her way out to the front yard, where David and father Mike Had been waiting, and as she made her way to them, David with his long dark hair and deep coal eyes, became so overwhelmed with such deep, warm, emotion that it seemed to wipe away all of the thoughts of his estranged youth, that he had been carrying with him for so long.

David was an orphan child. He was bounced from home to home and school to school, until he at the age of seventeen managed to land a job with a construction firm, where he, through hard work and schooling worked his way up to be the firms chief architectural engineer.

"David are you in there?" Elizabeth whispered.

"Yeah I'm in here, I was just thinking about."

"Are we ready?" Father Mike interrupted.

"Yes we're ready." David and Elizabeth replied simultaneously.

Turning towards each other while friends and family looked on, David and Elizabeth held each others hands and stared deeply into one another's eyes and then felt time stand still as the quiet, peaceful, presence of the lord fell over them. Hearing only the sound of Father Mikes deep voice while a warm breeze died down and the birds stopped chirping, David and Elizabeth, as a Beautiful majestic creature with long blond hair and eyes of blue contentment watched them from a unseen shadow, lovingly said their vows and Romantically Kissed while their two souls embraced and became one.

PART II

Findings

D.O.R North Atlantic
Deep Ocean Research for the Global Military
Submarine Osdel

"Captain!"

"Yes."

"I think you should come here and look at this."

"What the, How long have you been monitoring that?"

"Only a few seconds Sir, It just came up."

"Hmm, Helm all stop!"

"Aye, Captain, all stop."

"Commander, Keep monitoring that signal and notify me if it changes."

"Aye, Sir."

Making his way off the bridge and to his ready room while the crew felt his uneasiness, the tall, stocky, Captain, Jeff flyer men sat at his desk with a look of hardened steel and mumbled,

"Something tells me this isn't going to be good."

PART III

The Diary

A hand phone rings.

"Hello."

"Is this Doctor John Scott?" a woman's voice asked.

"Yeah, who is this?"

"I have a job for you. There are two men out front waiting."

"What if I don't want it," Doctor John replied as he looked out a window and quickly spotted a car sitting at the edge of his yard.

"Well then the two men out back with guns will probably take you by force."

Pausing for a moment while he heard his back door being kicked in Doctor John then replied in a quiet rhetorical snort.

"It sounds like I better take the job!"

PART IV

Findings II

"This is Captain Jeff Flyer Men of the submarine Osdel Transmitting on a priority channel security code 42376. Requesting permission to upload an unusual signal that we just picked up."

"Captain." A voice replied through a monitor, "Go ahead with the upload."

"Okay, Thank you. I'm uploading the signal now, please respond and verify when you have received it."

Sitting in seconds that seemed like long minutes to the Captain the monitor sat quiet then clambered back.

"Captain, we have received the upload, we are requesting for you to hold position and wait for instructions."

"Understood, Flyer Men out." Captain Flyer Men then sternly replied as a alarm sounded while a voice called through the ships intercom.

"Captain to the bridge."

PART V

The Diary

Global Military Base. Station 23. Oscoda Michigan

Half asleep as he arrived at the base, Doctor John gets out of the car and is warmly greeted by two people.

"Hello, you must be Doctor John Scott."

"Yes I 'am, that's me."

"Well I'm Lieutenant Michael Davis and this is Doctor Karen Omar, pleased to meet you Sir if you would just follow."

"Now wait a minute! I'm half asleep, I had to run out of my home to avoid being kidnapped, ride in a very uncomfortable car for 13 hours with two jerks from the Global Military, by the way they have real wonderful personalities! Oh and did I mention I really, really, really, really have to use the bathroom. Now I would like to know what's!"

"John," Doctor Omar interrupted with a smirking smile, "I'm sorry for your inconvenience, but if you calm down and come inside you will be fully briefed on what this is all about. Now please," Doctor Omar then stressed as she motioned John towards a building, "come with us. Oh and I promise Lieutenant Davis will find you a bathroom, won't cha Lieutenant?"

"Yes ma'am, I sure will."

"Okay then, shall We?"

"Well," Doctor John replied and said, "If you insist."

PART VI

The Beginning II

D&C Architectural Design & Building Firm
Billings Montana

Standing in his office and starring out a window, David turned around when he heard a female voice come through his computer monitor.

"David"

"Yes Christine, what's up?"

"You have an incoming call from Big Jim, would you like me to patch it through?"

"Yes please and thank you. Big Jim, what can I do for you?"

"David, man you have to get out here! You know that fool Carl hired two weeks ago."

"Yeah the one with the moe hawk right?"

"Yeah that guy, well anyways he came in drunk today and started rambling on about union dues and how are company's medical plan sucked and how he wasn't gonna pay for any of it. Then he started wrecking the place and I don't mean tossing stuff around I mean he really tore things up."

"Wow," David replied in a serious voice, "well you threw him out right?"

"Ha, Ha, Ha, yeah and I made sure he knew he was fired too."

"Well then what do you need from me? It sounds like you got it all under control."

Replying with a laugh Big Jim then said, "Yeah I do, except for the fact that our permits got tore up in the scuffle and the inspector just drove up."

"Ahh, got ya, stall him and I will be out with the duplicates in about an hour."

"Alright David I'll see you then."

PART VII

The Shooting

"Throw me out, make a fool of me! Ahh I don't care I didn't want to work for them anyways."

"Are you sure?" The beautiful, majestic, creature whispered, "have another beer, think about it. They made you look like a fool."

Cracking open and drinking beer after beer while the unseen, majestic, creature road by his side with a smile, the punk turned the music up and drove his pick up truck faster and faster, and the drunker he got the more agitated he became.

"I know," the creature whispered, "let's kill em."

"You know!" The punk then blurted out in a drunken slur, "I should shoot that dude! You know that black dude that put his hands on me! You know."

Grinning the unseen creature then whispered, "Yeah that sounds like a good idea."

"Yeah!" The punk then yelled in a loud, drunken slur, "I'm going to go back and shoot that black dude, mess with me. You know!"

Grabbing another beer, the punk then slammed on the breaks, guzzled the beer down and belched as he tossed the empty can out the window. Then in a dizzy, sloppy, drunken blur he managed to with the loud sound of screeching tires, spin the truck around while he drooled and then proceeded to recklessly drive back to the construction sight.

PART VIII

The Shooting II

"David," a voice called through his car's intercom, "where are you at?"

"I'm pulling in right now."

"Good! The inspector is getting ready to leave and Big Jim is still out front trying to stall him."

"I see them." David replied as he quickly parked his car.

Grabbing the permits from the passenger seat, David then got out of the car and ran to the inspector while he said. "Hey I have the permits right here, I'm sure Jim told you what happened to the original ones."

"Yeah he did," the inspector somberly replied, "but I'm in a hurry, taking my grandson fishing when I'm done. So common lets see em!"

"Grumpy grumpy," David whispered to Jim as he handed the permit papers to the inspector.

Looking over the paper work the inspector mumbled while he checked over them and then abruptly handed them back to David while he rudely said.

"Good day gentlemen, I'm gone fishing."

"He, he, he, he," Big Jim then snickered as the inspector made his way to his car, "I don't know who to feel more sorry for. The fish or his grandson."

"Yeah no kidding," David replied and said as he looked around, "lets step inside I can't believe how warm it still is."

PART IX

Findings III

Leaving his ready room and making his way to the bridge, Captain Flyer Men couldn't stop thinking that what was happening was some how going to affect life as he knew it and for some reason he and his crew just happened to be getting caught up in the whole thing.

"Captain on the bridge!"

"Commander report."

"Aye, Sir, we have two unidentified vessels holding position over our bow."

"What? How did they get in that close without us knowing? You weren't tracking them?"

"No Sir, they just appeared out of no where."

"Things don't just appear out of no where, Now I want some answers!"

"Captain! The radio officer clambered, were being hailed, audio only Sir."

"Put it through the con."

"Aye, Sir"

"Submarine Osdel, This is sub commander Zaron Bach. I'm speaking for the newly formed resistance against your global government. You will surrender your vessel to us and prepare to be boarded!"

PART X

The Diary

Global Military Base. Station 23. Oscoda Michigan

Hearing a knock on the door Doctor John said, "Yeah," as he looked around an empty room, "come in."

"Feeling better are we?"

"Doctor Omar, hi. Yeah I'm feeling better. A Bathroom, food and a couple hours of sleep can do wonders for the human body."

"Good I'm glad to here it, now tell me what do you remember from your studies when you spent some time with one of the last Native American tribes left on this continent."

"I remember a lot, why? And how do you know about my studies?"

"I work for the government John."

"Oh yeah," Doctor John replied as he turned towards a mirror that was obviously two way, "that explains it all. It also explains why all of my publications and transcripts were destroyed when you people erased them and there culture from existence! Admit it! You people destroyed them and everything I worked for!"

"John, Doctor Omar" stressed, "turn around and look at me. A lot of regretful things have happened through out human history. Things that none of us can change, or even explain. But right now we need your help, not a strife less argument about the past."

"Yeah ok," Dr John snottily interrupted, "spare me the lets be a good Samaritan speech I've heard them before! Just answer one question. Well maybe two. Why me and don't give me the I work for the government spiel again, and why did some one want to kidnap me?"

"Well let's just say I admired your work when I was in college. I even attended the lecture you gave back in 2019. You know the one that you gave on the pyramid that was found in California after the San Andres fault gave away?"

"Yeah go on"

"Well I found it interesting when you claimed that the symbols on the pyramid matched the symbols on the pyramid found by the Mars surveyor one year prior."

"Yeah I remember that. I also remember it all being discredited too. All because other scientist said the pictures from the Mars surveyor were inconclusive, they didn't show enough detail. Hmm go figure."

"You also claimed that the symbols matched an ancient form of a Native American language."

"Yeah but there were some differences. I claimed I could decipher the symbols by using their language key. That's why I spent so much time with them, but why did that interest you and why does it still?"

"Well just the thought of life existing on another planet has always intrigued me, but life on another planet that some how shared some similarities with us, well that's exciting and it puts a new perspective on the whole universe and I like you believe that there's far more to our reality then what meets the eye."

"Yeah ok and what of my kidnappers, why me?"

"I don't know."

"What do you mean you don't know, how did you know they were at my house?"

"Our officers tracked them to your house, but as far as knowing who they are and what they want from you, I or should I say we don't know, but I assure you that your safe here and we have some of our best people working on finding out what they wanted with you."

"Well that makes me feel safe," Doctor John muttered as a voice clambered through an intercom.

"Doctor Omar, please report to observatory three."

"John get some more rest," Doctor Omar then said as she headed out of the room, "we'll talk later."

"Rest yeah that's what I need more rest," Doctor John whispered to himself, as he sat down and thought while he put his head on a table, *they must have found something that proves my theory correct*, "why else would I be here?" he then mumbled as he fell asleep.

PART XI

The Shooting III

"Man what a day," Big Jim sighed, "one drunken fool almost ruined it all. If you wouldn't have had those extra permits printed David, that inspector would have shut us down for sure."

"Yeah no kidding," Don Mayor said as he butted in, "David saved the day again."

"Aw come on you guys," David laughed as he said, "can I help that I'm the only one around here that knows how to make good decisions."

"Yeah sure David" Big Jim sarcastically said as he grinned, "kind of like the time you lost the plans to the Davis project."

"Oh yeah, yeah, yeah, throw that in my face Jim, That's cool."

"He, he, he," Big Jim snickered and said, "well some one has to keep you on your toes. Mr. good decision maker."

"Woe" Don Mayor then jumped in and said with a look of concern, "wait a minute. You lost the Davis plans?"

"No Don. I didn't actually lose them, I misplaced em."

"Lose, misplace, what's the difference," laughed Big Jim.

"Yeah right, I mean no. There's a big difference, Jim I'm gonna get you later! Anyways they were found."

"Yeah in the bottom of your refrigerator."

"In your refrigerator, how the?"

"Look," David replied while he tried not to laugh, "I was up late, I ordered a pizza and when I went to bed I put the pizza in my brief case and the Davis plans in the fridge. Ok there you have it."

"So the Davis brothers got a pizza for their presentation?" Don asked with a half smile.

"No when I realized what I did, I called my wife before the meeting started and luckily she was home. So she fished the plans from the bottom of the fridge and kindly brought them to me."

"Elizabeth saved the day," Laughed Big Jim.

"Yeah she sure did," David then snickered and said, "speaking of her. What time is it?"

"It is 6:00pm," Don Replied.

"Hmm Six O Clock. I better get going, its Beth's night to cook and I don't wanna be late for that. She makes a great lasagna."

"Yeah," Don replied, "just make sure it doesn't end up in your brief case."

"Ah ha, ha, ha," David laughed and said as the room filled with laughter, "I will see you all later."

"Alright David, you have a good one." Jim replied while Don kept laughing as he waved David out of the office.

Making his way to his car while the breeze abruptly stopped blowing and the birds quit chirping, David looked around and thought as an eerie silence fell around the area, *wow that's weird it's a good thing I'm leaving*. Stepping to his car David then got inside and started to give his voice recognition code to the vehicle and thought as he saw an old style pick up truck recklessly drive up and stop.

Is that who I think it is? "It is," David then whispered as the door to the truck flew open while the punk came staggering out and began to slowly, stumbling towards the office.

"Hey Fool!" Big Jim then yelled to the punk as he came bounding out of the office, "I thought we went through this already!"

"Yeah!" The punk yelled back in a drunken slur, "we did!" Pausing and swaying for a moment he then yelled in a even sloppier tone, "but now I'm gonna end it!"

"End what? You just need to go home and pass out before I put you out!" Big Jim yelled while he firmly stood his ground.

Grinning with drool falling from his mouth the punk then sloppily replied, "Naw I'm gonna put you out!"

"Get the gun," the unseen creature whispered while he watched with a sinister smile, "SHOOT HIM!"

Reaching into his leather jacket while he stood and drunkenly stared at Big Jim, the punk then pulled out an old style revolver and slowly pointed it at Jim.

"Oh boy." David then said to himself as quietly slipped out of his car, "this isn't good. I hope Dons calling someone."

"What you gonna do with that!" Big Jim then yelled as he watched David slowly sneak up, "You gonna shoot me or something? Why don't you put the gun down and fight me like a man!"

"Naw," The punk slurred as he staggered back words while he spun around and pointed the gun at David, "I'm not going to shoot you, I'm gonna shoot him!"

"Woe," David calmly yelled as he held his hands up, "are you sure you really want to do that?"

"Well some ones gonna get shot," the punk then weirdly mumbled as he lowered the gun to his side while he staggered around and faced Big Jim again.

"Shoot him," the unseen creature then whispered while the punk stood still and looked like he was going to pass out, "Shoot him now!"

Lowering his hands and running full sprint David then tried to use this moment for an opportunity to tackle the punk and get the gun from him, but as soon as David started to run the punk woke from his momentary stupor and slowly raised the gun while he pointed it at Big Jim again.

Running as fast as he could, David put every ounce of heart full energy he had into getting to the punk before he pulled the trigger, but as David jumped towards the punks arm while he forcibly grabbed him by the waist it was to late. the gun went off and sent a bullet slamming, straight through David's left shoulder.

Then as David and the punk hit the ground, the gun went off while the two men rolled around and sent a bullet slamming straight into David's right hip.

"Now Shoot yourself," The unseen creature whispered while he watched with a wide smile, "do it. Do it now!"

Then with a quick blink of an eye, the punk grabbed the gun, stumbled to his feet and joyfully shot himself straight through the center of his forehead.

Slowly passing out from the pain that was now violently shooting through his bleeding body while the creature watched, David then Wearily saw a brilliant looking Indian man with long dark hair crouch down by his side and lightly chant while he mystically, waived smoke around David's wound's with a bird feather.

"Call Elizabeth, please call Elizabeth."

"Go to sleep, David Tall Tree," The Indian man quietly replied as he kept full eye contact with the unseen creature, "go to sleep and save your strength."

"Who are you?" David coughed.

"Sleep David." The Indian man said as he put his hand on David's head, "he's watching and I must not let him out of my sight."

Then with those final words David let himself fall asleep while the creature, knowing he couldn't get to David with the Indian watching over him. Shifted into a snake and ferociously hissed at them before he slithered away.

PART XII

Findings IV

"Prepare to be boarded. Are they kidding?" Captain Flyer Men Muttered, "I don't have time for this. Commander, what kind of a threat do those little pieces of junk pose?"

"None Sir. Unless they have something we don't know about."

"I was thinking the same thing. Send out a high amplitude pulse, once their power goes down take them into custody and then destroy their vessels."

"Aye, Capt. Weapons officer fire high amplitude pulse on my mark. Three, two, one Mark."

"Aye, Commander, firing pulse."

"Captain! Sonar reports two more ships just popped up! They came through some kind of vortex Sir and they just launched two C class torpedoes!"

"Sir," The Commander stressed, "If those torpedoes go off near this ship their pulse will render all of us unconscious."

"Red alert!" Captain Flyer Men Yelled, "all hands brace for a quick ride to the surface! Helm blow all ballast tank's now! Start your ascent and make it fast, all power to the main drive!"

"Aye, Captain, starting ascent with all power to the main drive."

"Captain! The torpedoes are moving in fast!"

"Come on girl rise, rise like you never have before." Captain Flyer Men whispered while the ship creaked as it shook. "Commander launch counter measures 90* vertical shot!"

"Aye, Captain launching now, 90° vertical shot."

"Captain sonar reports the torpedoes just went over our stern, there going after our counter measures Sir."

"Weapons officer once we're on the surface fire the upper bow laser on those fish when they go airborne, don't let them back in the water!"

"Aye, Captain."

"Sonar have our counter measures gone airborne Yet?"

"Yes Sir counter measures have gone airborne and the fish are still after the bait!"

"Surfacing now Captain!"

"All hands brace your selves."

Holding on tight while the ship violently slammed around as it broke the surface Captain Flyer Men then yelled, "Weapons officer Fire!" Then with a large burst of hot, red, energy the laser shot straight into the air and instantly with the loud sound of clapping thunder destroyed both of it's targets.

"Captain! Sonar reports all birds have been destroyed Sir!"

"Good." Captain Flyer Men replied, "well done, but this isn't over yet. Sonar where are the two subs that fired on us?"

"They broke off and split up when we launched our counter measures Sir."

"Commander, what about the ones we fired our pulse on?"

"The pulse rendered them powerless Sir."

"Well lets go get them and find out what's really going on."

"Aye, Captain. Helm once the ballast tanks fill make your dive and set course for the two derelict subs."

"Aye, Commander," the Helmsmen replied.

"Captain," The radio officer called, "you have an incoming message. It's on a priority one security channel."

"Put it through to my quarters. Commander you have the bridge."

PART XIII

The Diary

"John, John," a voice whispered, "you must let things happen the way their planned."

"Mom is that you? Where am I? I must be dreaming."

"Don't try to stop them John."

"Don't try to stop who?" Doctor John asked the hazy figure that stood before him.

"You will know what to do when the time comes."

"Mom?"

"Yes John, its me."

"How?"

"Don't be scared, let them succeed and I will see you soon."

"Who?" Doctor John tried to ask as be began to fall away from the ghostly image of his mother, while she smiled and waived good bye.

Desperately trying to reach for her he then found him self slamming onto his seat as he woke from the dream and said, "Wow, I must have been out for a while." Wearily standing up, he then walked around the room for a moment and then pored himself a cup of coffee while a man's voice called through a closed door.

"Doctor John, may I come in Sir?"

"Yeah go ahead, the doors open. Ah Lieutenant Davis. Didn't we meet not to long ago?"

"That was yesterday Sir."

"Yesterday. I slept that long?"

"About thirteen hours Sir."

"Thirteen hours, wow I must have been tired. So what can I do for you?"

"Well Sir."

"My names John, please call me John."

"Sorry. Doctor Omar was sadly killed in a bad car accident this morning so I've been assigned to assist you."

"Really, Wow that's to bad. Um ok. Assist me with what?"

"If you would please come with me, we can get started."

"I can see you don't want to answer that question." Doctor John then mumbled as he followed the Lieutenant out of the room.

Making there way down a long hallway Doctor John sipped at his coffee and thought about all of the things that Doctor Omar had said and how every inch of his being was telling him that the military must have found something that proved his theories. Then as they passed through a security door Doctor John began to tingle with excitement when his deep brown, puppy dog eyes spotted a small, diamond shaped box, sitting inside of a see through container.

"The pyramid." Did this come from the pyramid in California?"

"No," Lieutenant Davis replied.

Crouching down and looking closely at the box Doctor John then mumbled, "I bet it came from Mars then. Wow! This is made from a material that I've never seen before. "So," John then asked as he stood up, "where did it come from Lieutenant? Mars."

"That's classified John."

"Classified!"

"Yes that's correct. We were hoping you could decipher the writing for us. Any resources."

"Well!" Doctor John blurted out as he glanced at a camera while he rudely interrupted Lieutenant Davis, and firmly said. "I've already deciphered the writing, so your classification trash just got tossed to the curb. You see these symbol's right here, they say where it came from, they just don't say how it got here. So before we go any further would you like to tell me anything?"

"I'm sorry John, But I'm not authorized to tell you anything, I'm just."

"No, but I' am." a man interrupted and said as he entered the room, "Doctor John I'm General Henry Douglas. Lieutenant you're dismissed I will take it from here. You're right Doctor it did come from Mars."

"Was it in the pyramid?"

"No it was found a few miles from the pyramid. Anyways, the W.S.A Brought it back three months ago and it has sat here in containment ever since."

"The World Space Agency brought this back from Mars. How did you keep the public from finding out about it?"

"We have our methods."

"I bet you do," Doctor John mumbled while the General Asked.

"So what is it Doctor?"

"It's a diary." Doctor John replied as he pointed to some of the symbols, "to be exact." Doctor John then said as he walked around The container. "Its an audio diary and right here on this side are the directions on how to use it."

"I take it you've figured that out as well?"

"Yes I have, but the question is will it work? This thing has to be older then anyone can imagine. I can tell you one thing though who ever made this thing wanted it to be found."

"How do you figure Doctor?" The General asked as he stared at the box.

"Well you don't put a set of directions on something like this, unless you want it to be found."

"Good observation Doctor. Let's just hope your right and it is some kind of audio diary and not an ancient alien dooms day device. Because if it works and its not what you say it is, we could all be in serious trouble. So. Before we go any further with this thing, I'm going to report your observations to the President, let her decide what the next step should be. In the mean time, get yourself some lunch and have one of the duty officers outside assign you to a regular room. That's if you want to stay on with us?"

"Oh yeah General I would be honored to."

"Good, this is going to take some time. So I will see you in a while."

PART XIV

The Fall Of David

"Elizabeth," a automated voice called while she pulled a tray of food from the oven, "you have an incoming call from Don Mayor. Do you Accept?"

"Yes," Elizabeth replied. "Hello."

"Beth," Don Mayor's voice nervously responded, "there's been an accident. David's been shot and Big Jims dead."

Dropping the tray of food as her heart sank Elizabeth frantically replied, "What! How? I mean why?"

"I don't know, I was inside when it all happened. I didn't see or here anything. I'm at the hospital. They just took David into surgery. He took a bullet through the shoulder and one in the hip. The bullet that went through his shoulder apparently hit Jim in the head and killed him instantly."

Catching her breath and slowly walking around the room, Elizabeth thought about Big Jim and how his death was going to devastate his family, "That poor man," Elizabeth then whispered, "he was just recently married and trying to have children."

"Beth, are you there?"

"Yeah Don I'm here," Elizabeth softly replied as she wiped away some tears. "I'll be there as soon as I pull myself together."

"Okay I will see you then."

Slowly gathering her things together Elizabeth ended the call with a soft goodbye and slipped on her shoes while she wondered if all of this was what her grandmother had been talking about before she died.

"I hope so," Elizabeth then whispered as she rubbed her stomach, "that means David's going to be ok and you won't have to go through life without a father."

Not taking any notice to the tray of food that she dropped, Elizabeth left it lay on the floor as she made here way out of the house and to the car, where she got inside and cried before she left for the hospital.

PART XV

Findings V

Entering his quarters, Captain Flyer Men wiped some sweat from his forehead and then poured himself a drink. Sitting down at his desk he then took a few sips while he stared out a small window. Sighing he then set the drink down and answered the incoming message.

"This is Captain Jeff Flyer Men, message on main viewer. General Douglas, what in the worlds going on! Why was my vessel just attacked? And who is this group that's calling them selves the newly formed resistance against the global government. Does this have anything to do with that odd signal we picked up?"

"No," the General replied, "its."

"Well then what's it about!" Captain Flyer Men yelled as he cut the General off, "And why is this happening?"

"Jeff! Will you calm down and let me speak please! We know about the attack on your vessel and we know why you where attacked. It seems that a crazy religious faction has taken over the Helium three mines on the moon. They stole one of the reactors and managed to get it to the Jupiter moon base on Europa, where they somehow managed to convert the reactor into an under water porthole devise which allowed them to go from Europa to Earth instantly. They attacked your ship hoping if they took it over they could some how make their way into one of our stations and start an invasion. We have two men and their hijacked subs in our custody. Now, we've managed to take the Europa base back.

"So do we have the porthole devise?" Captain Flyer Men Interrupted with concern.

"No. They blew it up when the fire fight broke out. That devise took out half the base when it went off and it killed a lot of people. Jeff if we don't get the moon back I'm afraid more people are going to die."

"Wow," Captain Flyer Men Muttered and said with agitation, "and every one wonders why a united planet still has to have a military. It seems like every other decade some crazy group of nuts comes up with a wacky idea and they think they have to start a war in the name of some false god and then innocent people have to get caught up in it. Does the public know about all of this?"

"No and we would like to keep it that way, you know what kind of chaos this would cause if it all leaked out.

"Oh yeah General, I sure do. So what would you like us to do?"

"Remain on full alert and return to your original coordinates."

"What about the two subs we rendered powerless. Do you want them taken into custody?"

"No. Destroy their vessel's and take no prisoners, Douglas out."

PART XVI

The Fall of David

"Mrs. Leviticus."

"Yes."

"I'm Doctor Irvan, pleased to meet you. The surgery to fix your husbands shoulder was successful. Luckily for him the bullet only went through the skin that's close to the underarm. It caused minimal damage. How ever, the one that impacted into his right hip severely shattered your husbands Greater Trochanter which required a total reconstruction.

"So he's going to be okay?" Elizabeth tearfully interrupted.

"Yes he's going to be fine. But its going to take at least three months for a full recovery and he will probably walk with a slight limp for the rest of his life."

"Thank god, that's all. Can I go and see him Doctor?"

"You can go see him in about an hour, he's still coming out of the anesthesia. If you would like to wait here I'll have a Nurse come and get you when he wakes up. Would you like me to do that?"

"Yes please, that sounds good."

"Okay then, good luck and I will see you soon."

"Thanks again," Elizabeth softly said as she shook the Doctor Irvan's Hand while Don Mayor

Patted her on the back and asked.

"Do you need me to do anything?"

"No I think I'll be alright, at least he's still alive."

"Yeah," Don sighed and then said, "I should probably get going then. I called Jims wife after I called you but there was no answer, so when I get home I'm going to try again."

"If you get a hold of her, will you have her call my Pocket monitor?" I'm sure she's going to need someone to talk to."

"Yeah Beth, I sure will."

"Thanks Don."

"You bet Beth, and I will see you later."

PART XVII

The Fall and Rise of David

"David Tall Tree. Come and walk with me."

"What where am I, am I Dreaming?"

"Come," The Indian man said again, "rise and walk with me."

"I can't." David replied as he looked around the hazy hospital room.

"Yes you can, now rise from yourself and walk with me. You have a long journey ahead of you David Tall Tree."

"Who are you, what journey and why do you keep calling me David Tall Tree?"

"Because, That is the Earth name your mother gave you when you where very young."

"My mother?"

"Yes your mother."

"My mother's dead, and how would you know what she called me?"

"We know many things David Tall Tree."

"We, who's we?"

"The spirits of your people."

"The spirits of my people?"

"Yes, your people," The Indian man said as he made his way to David's side, "now come, let me show you."

Rubbing his hands together and chanting the Indian man then clapped Three times and said as he put his hands on David's forehead, "Sleep and awaken again."

Falling into a dream inside of a dream, David then found himself standing in a field of summer green.

"I got a flower for you mommy, Its pretty like you."

"Thank you David Tall Tree. Now run along and play while mommy watches."

"Ok mommy."

"Is that my mother?" David then asked as he turned towards the Indian man.

"Yes and the little boy is you."

"Man This has to be a dream. But how? This seems so real. I can feel the air, I can smell the flowers and I can hear the birds chirping. My mother, she was a full blooded Native American?"

"Yes."

"So that makes me half, right?"

"Very good David Tall Tree," The Indian man replied while they watched the little boy chase after a butterfly, "you are all that remains of what was once a very wise and noble people."

"Why were they all destroyed, do you know?"

"Well David Tall Tree when you figure out why a frightened and paranoid culture always has to impose them selves onto a much wiser one. Then you will know the answer to your question."

"Hmm I never thought of it like that. My father what about him, can you show me what he looked like?"

"He was a white man killed in battle before you were born."

"Well yeah, that's obvious, but can you show me?"

"No I'm sorry I can't. You have no memory of him."

"Well how are you showing me this?"

"I'm not, your showing yourself all of this. This is your memory, I only opened the door for you."

"Why?"

"Because you have a long journey ahead of you David Tall Tree, a warriors journey. You must find peace with your past and yourself before you can make the journey."

"What journey?"

"David."

"Yeah mom."

"She cant hear you David Tall Tree."

"David Tall Tree, Its time to go."

"Okay mommy, But who is that man?"

"What man David?"

"That man standing over there."

"I don't know sweetie but we better get going."

"Okay Mommy."

"Yeah," David then said and asked as he turned towards the Indian man again, "who is that? He's been standing there watching us the whole time we've been here."

"That is the Serpent Creature, he's been watching you for along time David Tall Tree. He doesn't want you to complete your journey. Come we must go before he realizes we're here."

"How could he?"

"Come David, no more questions we will speak again. HI YE NI YA!" The Indian man then spoke as everything quickly faded to black while David woke to the sound of Elizabeth's warm and heart full voice.

"David, David common honey it's me your blond haired bimbo. Wake up and give me a kiss."

Slowly turning his head towards the hazy image of Elizabeth while he slowly opened his eyes David then quietly whispered, "oh Beth you're a sight for sore eye's, man I had the strangest dream."

PART XVIII

The Diary

"Doctor John."

"Yeah come in, General Douglas how are you?"

"Things could be better. I've spoken with the President and she has given us the go ahead on the Diary Devise."

"That's great, so when can we get started?"

"ASAP, but before we do we need you to look at something else."

"Something else?" Doctor John asked with a puzzled look on his face.

Slowly walking around the room with his hands behind his back General Douglas took a deep breath and then sighed, "along with the Diary Devise the W.S.A. also brought back six stone tablets from the Mars expedition. They were found inside of the Cydonia pyramid and we have them here as well."

"Strange"

"What's that Doctor?"

"Well The W.S.A. finds a strange box on Mars, the Military request my knowledge to decipher the thing and now I'm being asked to look at some stone tablets. Is there anything else I need to know General?"

"Doctor. You know were not always a loud to give up information freely, especially on matters such as this."

"Oh," Doctor John Mumbled under his breath, "you won't tell us anything but you have no problem taking our tax money."

"What's that Doctor?"

"Nothing, um I don't get it. The military is sitting on one of the greatest discoveries possibly known to the inhabitants of this planet and you all want to keep it a secret."

"John I don't think you have any idea of what's all at steak here. If these things fell into the wrong hands."

"You don't even know what they are!" Doctor John loudly interrupted and then asked as he cut the General off, "or do you?"

"We know very little," General Douglas somberly replied and said, "Doctor Omar was only able to decipher a small portion of the tablets. She thought they might be some kind of instructions on how to build one of the greatest sources of energy ever known to man. Now I know your not aware of this, so right now I'm going to tell you because we need your Fucking help Doctor and I don't have time for a god dam debate! You see a crazy religious faction has taken over the Helium three mines on the moon. They attacked one of our submarines and they also blew up half of the Europa out post and now there threatening to blow up the mines one the moon, so you can see why we choose to keep some secrets. If something like those tablets fell into the wrong hands, well you know as well as I do the consequences could be disastrous."

"Yeah no kidding General. I'm sorry I had no idea. This sounds bad."

"Yeah its bad alright and its only going to get worse. If those people succeed a lot of innocent people could die, there are over 400,000 living on the moon. 180,000 alone in the dome city of Montes Jura."

"Montes Jura, isn't that where the mining headquarters' is at?"

"You got it Doctor, and that's where they have taken hostages. We're desperately trying to take the city back but are attempts keep failing. Earth can't afford to lose those mines."

"Hmm it looks like I'm the back up plan." Doctor John then mumbled.

"What's that Doctor?"

"Well if they succeed I must be the back up plan. Those Helium Three mines supply 65% of the worlds energy with out them we would be in big trouble, so if you want to show me the way to the tablets I would be more then happy to help out."

"Thank you Doctor, If this all works out humanity is going to be greatly indebted to you."

"Well I'll do my best General."

PART XIX

Dome city. Moon Base Montes Jura

H'3 Main Head quarters
Tower one

"Colonel. What's your situation? Over."

"There's three men guarding the northern end of the room Sir, they have ten hostages on the floor. We have a clear shot to take them down. Requesting permission to engage, I repeat, may we engage? Over."

"Colonel, you have the go ahead. As soon as your snipers take them down get the hostages out and move your men up to the next level."

"Yes Sir." Colonel Devon Rells replied into his head set as he gave hand signals while he motioned his men into position. Then as they lined up to take their shot, a female hostage got up and started screaming.

"Please let me out, I can't handle this, Please! I want to go!"

"Get back on the floor lady!" One of the men in the room yelled as he made his way to her while he pointed a gun at her head, "get down, Now!"

"No! Let me go I want to leave now! You have no right doing this!"

"I have every right . Now get down! Or I will!"

"Or you'll what? Kill me, Beat me, What? You aren't so tough! Your just another stupid punk with a gun."

"Colonel. Do you see that?" One of the men called thorough his head set as the man in the other room began to raise his fist to the frantic woman's head.

"Yeah I see it," Colonel Rells replied and said as he steadily aimed the scope of his rifle while he took a deep breath and carefully gripped the trigger, “If your ready gentle men lets send these pieces manure back to the shit farm that they grew from, remember shoot to kill, one shot in each of their heads should do it. On my mark, three, two, one mark.”

Then with those words spoken, Colonel Rell’s men quickly squeezed the triggers on their silenced rifle’s and sent their forged bullets of flawless steel flying into the room. where they instantly with the loud sound of bloody, shattering, flesh, slammed into the three captures skulls and smashed their brains to peaces as the hostages watched in horrific surprise, and the captures silently died as they fell to the floor.

PART XX

Findings VI

Making his way to the bridge Captain Flyer Men stopped in front of a large port hole and took a moment to watch a couple of humpback whales peacefully hover in the water.

"You guys know what's happening," Captain Flyer Men then whispered as he looked into one of the whales deep, dark eyes, "I sure don't, I mean I know what's going on. I just don't know why. I bet you do. If people would only learn to communicate better we wouldn't have these problems. You obviously don't, you've earned your place my friend. You where here way before man and you managed to survive centuries with no war, no religion, no struggle for financial power and I know you don't know anything about substance abuse. Man could learn a lot from you my friend."

Resting his hand on the port hole Captain Flyer Men then let out a big sigh and blankly watched the whales swim away.

"Captain," a voice then called through the ship's intercom, "We've reached the two derelict subs. Would you like us to take them in toe?"

"No Commander, hold your position. I'm on my way."

"Aye, Captain."

Walking swiftly, Captain Flyer Men thought deeply about his orders and what he must do to carry them out. Then as he made his way onto the bridge while the crew sat with a séance of uneasiness he quickly realized what he had to do.

"Captain on the bridge."

"Weapons officer," Captain Flyer Men called as he made his way to the weapons station. "Stand down, your temporarily relieved."

"Aye, Captain."

Looking over the firing panel, Captain Flyer Men checked over some readings then fired the ships bow lasers onto the two derelicts subs and instantly destroyed them.

Turning to the bridge crew he then said with a stern voice. "If anyone of you disagrees with what I have just done, please speak now and I promise any objections you have will not go onto any of your permanent service records. But before any of you do, you must first understand that I'm acting under strict orders and this was my responsibility to bare not yours. So, anyone?" Captain Flyer men then asked as he looked around at his silent crew, "no. Very well then. Weapons officer you may return to your station. Your no longer relieved."

"Aye, Sir."

"Commander, are we still receiving and monitoring the abnormal signal?"

"Yes Sir, its gotten weaker but we still have it."

"Good. Helm start tracking the signals location and plot a course to intercept. Lets see what's creating it."

"Aye, Captain. Tracking now and plotting course."

PART XXI

Home I

"Mr. Leviticus," a Nurse said as she entered David's room, "Guess what? Today's your lucky day, you get to go home."

"Oh Yea," David replied as he slowly sat up and carefully slid to the edge of the bed, "it looks like you have a pile of paper work for me to sign."

"I sure do."

"Well considering my left arm is in a sling, I think that's going to be a little difficult. Don't you?"

"Yeah, that's not going to work to well. Hmm," the Nurse then thought and asked as she turned towards Elizabeth, "you're his wife right?"

"I sure am."

"Well you can go ahead and sign for him."

"My pleasure," Elizabeth replied as she stood up and made her way to the Nurse.

Grabbing the clip board that was full of paper work, Elizabeth then laughed and said as she began to sign each piece of paper, "Whew David, this is heavy stuff. I sure hope I don't miss something and sign our butt holes away."

"Ha, ha, ha," David laughed, "very funny."

"Well some one has to make a joke out of this," Elizabeth replied and said as she handed the clipboard back to the nurse, "you know they certainly won't."

"Okay," the nurse the then said as she motioned to Elizabeth, "If you'd like you can go and get your car and I'll get a wheel chair and wheel him out to you."

"Okay, that sounds good, David do you want me to help you get dressed?"

"No Beth I think I can manage."

"Okay then, I'll see you in a few minutes."

Leaving the room and making her way out to her car Elizabeth franticly thought while her mind raced with wild emotion. *How am I going to tell him, is this a good time. How is he going to react? Man I just don't know*. "Okay Elizabeth, calm down," Elizabeth then whispered to her self, "I can do this."

Getting into her car, Elizabeth then sat behind the wheel, took a quick look at her self in a mirror and said, "Okay lets go."

"Okay Mr. Leviticus here we are. Are you happy to be going home?"

"Oh yeah most definitely, it would be nice if it were under different circumstances, but hey. I'm still alive right. And it looks like it's a nice day out, it could be raining or something."

"This is true," the Nurse replied as she wheeled David out of the room, "you should always look on the brighter side. Especially when these kind of things happen. "Wow," she then said as she wheeled David outside, "it looks like your wife beat us here."

"Yeah she's like that, she moves so quick, sometimes I can hardly keep up with her."

"Well don't try to run after her any time soon, you have to let that hip heal first."

"Believe me I don't plan on it, may I take this sling off though? I don't think I can motivate this walker again with it on."

"I don't see why not, just make sure you have it on when you're not up and about."

"We'll do. Elizabeth will you take this please?"

"Sure David, But let me help you get up."

"No, I think I can do it, just make sure the door doesn't come down on me. I'd hate to add a head injury to the list. Well here it goes."

Slowly reaching for his walker David then painfully pulled himself up and made his way into the car where he sat and said, “whew that almost took my breath away”

“Are you okay Mr. Leviticus?”

“Yeah I’m fine, I just need someone to help me swing my legs in.”

“I got it.” Elizabeth said as she jumped in front of the Nurse.

“Are you sure?”

“Yeah.” He wouldn’t let me help him up, so it’s the least I could do.”

“Okay then, You two have a good afternoon and well see you in three weeks.”

“Alright and thank you for your help.”

“You bet.”

“Alright Mr. stubborn, lets finish getting you in here.”

“Yes Mother.”

PART XXII

Home II

"David. What's on your mind?"

"Not much of anything, I just want to get home and lay down. The medicine that the hospital gave me for pain is really making me feel real dizzy. Do me a favor."

"What's that?"

"Don't have the script filled."

"Are you sure?"

"Oh yeah I'm sure. I can deal with a little pain and stiffness but I can't deal with this. Its truly amazing that people can get addicted to that garbage, hmm especially when it makes you feel like this."

"Yeah no kidding," Elizabeth replied and said, "well I got some news that might make you feel a little better."

"What's that?"

Squeezing the steering wheel while she bit her lower lip, Elizabeth started to tingle with so much warmth that she became filled with red, loving emotion as she tried to get the word's to come out of her mouth.

"Beth," David then asked while he stared at her blushing face, "are you in there? What is it?"

"I know who's going to be a daddy." Elizabeth finally whispered while she tingled.

"Who? Me?"

"Mm hmm."

"Wow!" That's great David shouted, "oh ouch that hurt. I better calm down before I rip my strips out. No really Beth that's wonderful,

I didn't know I had it me. Now I'm not only stoned on pain killers, now I'm also stoned on you."

"I love you David."

"I love you too, you know. Hopefully I make a speedy recovery. So we can have some fun with your new condition."

"Yeah okay Mr. Perv, Just don't push yourself and make things worse."

"I wont, I promise and why did you call me a perv?"

"You Know why."

"No I don't Beth."

"Oh okay, If you say so."

"I have to do something."

"What's that?"

"Are you ready?"

"Sure David, have at it."

"Okay here it goes. Passenger window down. WHEEEEEEEEEE EEEEEEEEEEEEEEEEW!!!!! There. Aw man that hurt. Passenger window up."

"David. Calm down," Elizabeth said as she laughed, "people are staring at us."

"Sorry Beth I couldn't help myself. Are we home yet? I really need to lay down now, I think I just used up my last bit of energy. Oh man Its going To be great, I just know it. Oh look, is that our house?"

"Yes David, that's our house. And look here's the driveway."

"Oh boy, getting from the car to the bedroom is going to be fun. Isn't it?"

"Just remember sweetie, one step at a time."

"Got cha."

"Vehicle off, doors open. I'll be right back David. Don't go any ware. Okay."

"Oh, okay. I won't."

"You better not."

Slowly swinging himself around while Elizabeth went into the house, David then called out when he wearily saw the Indian man quietly chanting as he mysteriously waived smoke from a smoker around a window with a bird feather, "What are you doing? I said, hey, what are you doing?" Repeating himself David said again, Hey. What are you doing?" But the man didn't answer he just kept on chanting and waiving smoke.

"Alright I'm back. Here's your walker."

"Do you see him?"

"See who, David?"

"The man in the yard, he was in my dream. I think?"

"No, David. There's no one in the yard."

"That's strange. Man I swear I saw someone."

"It must be the med's David."

"Yeah Beth, Your probably right, anyways are you ready to do this?"

"Only if you are."

"Yep I sure am. so lets go," David then grunted and said as he slowly stood up. "I can't wait to lay in a real bed."

PART XXIII

The Diary

"Hello John."

"What! Who are you and where am I?"

"This is my world. Stop them and you can have anything you want, all you have to do is ask," The serpent creature said as he made his way towards Doctor John.

"Ask, I already did. Who are you and where am I?"

"Your sitting In a chair John. All safe and sound while you sleep in this place. This disgusting, tasteless place made for the precious humans when they need their precious little naps.

"That wasn't my first question."

"Always the wise guy, aren't cha John?"

"I try."

"Let's just say that I'm some one that can help you fore fill all of your desires."

"G thanks, but I think I can manage that on my own."

"Yeah, Yeah, Yeah, I've heard that from so, so many people, that I finally lost count."

"Oh so let me guess," Doctor John said and then asked, "you're the biblical devil that people have been writing about for so many centuries?"

"Please John I've been called many things but biblical devil now that might be a first. You know I helped write that book and all of the others that followed, Oh and guess what? I even helped create all of the religions that your pathetically, blind species likes to, so lovingly base there stinking lives around. So A devil, no I'm not. You want to see a devil. Look in a mirror, grind out your Genetic code then stick under a microscope and look at it. Now that's a devil, not me. So don't even try to make me out to be the bad one."

"Well some how I get the feeling that you're not the good one either, You said ask and I'll have anything I want. Did Hitler ask or did you give him an ultimatum as well?"

"Hitler, you mean old Adolf, please. I gave him what he wanted. and I knew what he wanted. Guess what? I even knew what the church wanted when they killed Hypatia of Alexandria."

"Like I said, you're not the good guy."

"Please, when your people couldn't figure out how to sufficiently sustain a solid economic structure I was the one that helped your freemasons create the system of currency you all are still living under. So stop saying I'm the bad one."

"Well you're most definitely not the good one, remember what you just said about Hitler?"

"Ha-Ha, Ah ha, ha, ha," The creature laughed and said. "I gave him what he wanted, So what's so bad about that?"

"Well for starters, Millions of people died under his command and in the end he killed himself."

"I didn't do any of those things John. I gave him his rise to political power and the rest he did on his own. You know!" The creature then said with an eerie snarl, as he levitated John off from his feet while he put him in a trance with the wave of his hand, "I've had enough of this small talk." Stepping in closer to Doctor John the creature then said, "Now you see Johnny boy, Hitler was no different then your beloved Kerri Ash bury, Millions died under her rule. Millions died under his rule, things die all the time and I don't really care. But what I do care about is the planet you live on. It's mine, always has been always will be. Earth, is kind of like my playground and if you let them people succeed, I'm not going to have a place to play. If you stop them, well you and I can have a lot of fun!"

"You have nothing to offer." Doctor John Mumbled back in sarcasm."

"Oh I think I do," The creature replied as he snapped his finger and said, "Does your mothers execution ring a bell?"

"Stop!" Doctor John then screamed while his mind filled with uncontrollable horror.

"Didn't she murder two men after they brutally had their way with you? Didn't she!"

"Stop!" Doctor John yelled again.

"Oh what's wrong, does that hurt? You still want revenge. Don't you!"

"No!" Doctor John screamed in horror, "I hate them! I hate all of them! Why, Why did she have to die!! My mother did nothing wrong, she was only protecting me. You Can't do this," Doctor John then loudly cried, "The visions of her death, I was so young. I can't take it anymore, Make it stop! Make it stop!"

Violently shaking and spitting while the creature watched with a bright smile, Doctor John then became extremely overwhelmed with deep dark anger and feverishly spoke in tongues while he viciously said, "I'll kill elm, I'll kill all of them!"

"Oh, are you angry John?"

"Yes and it feels good. I can see them. All of them suffering. The woman, the children, the filthy men with their stinking cities and their bars built for the innocent. I wanna see them burn! All of them!"

"If that's what you want John. I can give it to you. Just Ask and we'll burn them together."

"No, I can't," Doctor John then feverishly replied In emotional confusion, "In the end I'll lose, we'll lose."

"There is no such thing as losing John. Only victory."

"No I can't, the end will come and I'll have nothing."

"There's no ending John, Only new beginnings."

"Don't listen to him John." A female voice called while the creature began to nervously look around, "don't let him win."

"Who is that? Who's there!"

"Mom is that you?"

"Don't listen to him John, you must not let him win."

Struggling with his emotions, Doctor John repeatedly whispered, "I won't, I won't." While the serpent creature said.

"Oh but you will John. Ask! Ask now!"

"No!" Doctor John screamed while the female voice called again.

"Break his spell John, He can't hurt you."

"Mom, I'm so scared he's to strong."

"Ask me Now!"

"No he's not John, you can do it."

"Yes John, Yes you can." A Second voice called while the creature looked around and said again.

"Who are you? Show yourself. Show yourself, Now!" The creature then demanded while the sprits of Doctor Omar and Doctor John's mother appeared between him and Doctor John.

Struggling even harder with his emotions Doctor John then managed to break the creatures spell and fell to the floor. Hitting the ground he then faintly saw the two sprits and watched the creature shift into snake form and slither away into the darkness of the dream realm that he once stood in. Passing out Doctor John then heard his voice being called again.

"Doctor John, Doctor John."

"Yeah mom?"

"Doctor John, Wake up!"

Sitting up fast and knocking over a cup of coffee as he wearily shook his head, Doctor John then said, "what a nightmare. Marcy, how long have you been trying to wake me?"

"About Five minutes, you fell asleep here last night, so I just left you."

"Did we get the diary devise to load?"

"Yeah as a matter of fact we did. We started the transfer before you fell asleep."

"Good, lets go and get something to eat and then check out what we got. Sound like a plan to you?"

"Yep. It sure does."

PART XXIV

Dome City. Moon Base Montes Jura

H'3 Main Head quarters
Tower one

"Captain, Have any of the other teams located the explosives yet?"

"Negative Colonel, the other six teams are in the mines right now and there not turning up anything. What's your position?"

"Where almost at the top floor Sir. Just a few more levels to go."

"Good keep me posted and I'll do the same. Captain Wayne Beck out."

"Colonel Rells, I think you should look at this. According to these readings there's a signal coming from one of the rooms above us. It looks like its short wave Sir."

"Short wave," Colonel Rells replied and said, "That's the kind of signal you'd use if you wanted to set off a bomb."

"I don't think so Sir. The band width is to narrow. The signal won't go much farther then this."

"Well what ever it is, we know are boy might be close by."

"Mean While in a hidden location."

"If where going to die! We all die as brothers and sisters, for the mighty Gealeha! The outsiders may have defeated us but they will never take us! What do you say people!" A man standing in front of his crowd of followers shouted, "May I get a Alee!"

"Alee!" The crowd then shouted back.

"I couldn't hear you! I said may I get an ALEE!"

"Alee! Alee! Alee! Alee!" The crowed roared until the man in front raised his hands and said, "Brothers and Sister's of Gealeha's Kingdom of Light. Let's pray. Oh mighty Gealeha in our final hours, please grant us the strength to journey in to your mighty kingdom. Grant us the wisdom to find our way. Shine your light onto our fallen brothers, so they too can find their way into your kingdom. And please warm and watch over our children as they also enter into your Holey Kingdom of light.

"Mommy I want to go home, I'm scared." A little boy in the crowd said while their leader kept speaking.

"Shhh, it's ok Bobby. We'll be home soon."

"No I want to go now, I want to go back to Earth and see daddy."

"We're going to see daddy real soon," The little boys mother whispered to him as she tried to calm him, "but we're going to see him in a different place and it's not going to be on Earth Bobby, its going to be at Gealeha's kingdom and I know when we get there, daddy's going to be real excited when he sees you."

"Really?" Bobby replied with a smile.

"Oh yeah, now lets wipe away them tears. It sounds like we're all going to sing a song."

Wiping Bobby's tears away his mother then set him on her lap while the crowd started to sing.

"In his name we will follow"

"In his name we will triumph"

"In his light, we, will, shine, through out his, holey, kingdom and Slowly making his way around the singing crowed, the serpent creature who'd been watching them with glee, Hid away from the adults eyes, then smiled and waved to the children as he made his way around and mocked the singing crowd.

"Mmm, Hmm, Ha, Ha, Ha, Fools. This was almost to easy, Neh, Neh, Neh. In his Name your all going to die and be gone, gone, gone. Then all of the energy will be mine, mine, mine."

PART XXV

Dome City. Moon Base Montes Jura

H'3 Main Head quarters
Tower one

"Lieutenant report. Has your team finished their sweep yet?"

"Yes Sir," Lieutenant Karley Ashton replied into her head set, "and I'm happy to say that we haven't found anything Sir, just a few deactivated mining drones. If the resistance put bombs down here they did a real good job of hiding them. Have any of the other teams found anything?"

"Negative Lieutenant, they haven't found anything either. All we have is three men dead and two back on Earth that refuse to talk, so, once your packed up and ready to go I want you and your team to assemble with the other teams. Find the resistance and take them into custody, use force if necessary."

"Understood Sir, Ashton out."

"Colonel Rells this is Captain Wayne report. Have you reached the top floor?"

"Yes Sir we sure have and we've also been tracking a short wave signal that appears to be coming from one of the room's. It's possible the signal could be a link to the resistance's Bombs."

"If there are any," Captain Wayne Beck interrupted.

"What do you mean Sir?"

"I mean this whole thing could be a bluff, all of our teams haven't turned up anything. Not even a hair follicle."

"Well Sir I highly doubt there bluffing. Why would they go through this much trouble?"

"Wouldn't you if you wanted to send your enemies in the wrong direction?"

"Yeah I guess I would Sir, but I really don't think that's the case."

"And whys that Colonel."

"Because we just found the room where the signal is coming from and it looks like there's someone standing in it holding a detonator. I'll get back to you Captain, Rells out."

"Okay Team, lets put our heads together. How are we going to get in there with out them knowing?"

"Colonel. Why don't we send in a spider drone and just stun the guy?"

"That's a good Idea Lieutenant, the drone's venom will paralyze him just enough to keep his hands from activating that detonator."

Pulling a silver case from one of his vest pockets Colonel Rells smiled and then said, "I've been wanting to use one of these things for a long time. I've seen them tested but I never actually got use one."

"Not even in training Sir?"

"Nope. We were given operating instructions and that's it. So here we go. Hold out your hand."

"What? Why?"

"Just do it."

"Alright if you insist."

Nervously holding out his hand the young lieutenant stood real still while Colonel Rells put the case in his hand and said, "now press your index finger to the middle of the casing."

Pressing his finger to the center of the case while the team watched, Lieutenant Bargemen then nearly jumped out of his skin as the top of the case slid open and a small robotic spider jumped out an started hissing at him.

"Alright Colonel, any time your ready."

"I promise she wont bite Lieutenant."

"I hope not." Lieutenant Bargemen replied as he set the robot on the floor.

Pressing some buttons on an illuminated key pad Colonel Rells then proceeded to maneuver the spider under the door and into the room. Watching a small view screen he then programmed the robot to strike its target while he said, "once our little spider girl takes her bite I want every one on my signal to rush the room. Bargemen its going to be your job to secure the detonator. You got me."

"Yes Sir understood."

Holding his hand up Colonel Rells then vigorously stared into the small view screen and watched the room from the robots point of view. Then as the robot climbed up its target's leg, Colonel Rells heart raced with adrenaline while the drone viciously drove it's steal fangs into its target as he quickly yelled, "NOW!"

Forcing their way through the door, Colonel Rells three man team then quickly moved in with their rifles drawn and swiftly secured the room.

"Bargemen! Secure that detonator!"

"Yes Sir, one step ahead of you."

Reaching for the detonator Lieutenant Bargemen's look of seriousness quickly turned to one of confusion while Colonel Rells watched and asked, "What's wrong Lieutenant?"

"This things a dummy Sir, its not real."

"Are you sure?"

"Oh yeah I'm Sure."

Lowering his rifle Colonel Rells motioned his men to stand down while he said, "I don't believe this! Maybe this whole thing was a bluff? Hawk is it still giving off a signal?"

"No Sir the signal has subsided."

"I don't think it ever gave one off." Lieutenant Bargemen mumbled under his breath while he stared at the dummy.

"Do you care to share that with us Lieutenant?"

"Well look at it Sir it's a rubber dummy. How could it give off a short wave signal. It has to be some kind of a trap."

"I agree with Bargemen Colonel, lets get out of here and forget about this stupid thing."

"No, there might be something inside of it."

"Inside of that, come on Colonel I highly doubt it. Here watch I'll prove it to you."

"Hawk! Don't touch it, that's an order," Colonel Rells yelled as he swiftly walked and tried to stop Hawk, "I said."

"See," Hawk then said as he interrupted the Colonel while he knocked the dummy over, "its nothing but a stupid rubber dummy. Oh wait a minute," Lieutenant Hawk then said with fear in his voice while he looked down, "Why's the chest lighting up? Man! I'm getting out of here."

"Yeah," Colonel Rells replied in a soft somber voice then yelled, "that sounds like a good idea, come on men lets move it!"

Moving as fast as they could Colonel Rells team quickly scrambled out of the room and franticly ran through a hallway while Captain Wayne Beck, totally unaware of what had just happened, tried to radio Colonel Rells and quickly found out that his signal was being Jammed.

"What's going on? Why Can't I get through and why are those security drones coming back on line?"

"I don't know Sir."

"Well boost the signal."

"I'm trying to Sir, but something is draining our power and its making it really to difficult to raise the main linear boost."

"Well keep trying."

"Mean while."

"Lieutenant Ashton, I think you should come up here and see this. The mining drones are coming back on line."

"That's impossible, they were supposed to be completely shut down."

"Well as you can see their not."

"Captain Wayne. This is Lieutenant Ashton do you read me? Why are the mining drones being activated? I repeat why are the mining drones coming back on line? Please respond."

Pausing while she waited for a response Lieutenant Ashton's eye's grew wide when she noticed a small round glow coming from the drones chest.

“Mark, do you see that?”

“I sure do.”

“Assemble the team Mark, I think we should get out of here.”

“Don’t you think we should wait for new orders?”

“No, I’m not getting a response from base, all I’m getting is static and I think what ever is going on is some how affecting our communications so go, go and assemble the team so we can get out of here.”

“Yes Ma’am, I’m on it.”

“My brothers, My sister’s it’s time. Gealeha’s light is upon us. Let’s all kneel and hold hands while we await his arrival.

“Daddy,” a little girl in the crowd of followers said, “your chest is glowing.”

“Yeah I know honey, so is yours.”

“Why?”

“It’s Gealeha’s light sweetheart, look around it glows in all of us.”

“Why does it glow Daddy?”

“Because it’s his way of letting us know that he’s ready for us, now common. Kneel with me and hold my hand while we wait.”

“Okay Daddy.”

“Captain!” Colonel Rells yelled as he banged on the side of a ship with his fist, “open the door.”

Running to the door, Captain Wayne Beck then force fully removed a latch and swung the door open while he hurried Colonel Rells inside and said as he slammed the door shut, “Colonel. what’s going on, where are the rest of your men?”

“The security drones,” Colonel Rells replied as he tried to catch his breath, “they opened fire on us. I was the only one that was lucky enough to get away. After Lieutenant Hawk knocked over what appeared to be a decoy everything just started going crazy. I suggest that we move the ship and send in a E.M. Pulse drone. It should be able to take the security drones out.

“I was thinking the same thing Colonel. Pilot! Get this tub off the ground and far away from that tower.”

“Yes Sir.”

"Rells, try to reestablish communications."

"Already on it. Sir! Woe, communications are back up. Its like they never went down."

"Good, establish a link back to earth and Inform them of our situation. Let them know that plans have changed."

"Yes Sir."

PART XXVI

The Final Call Home

Sitting in his office and having a video conversation with his granddaughter General Douglas is abruptly interrupted by an incoming communication from Montes Jura.

"Sweetheart Grandpa has to go back to work now. I will try and see you this weekend, okay."

"Okay, bye Papa."

"Douglas here!"

"General, this Colonel Devon Rells. The situation up here has been compromised Sir. Some how all of the security drones have come back on line and they just started attacking us."

"What about the mining drones have they come back on line as well?"

"Were not sure Sir, we haven't been able to establish contact with. Wait a minute," Colonel Rells then said as he stopped in mid sentence, "Captain can you hear that, it sounds like laughter?"

"Yeah," Captain Wayne replied, "I can hear it and it sounds like it's getting louder."

"General, are you picking that up?"

"Yes I' am Colonel, it sounds like there's a carrier wave riding on top of your signal."

A carrier wave on top of our signal, Colonel Rells thought to himself while the General patently stood by, *that's it the explosives are inside of the drones and they're using our signal to coordinate an attack.* "General we have to go. Rells out."

"Colonel what are you doing, why did you just cut the general off like that?"

"I had to Sir, I have a hunch. I think I know what's going on."

"Well go on, explain."

"You see Sir, if there's a carrier wave on top of our signal they could be using our signal to boost theirs and that's how they plan on detonating their bombs."

"Their bombs where never found Colonel."

"Yeah I know they were never found, that's because they are more then likely hidden inside of the drones Sir. It's a good thing I cut the General off when I did, if that carrier made its way into the systems on Earth, there's no telling what might have happened."

"Yeah no kidding Colonel. Well what do we do now?" Captain Wayne asked while Colonel Rells walked around and thought for a moment.

"We have to go back and blow the tower up. This whole thing started when Hawk knocked that decoy dummy over, I bet that's where the signal is originating from."

"Are you sure Colonel? I wouldn't want to be us if you're wrong."

"Well Sir the only other option we have is the E.M. pulse drone, but that will take to long to get here."

"I agree. Pilot turn this tub around and take us back to the tower! Prepare to drop some bombs, I want that building leveled!"

"Yes Sir," the pilot replied.

Turning the ship around and maneuvering it back through the city's protective dome the pilot then flew the ship as fast as it would go but before they reached the tower it was already to late, the drones while the small crew on the ship watched in silence, had already began to blow up. One bye one they exploded and brought the mighty tower crashing to the ground, while the remaining drones relaye, d their signal to all of the mining drones and then finally to the resistance where the glowing explosives that where surgically implanted into their chest, violently blew all of them and everything thing in the mines to pieces.

"Pilot! Get us out of here before the dome collapses and we get sucked into space! Then set your course for Earth and take us to Base station 23!"

"Yes Sir."

"The worlds gonna have to know what just happened."

PART XXVII

Good Bye To Old Friends

"Every one please be seated. Thank you. I would like to start by saying its nice to see that my cousin had so many friends, much to often most of us walk through life without them, its obvious Jim never did, and that's why we're here today, to give honor not only to a man that had a lot of friends but to honor a man that was a friend to a lot of people. Jim or should I say Big Jim was one of the most kindest gentlest men you could meet. Underneath his hard and heavy looks stood a very humble man who would have done anything for anyone with no thought of reward. The bible says In Peter 5:14,Act 5.6. God resist the proud but gives grace to the humble. Well my friend," Father Mike said as he tearfully turned to Big Jim's casket, "God didn't resist you one bit, instead he gave you all the seeds you needed for planting a fruitful life and through hard work and determination you managed to plant your seeds well. Especially into the hearts of everyone that loved you." Turning back around and wiping away his tears Father Mike then said, "I know some of you right now are probably saying to yourself. If there's a god in this universe, how could he let something like this happen? Well I don't know how to answer that. But I can tell you this, you people here today, you are living proof of gods existence. Never before in all my years of ministry have I felt a room full of so much love and that love people is gods weapon against darkness! When the lord knows we're falling into darkness he shines his ever lasting love on us. Lifting us from the darkness and guiding us into the light! Jim Odowel was that light. A light that shinned brightly on all of us. And even though Jim's gone from us his light will keep shinning on. Let us pray together. Taken from the Holy Bible, the lords praye, r."

Our Father who art in Heaven
Hallowed be thy name Thy Kingdom come
Thy will be done on earth as it is in heaven
Give us our daily bread and forgive us our trespasses as we forgive those
Who trespass against us and lead us not into temptation
But deliver us from evil

"A men."

"A men."

"Now before we do one of Jims favorite past times, which happens to be eating a good meal with his friends and family, one of Jim's close friends would like to say a few things. David when your ready."

Grabbing his walker, David then stood up and made his way to the front of the room while Don Mayor whispered to Elizabeth, "He's motivating that thing pretty well, isn't he. He'll be back to work in no time."

"Yeah well don't rush it." Elizabeth replied and said, "until his doctor's say he's fully recovered, he's not going any ware or doing anything that requires the four letter word work, understood."

"I know, I know. I just wanted to comment on how well he's moving."

"Shhh." Don mayor's wife butted in and said "David's starting."

"Hello. Some of you here know me and some of you don't. For those who don't, I'm David, Jim and I worked together for a short time. And if you ask me it was to short of a time. From time to time my wife and I would get together with Jim and his wife. Sometimes we would cook out, sometimes we would go out for a night on the town or we would just hang out and talk for hours . But what ever it was we did, we always had a good time." Pausing for a moment David then said, "You see I grew up an orphan. I had nobody until I met my wife, not even a brother and to me Big Jim was more then a co worker or a weekend friend and whether he knew it or not he had become the brother that I never had. That's why I wrote this letter Jim, I wrote it for you." Tearfully reaching into his pocket, David then pulled out a piece of paper and started to read.

"What a brother is to me. A brother is someone that will catch you when you fall, a brother will be there when you have nothing at all, a brother will teach you when you need to be taught, a brother to me is someone that can't be bought. Big Jim. I will never again see your smiling face or hear the warmth of your voice on a cold day. I will never again see you standing so mighty and true but I will always hold you in my heart and remember you as the only brother I ever knew. Thank you for being a part of my life."

Slowly making his way to Jim's casket, David then folded the letter up and tearfully said as he placed it in Jim's Hand, "good bye my brother I will always remember you." David then turned and made his way back to his seat where Elizabeth rubbed his shoulders as she put her arms around him while she kissed his cheek and said, "well done sweetie, I think Jim would have appreciated that."

"In honor of Big Jim will everyone please rise for a moment of silence," Father Mike then politely requested, "and remember the man that has moved onto god's kingdom, thank you."

Silently rising and bowing their heads, everyone in the room quietly wept as they stood in the silence of their lost loved one.

PART XXVIII

The Day Earth Got The News

The day Earth got the news was a day like every other day the weather was warm in some places and cold in others. Some places it was night time. Some places it was day time. Some places it was raining. Some places it was snowing, and the people of Earth had been going about their business as usual. Then when the announcement was made, every television broad cast, every radio broad cast, every internet connection and even your personal phone conversations got interrupted when the President went on the air. People then all over the world abruptly stopped what they where doing to listen.

"We interrupt your normal communications network for a special news report from the capital building in Mexico City. President Debra Conley."

"People of Earth a terrible tragedy has fell upon us. A short while ago the mining city of Montes Jura was lost to the hands of terrorist, the city the mines everything gone. Nothing left but the fallen ruins of what was once one of man kinds greatest achievements. In these dark hours our deepest thoughts go out to the families that have lost loved ones due to this tragedy, they most certainly won't be forgotten. As most of you know Montes Jura was the main supplier of Helium3, the fuel we use to power our reactor's. With out it the wonderful civilization that we've built together could easily collapse, that's why I ask you this. Until we can get one of the other facilities on the moon up and running would everyone please try to conserve as much energy as possible.

I ask this of you not as the world's President but as a citizen of a great planet, where in troubled times I know we can come together as one and prevail over the hardship that has been laid before us. Thank you."

PART XXIX

Big Jim's Wake

Walking over to view screen that some people had gathered around during the President's speech, Don Mayor rudely shut it off and said, "Wow, I can't believe it. What kind of person would do something like that? Let alone how could they."

"What do you mean?" Father Mike asked.

Taking a bite of his food Don Mayor quickly chewed it up and swallowed then said, "Well the global military is paid very well to protect us from this kind of thing. So how could it have happened?"

"So what you're saying is, people with a big paycheck will always defeat those with a small one?"

"Well yeah," Don Mayor replied as he took another bite, "More money means you should have access to the best resources, and with that how could you fail. Isn't that right David?"

"Yeah but sometimes a strong belief in a crazy idea is the only thing you would need to pull something like that off, regardless of your finances or your resources."

Wiping his face with a napkin Don Mayor then replied, "So you mean to tell me that a strong belief is the only thing a person needs to succeed."

"No but it's a good foundation to build on."

"I think I know what David's trying to say Don, Money and financing can only take you so far. But when you strongly believe in an Idea, then you posses the power to do almost anything."

"If that's true," Don Mayor replied and said as he finished eating, "This is the first time I've seen it. Now if you'll excuse me gentlemen, I have to get me some cake."

"Boy he's a character," Father Mike then said as he turned to David, "he must be a real joy to work with."

"Yeah that's Don, he'll strike a financial debate on just about anything. You should hear him when his wife makes out a grocery list."

Laughing, Father Mike replied, "no thanks I get enough of that from my wife when I make a grocery list."

"I heard that." Father Mike's wife said as she snuck up from behind while she startled him.

"Huh, Andrea. Hi, I was just kidding."

"M, hmm. Sure you were. Here I brought you guy's a piece of cake."

"Mm, Thanks."

"Yeah thanks." David said and then asked, "have you seen Beth?"

"Yeah." Andrea replied and said while Father Mike ate his cake, "she's in the kitchen helping Diane clean up."

"Beth I don't think I will ever be able to thank you enough. All the support you and David have given me through all of this means so much to me and I. Oh here it goes again here come the tears."

"It's going to be okay." Elizabeth replied as she set a stack of dishes down and put her arms around Diane, "were here for you and Jim is too. All you have to do is remember that."

Squeezing Elizabeth tight Diane then cried hard while she said, "yeah I know but it hurts so much right now, this wasn't supposed to happen we were trying to have a baby. You know what the last thing he said to me was?" Pausing and trying to get her words out Diane then cried harder while Elizabeth softly said.

"Shh, what was it honey? Let it out that's what I'm here for."

"He said to me. God gave me the perfect wife, the perfect home and the greatest friends, now all I need is a child. You think the lord will do that for me. Maybe if I pray real hard he'll help me out. What do you think baby, You think he'll listen? That was the last thing he said to me. You know my husband had almost everything he wanted and now he's gone. Gone because of some selfish jerk with a gun. The world isn't ever going to change, is it?"

Lifting Diane's head while she put both of her hands on her face,

Elizabeth looked Diane in the eye and replied, "no honey the world isn't ever going to change. That's why you have to be strong. When the world throws something like this at you. You have to be strong enough to throw back, because if your not. Your life will pass you by and all you'll have is an unforgiving memory of what could have been." Removing her hands from Diane's face and placing one on her chest, Elizabeth then said, "Jim's right here inside of you and no matter what happens no one can take that away."

"Not even a jerk with a gun?" Diane asked as she slowly smiled while she wiped away her tears.

Half crying and half laughing, Elizabeth replied, "no. not even a jerk with a gun. Now give me another hug."

Reaching out to give Diane a hug Elizabeth then all of a suddenly became real dizzy and stumbled back words while Diane's look of confusion turned to one of concern.

Quickly grabbing Elizabeth by the arm Diane then asked, "Beth are you alright?"

"Yeah I'm fine, just a little dizzy."

"Just a little. You almost fell over. Here grab a chair and sit while I get you a glass of water. Have you eaten anything today?"

"Oh yeah. As a matter of fact, ever since I found out I was pregnant I've been eating like a horse."

"Well Diane," said as she handed Elizabeth a glass of water, "dizzy spells aren't uncommon during pregnancy."

Taking a few sips and setting the glass down, Elizabeth replied, "yeah that's what I've heard. I just didn't think they would feel that weird."

"Well you just take it easy you hear. We don't need you falling and busting your head, adding another casualty to the list isn't a good idea."

"Yeah. No kidding." Elizabeth replied while Don Mayor walked into the room and said,

"Ladies. How are we doing, are you two behaving?"

"No." Diane replied, "We're causing trouble as usual. Isn't that right Beth."

Getting up and finishing her glass of water, Elizabeth then

sarcastically replied, "That's right and unless you want some you'd better take a hike."

"Woe." Don then laughed, "it sounds like I came into the wrong room."

"Well you asked," Diane replied and said while she patted Don on the shoulder, "Beth if you don't need anything I'm going to tend to the rest of the guest?"

"Nope I'm fine. Oh, will you let David know I'll be out as soon as I finish loading these dishes?"

"I sure will."

"Thanks."

Grabbing a stack of dishes Elizabeth paused for a moment then turned to Don and said, "Here hold these please. I think I should read the instructions on that dishwasher before I try and use it. The one David and I have at home is controlled by voice command."

"Yeah so is ours"

Walking over and putting her index finger on the dishwasher's touch screen. Elizabeth quickly found the operating instructions and started to read them, but before she could finish. The words became blurry.

"Hmm," she then said, "something must be wrong with the screen. Don do you see this?" The words just went out of focus."

Setting the dishes down and walking up from behind, Don then became overwhelmingly, intoxicated by the smell of Elizabeth's hair. Slowly looking down in a daze while he stared at the soft, round outline of her behind Don then calmly said, "the stress you've been under lately must be playing tricks on your mind, because everything looks fine to me."

Squinting at the screen and trying to read the words Elizabeth asked, "you think so?"

"Oh yeah," Don replied as he stepped forward and pressed the full hardness of his now fully erect manhood between the two soft cushions of Elizabeth's meaty behind, "and I also think while David's out of commission we could find away to relieve some of that stress."

"Oh really," Elizabeth replied in a soft, sexy voice, "just how would we do that?"

"Well maybe when things become blurry, I can help bring them back into focus. All you have to do is ask and I will be ready and willing to help."

Slowly turning around Elizabeth put her arm around Don and firmly pressed her soft, warm, mound of moist femininity against his throbbing manhood and licked her lips as she passionately looked him in the eye while she softly said, "mmm. That sounds good. Accept you forgot one small detail."

"Oh yeah, what's that?"

"Well!" Elizabeth then yelled as she grabbed Don by the back of his head and clutched it with all of her might, "I'm married you asshole and I love my husband!" Elizabeth then quickly jerked Don's head back, stomped the top of his foot with the heal of her shoe and kneed him in the scrotum with such force that it sent Don screaming to the ground like a wet paper doll.

Straightening up and catching her breath Elizabeth then stepped over Don's wheezing body and started to make her way out of the room, but before she left Elizabeth grabbed a wet dishcloth and threw it in his face as she viciously kicked him in the stomach while she said, "If you ever touch me again your wife will hear about it, and I will tell David and believe me the beating you'll get from him will be far worse then the one I just gave you."

"Your gonna pay for this bitch," Don wheezed as he clutched his stomach while he tried to get up, "your gonna pay."

"Oh I'm really scared little man. What cha gonna do? Tell everyone, you know I went to Big Jim's funeral yesterday and at the wake while my wife was in the other room, I decided to come onto Elizabeth. I didn't think she'd mind, you know her husband David is the loyalist employee I have ever had. So I um, well you know I thought it would be okay, but apparently it wasn't because Elizabeth beat me down like the lying, dirty piece of scum ball, perverted, adulated trash that I' am. Yeah that will go over really well," Elizabeth then laughed as she poured a glass of water and said while she dumped it over Don's head, "now cool off you over confident baby, because you aren't going to do anything."

Doing a quick about face Elizabeth then loudly laughed and walked shamelessly out of the room. Stopping to straighten her self up, she then spotted David and tingled with the same loving emotion that had burnt into the core of her very souls since the day they met, and with that feeling coursing through her veins Elizabeth confidently made her way to him and quickly forgot about what had just happened.

PART XXX

The Six Stone Tablets

Listening to the upload from the diary and studying the six stone tablets, Doctor John is completely amazed by what he sees and hears.

"Marcy can you believe this?"

"Believe what?"

"That the diary actually worked, its amazing. The military did a carbon radio test on it about a month ago, they estimated it to be at least 100,000,000 years old. And these tablets have almost the same writing found in the San Andres pyramid. I wouldn't be surprised if these people were some how traveling back and forth between the two planets and some how using the two pyramids as a mass transportation depot."

"That's possible," Marcy replied, but if that where true, wouldn't the language be the same?"

"Not necessarily. Its possible that over time the two places just developed two different languages."

"I don't understand, what do you mean Doctor?"

"Well think about it, we live under a one world government and right now we're in the province of Michigan. A few hundred miles away is the upper peninsula but even though we're that close there are some differences in the language used here and the one used there. Aeh."

"Oh I get it," Marcy laughed and said, "its kind of like the old saying. I say tomato you say tama to."

"Exactly," Doctor John replied with excitement, "now you're starting to think like a true anthropologist."

"Well I do my best," Marcy laughed and asked as she began to take pictures of the six stone tablets, "so Doctor. Do you really think these are some sort of building instructions?"

"Oh yeah definitely. But on what I have no idea, Doctor Omar thought they were a schematic for an unimaginable power supply, but I'm not so sure of that yet. Its gonna take some time to decipher all of this. Once you get the photos done we should be able to move a little faster. Until then I'm going to keep listening to the diary's up load. There's a lot here and I'm having trouble making out the words. The language is close to an old Native American style but the dialect is unlike anything that I've ever heard. The only thing I've gathered is it's a child doing the talking."

"Wait a minute," Marcy said as she set her camera down and handed Doctor John the camera's memory chip, "Not to long ago I was assigned to a team and our job was to study the sound of the human voice, we were supposed to be looking for compressive change in vocal tonality. You know for when someone wasn't telling the truth. Basically the military wanted a better lie detector, anyways. When we ran our test we surprisingly found sub frequencies inside of the normal vibrating frequencies created when some one speaks. And can you believe it when we looked further we found that every spoken word no matter what language it is always vibrates on the same sub frequency."

"Really," Doctor John replied and said as he stopped the audio play back while he removed a ear phone from his ear, "so your telling me that if I say any word like uh, the word apple. Lets say in six different languages that its always going to vibrate on the same sub frequency and by identifying this frequency you'll know the word is apple, no matter how its said? Common if that's true why didn't you create a universal translator and. Oh wait a minute you did. Didn't you? You created a universal translator."

Grinning from ear to ear Marcy replied, "well not exactly. I started to create one but when the military heard they wasn't going to get a new lie detector, they scrapped the whole project and I never finished it."

"But you started it right?"

"Oh yeah," Marcy replied as she reached into her pocket and pulled out a small flash drive, "I have the proto type right here. Give me a couple of hours and I'll have it up and running, hopefully we can use it to decipher all of this."

"Yeah," Doctor John replied as he poured himself a glass of water and loaded the pictures of the six stone tablets into the computer, "that would be great. Man this is so weird, I can make out the writing but I cant make out what the child is saying."

"Maybe it's that difference in language thing you where talking about earlier," Marcy replied and said as she began to work on her translation program, "you know tomato, tama' to."

"Yeah that's true," Doctor John replied and said as he flipped through the pictures of the six stone tablets, "that just makes me wonder where the child might have came from. The markings on the diary clearly say it came from Mars but its possible she didn't." Pausing for a moment Doctor John then read some of the writing on one of the pictures and mumbled, "here we go."

Lining the photographs up and putting them in a row Doctor John then said to himself, "Doctor Omar was right. These are a schematic for an enormous Power supply. How it works though I have no idea? But she was right." Doctor John then blankly stared at the first picture and started to mumble the translations to him self as he wrote them down and then found himself being startled buy General Douglas's voice.

"Doctor John. How's it going?"

"General, I didn't hear you come in. What can I do for you?"

"I just came to check on your progress. You've obviously heard about what happened to Montes Jura, didn't you?"

"Yeah" Doctor John replied as he stopped writing and turned around in his chair, "as a matter of fact I did and I think it's a shame. I still cant believe it happened."

"Neither can we," the General replied and said as he grabbed a chair and sat down, "Its gonna take at least three months to convert one of the other moon facilities into a functional headquarters and another six to get the mines up and running again. Hopefully we have enough H'3 to last. The secretary of energy says we do but I'm not to sure. You know I don't understand why we ever converted to that junk anyways. There's enough energy coming from the sun to for fill our energy needs on this planet until it doesn't exist anymore and with the right solar grid put in place we wouldn't have to worry about them ridiculous mines.

"Yeah that's true General but you know as well as I do H'3 is big business and If you try and shut it down you'll probably have another war on your hands. You remember what happened when the petroleum industry finally went under."

"Oh yeah I remember that day all to well. Auto Makers announced the introduction of the permanently fixed magnetic engine and President Asbury of Russia gave a speech on H'3 and explained how it was going to save us all. Shortly after that world war three broke out. Two Billion dead, all because people had become so afraid of change."

"Well," Doctor John interrupted as he spun back around in his chair, "You better find a way to keep this thing quiet, well that's if the government wants to build it and bring it on line. Because if I'm reading correctly, this contraption is capable of producing more energy then solar power and H'3 combined. Well at least that's what I've gathered from this first tablet. I won't know for sure until I finish reading the whole thing."

"So it's defiantly building instructions?" General Douglas asked as he got up and walked over to Doctor John's side.

"Oh yeah, most defiantly. Well at least the other five tablets are. This one just says what it is."

"Doctor John." Marcy interrupted, "I'm gonna go get something to eat. You want anything?"

"No thanks Marcy. I'm fine."

"General, How about you?"

"No thanks I'm good."

"Okay then I'll be back in a few."

"Okay Doctor. What Is it?" General Douglas then asked as Marcy left the room.

"Well it's a device that supposedly channels a planets EM field and centers it through a crystal and then forces it through the reverse poles of powerful super conducting magnets, thus creating a huge fountain of flowing electrons. But by the looks of it we'll never be able to build it. Aside from the magnets this thing would have to be built from a material that's not available on Earth and the crystal, well. The story behind that is amazing."

"Whys that? Crystals can be found almost any ware."

"Not like this," Doctor John replied as he pointed at the view screen and said, "This ones very unique."

"How so?"

"Well according to this the crystal was discovered around the time these people converted all of their transmitting technology from digital to reciprocating digital, something we've just recently started to do, anyways when they started to use this new technology they discovered an unknown signal coming from one of their oceans and when they tracked its place of origin they found this crystal. Performing scientific experiments on it they soon found out that the crystal was capable of collecting EM particles through one end while it sent them through the other end at an outstanding velocity and."

"Wait a minute," General Douglas interrupted and said as he pointed at the screen, "that crystal transmits some kind of signal."

"That's what the tablet say's," Doctor John replied as he got up and stretched for a moment then asked, "why, does that seem strange to you or something? Crystals have been know to resonate certain sound waves and transfer them into short wave or long wave signals."

"Well its more coincidental then strange."

"Whys that?"

"Because we have a sub in the North Atlantic that was just recently fitted with the new reciprocating technology and right before they were attacked, the crew picked up a strange signal. So strange that it had most of the crew baffled, even the Captain. So he up loaded it to one of our analysis teams and they can't figure it out either. Do you think it's possible there's a crystal like that in one of our oceans as well?"

"Well General we're looking at 100,000,000 year old writings from Mars and I just started to listen to what appears to be a child's diary that came from Mars as well. So you tell me if its possible, probable is more like it."

"Yeah your probably right Doctor. I had better get Captain Flyer Men on the horn and let him know what's going on. Care to take a walk with me?"

"Sure I'd be glad to. Just let me leave Marcy a note, I'd hate to have her wonder where we went."

Grabbing a piece of paper Doctor John then jotted down a few words and stuck a note on Marcy's desk then said as he followed the General out of the room and through a hallway, "Coffee I need coffee, since all of this began I don't think I've had more then Four hours of sleep a day. I'm starting to feel sluggish, a good cup of coffee always snaps me out of it."

"Yeah I know what you mean," the General replied and said as they entered his office, "I think I've lived on cat naps for the past three years. Have a seat and I'll pour the first round."

"Thanks General." Doctor John replied as he sat down and patiently waited for the General to pour him a cup of coffee.

"Cream and sugar Doctor?"

"Yes please." Doctor John replied while he looked around the room and fumbled though a book.

"Ahh here we go," General Douglas then said as he turned around and handed Doctor John a warm steaming cup of coffee, "Here's to the people of Montes Jura. May they rest in peace."

Setting the book down and grabbing the cup of coffee Doctor John then toasted the General, took a sip and said, "here, here."

The General then took a couple of drinks, walked to his desk, set his cup of coffee down while he looked at a view screen and said, "monitor on. This is General Henry Douglas. Transmit and open a priority one channel to Captain Jeff Flyer Men of the North Atlantic Submarine Osdel."

"Channel open." An automated voice replied.

"Captain Flyer Men."

"General Douglas, What can I do for you."

"Well you remember the odd signal you sent to our analyses team?"

“Yeah, did they figure out what kind it is?”

“No Captain they didn’t but one of our Doctors did.”

“One of your Doctors?” Captain Flyer Men asked with a puzzled look.

“Here Jeff I’ll let him explain. Doctor John when ever your ready.”

“Oh sure,” Doctor John replied as he got up and made his way to the view screen and said while he stood in front of it, “Captain Flyer Men hi. How are you? I’m Doctor John.”

“I’m fine Doctor. Now what’s going on?”

“Well the signal you picked up is being transmitted by a very powerful crystal, we think. Anyways we don’t know why it emits the signal but we do know that without the new reciprocating digital technology you would have never picked it up.”

“So what now?” Captain Flyer Men sternly asked.

“Well uh, I don’t.” Doctor John mumbled as General Douglas Interrupted him and said.

“Your still tracking the signal aren’t you?”

“Yes Sir we sure are and we’ve already set a course to its place of origin.”

“Well then you know what to do, retrieve the crystal if there is one and bring it back to this station. Douglas out, oh yeah Captain one more thing, mums the word.”

“Understood General. Flyer Men out.”

PART XXXI

Retrieval

"You heard the General gentlemen, mums the word. Helm how close are we to the signals point of origin?"

"About two miles Sir. It appears to be coming from one of the New York city caverns."

"Can you tell witch one?"

"No Sir we're still to far."

"Commander. Do you still remember how to pilot the mini diver?"

"Yes Sir I sure do."

"Good. Go get suited up and prepare to take it for a swim."

"Aye, Sir."

Making his way off the bridge and through a hallway, Commander Mark Tomas glowed with excitement and as he stopped to wait for a elevator to take him to a different level of the ship he began to Hum.

"Hm hm hm mm doe re me fa sue I'm so in love with you."

"Commander," a young female Ensign said and asked as she walked up from behind, "Are you alright?"

"Ensign Joyce Pertson. Yeah I'm fine, I'm just a little excited its been a while since I've taken the mini diver out. Would you care to join me?"

"I would love to," Ensign Pertson replied as they entered the elevator and made their way down to level twelve while the helms men called to the Captain and said,

"We have a complete lock on the signal Sir, it's coming from the center cavern and it's approximately three miles down on the other side."

"Three miles down," Captain Flyer Men Said, "That's almost inside of the old New York cities time square."

"Actually Sir according to my calculations it's right below it."

"How fare below?"

"About 50ft Sir. Its' a good thing the mini diver is equipped with a drilling laser."

"Yeah no kidding," Captain Flyer Men replied and said, "lets just hope its telescoping arm will reach that far. When we get closer, put the cavern on main viewer and park us right in front of it."

"Aye, Sir."

"This is gonna be fun," Ensign Pertson said with excitement as she climbed into the mini diver and pressed some buttons to seal the hatch, "I've never been inside of one of these things. This sphere is amazing. I can't believe the whole thing is made from glass."

"Yeah high pressure engineering has come along way," Commander Tomas replied and said as he sat down and hooked his suit up to the mini diver's on board computer's, "I just hope my driving skills have gotten better."

"Whys that?" Ensign Pertson asked as she sat down and strapped herself in.

"Because," Commander Tomas replied while he pressed some buttons on his suit, "the last time I took one of these things out I crashed it into the side of the Osdel."

"Thanks for the warning!" Ensign Pertson then yelled as Commander Tomas flipped a switch that opened a large door while the mini diver quickly launched and sped through a flooded tube at a extremely high velocity.

Quickly reaching the outside ocean and clearing the back of the Osdel while Ensign Pertson held on tight, the mini divers intercom then clambered with the sound of Captain Flyer Men's voice.

"Commander."

"Yeah Captain, go ahead."

"We're up loading the signals point of origin into the diver's main computer. Once the upload is complete she should take you right to it. Let the diver do the driving Mark and we'll monitor your progress from here."

Looking over some readings on the diver's monitors Commander Tomas then replied, "understood Captain, but it looks like we're gonna have to dig."

"Yeah you are." We figured you could use the drilling laser for the first 49Feet and then let the arm do the rest. Does that sound easy enough for ya?"

"Oh yeah it sounds like a piece of cake Captain. Just one thing."

"What's that Mark?"

"Well," Commander Tomas Laughed and said, "if the diver gets to do the driving, does she also get to crash into the side of the Osdel?"

"I hope not," Captain Flyer Men replied in a laugh and then said, "good luck Mark. Flyer Men out."

"Wow is that the lady Liberty?" Ensign Pertson then asked as she spun around and gazed at the face of a large, leaning statue.

"Oh yeah, that's her," Commander Tomas replied and said while he turned around to take a look, "yep she's all safe and sound lying peacefully on the ocean floor. Its hard to believe that all of this was once above the water."

"Actually Commander according to a article I read in the Earth's Times, half of the statue was above the water. It wasn't until recently the whole thing had finally went under."

"Yeah I read the same article, some company tried to raise her but instead they accidentally knocked it over and sent it straight to the bottom. How would you like to have that on your resume?"

"Um no thanks," Ensign Pertson replied and asked as they sped past the statue and made their way into the cave, "is that kind of like having a diver crash on your resume?"

Laughing Commander Tomas replied, "I can see I'm never gonna live that down."

"Just kidding Commander. You know me I'll take a cheap shot When ever I can."

"Cheap shot," Commander Tomas Laughed again, "I think that was as cheap as they come."

"Well I try." Ensign Pertson chuckled while she stared through the glass sphere and became internally excited as they emerged from the cave and hovered over an old building, while she gazed out and saw the flooded ruins of the once mighty dry, city, That now stood silently, sinking into the deep waters of time.

Pressing some buttons Commander Tomas then said, "hang on Joyce," then without a flaw the mini diver quickly, dove deep into the city.

Weaving in and out of some dilapidated buildings the diver then quickly located its target, and with the precision of an acrobat landing on a tight rope, it swiftly descended and Hovered a few inches from the ocean floor before it softly touched down.

"Ah here we are," Commander Tomas said as he put his hand on a touch screen and pressed some buttons. "The crystal. If there is one? Should be directly below us."

Spinning his seat around Commander Tomas then lowered a consol from the ceiling and pressed some buttons while he said, "Joyce, signal the Osdel. Let them know we've arrived and we're ready to start Drilling."

"Aye, Commander."

Turning a dial and pressing an illuminated switch Ensign Pertson signaled their mother ship, "Submarine Osdel this is diver one, we've reached our destination and we're ready to commence drilling."

"Diver one this is the Osdel, you may proceed when ready. Osdel out."

"Well you heard the man," Ensign Pertson said and then laughed as she shut the communications channel down, you may fire when ready."

"What's so funny," Commander Tomas asked while he imitated the radio officers voice as he fired the drilling laser and said with a chuckle, "It sounds like I'm gonna have to adjust the air mixture in here. I think your getting way to much oxygen."

"No I'm not, that mans voice just struck me funny and besides I've heard I'm not the only one that's happened too."

"No your not," Commander Tomas replied and said as he monitored the laser's depth, Lieutenant Offermen's voice has been known to have that effect on people. We've tried to politely let him know about it, but as you obviously heard our attempts failed, so we just go with it."

"That's probably the best thing to do," Ensign Pertson said as she laughed, "next time I'll try to keep it to myself. I'd hate to get a reprimand from the Captain for laughing at the wrong time."

"Or in the wrong situation," Commander Tomas interrupted and said with a sly snicker, "ol Captain Flyer Men's a real stickler to that type of thing."

"Oh I've heard," Ensign Pertson replied as she looked at the laser's depth and said, "it looks like we're almost there."

"Yeah just a couple of really big rocks to cut through and we'll hit our mark."

"Do you think they'll pose a problem Commander?"

"Nah, When the laser starts to cut through em we'll probably pick up some vibrations from the rock's resonant frequency."

"But that's only if the laser vibrates on the same one."

"Very good Joyce, I'm impressed, you've done your home work and that means I don't have to tell you what could happen to us if the laser and the rocks have the same resonant frequency."

"No you don't," Ensign Pertson replied as she watched the laser slowly descend through the rocks, "I'm very aware of what could happen and by the looks of these readings it just might."

"Nah," Commander Tomas said we'll be through the rocks before things start to shake."

"I sure hope so." Ensign Pertson replied while she felt the floor of the mini diver start to vibrate, *I hope so*, she then thought, *cause if we're not we're in serious trouble*.

Standing real still, Ensign Pertson then nervously looked around the mini diver while the serpent creature who'd been fast asleep in his bright, white, realm of soft, lustrous satin is abruptly woken by the laser's vibrations.

Rising up and peering into the murky water that floated above him, the creature then quickly spotted the outline of the mini diver and became filled with jealous rage. Loudly screaming he then transformed himself into a giant snake like creature and slithered up through the water. Slowly moving like a cat waiting to pounce on its prey the creature then made his way into a small cave and Watched the mini diver with green, glowing, eyes of lustful resentment while he patiently waited in the dark and mindfully planned his attack.

Unaware that they were being watched Commander Tomas shut the drilling laser off and started maneuvering the diver's telescoping arm down the 49 foot shaft while he said, "see nothing to worry about. Lets just hope the arm will reach."

"Why wouldn't it?" Ensign Pertson asked and said as she looked at the screen that monitored the arms progress, "I know the arm is only rated at 49 in a half feet, but if you can grab onto what is obviously now a crystal with the claw we should be good. It'll be just like playing a crane game at a fair."

"Yeah," Commander Tomas replied and said as he watched the arm descend, "your right. Except I was never any good at those things."

Laughing Ensign Pertson replied, "Well Commander now's your chance to get better."

"I tell you what Joyce, if I bag this the next time we're on leave we'll hit a carnival and play every crane game they have. Sound like a deal?"

"Sounds more like a date Commander."

"Well it could be a date, but doesn't that also require dinner?"

"Commander, are you asking me to dinner as well?"

"You catch on quick," Commander Tomas snickered as he watched the arm hit bottom and slowly push its way into a half of foot of mud before it stopped. "Well that's it 49 in a half feet. Time to test my skills.

Flipping a switch and squeezing a trigger, Commander Tomas opened the claw and slowly released it. He then cautiously inched it through the mud and said, "I think we're gonna get it. Yep!" Commander Tomas then yelled as he let go of the trigger, "got it! It looks like we have a datc Joycc."

"Well Commander, it would appear that way. But you haven't brought the crystal aboard yet."

"Oh was that part of the deal? I thought I only had to snag it."

"Common Commander, did you really think you were gonna get off that easy?"

"Hey," Commander Tomas replied and said as he watched the arm slowly make it's ascent, "You cant blame a man for trying."

"No you can't," Ensign Pertson chuckled as she prepared a container for the crystal, "a little dreaming every now and then is always good for the soul."

"That is so true," Commander Tomas replied as the both of them watched the arm emerge with a foot ball shaped and sized crystal, that glowed with such a brilliant, bright, hue, that it instantly filled the cabin of the mini diver with a deep, blue, shimmering light as it slowly emerged from the hole and quickly lit up the ocean floor.

"Oh my god Mark," Ensign Pertson then said while she stood in aw, "it's beautiful. Where do you think it came from?"

"I have no idea." Commander Tomas quietly replied as he stared at the crystal while he slowly lowered it into the divers sample drawer, "one things for sure though, it's gonna have some kind of impact on humanity."

"You think so?" Ensign Pertson asked as she slid the prepared container into the sample drawer.

"Oh yeah I can feel it in my gut. Don't ask me how or why. But I just have that feeling."

"Well," Ensign Pertson said as she used the diver's small robotic hand to pull the crystal from the sample drawer into the container, "just so you don't feel alone I have the same feeling."

Sliding the container back inside, Ensign Pertson then dried it off and secured it to the floor and said, "There we go I'll signal the Osdel and let them know we have our package."

"Okay," Commander Tomas replied as he prepared the diver for departure, "Just don't tell them about our date."

"And why not Commander? I'm sure they would love to know all about it."

"Oh yeah," Commander Tomas laughed, "them and the rest of the world would probably love to know. I can see the headlines now. A high ranking Commander and an Ensign from the mighty submarine

Osdel caught fraternizing, story at six. Oh yeah that would go over well."

"Just like a brick in the toe, Commander."

"You are so right Joyce. Just like a brick in the toe. I like that one, I'm gonna have to remember it."

"You've never heard that one?"

"No Joyce. I've heard a lot of em, but I've never heard that one."

"Well," Ensign Pertson said as she radioed the Osdel, "I'm gonna have to see if there are any other sayings that you don't know about. Sound good to you?"

"Oh yeah that sounds good to me." Commander Tomas replied as he finished preparing the diver for departure.

Strapping himself in while Ensign Pertson finished radioing the Osdel Commander Tomas then Asked, "Are we ready Joyce?"

"Oh yeah, I'm ready."

"Lets do this then," Commander Tomas replied while the serpent creature slithered

Out of the cave and reared up as he closely watched the mini diver start to make its ascent.

Totally unaware that deep under ground the Indian man had been peering into the white swirling smoke of a sacred fire and watching his every move, the serpent creature then quickly swam after the mini diver.

Catching a vision of what was about to happen, the Indian man quickly rose to his feet, jumped through the fire and became one with the smoke. Swiftly ascending to the surface and emerging from the center of the swirling, white, smoke as a brilliant, red, yellow and blue winged hawk, the brilliant, bright, bird then softly landed on the ground and perched himself while he called out in a loud screech and awaited the serpent creatures next move.

"Commander!" Ensign Pertson called out as she switched the diver's small sonar screen to a large holographic image, "look."

"What the!" Commander Tomas yelled as he quickly leaded forward and said, "That thing is huge."

"Yeah no kidding Commander and it looks like it's following us."

"You know what Joyce?" The Commander replied as he leaned back and watched the creature lunge at the back of the diver, "your right!"

Quickly Spinning out of control from the wake of the creatures now circling strikes the Commander then said, "it also looks like it's hungry. Strap yourself in Joyce I'm gonna take this thing off from auto pilot and try to out run that snake."

Quickly pressing some buttons, Commander Tomas's chair then raised upwards while a black video visor fell over his face, but before he became one with the mini diver's systems the serpent creature swiftly moved in and struck again. Just like a cat playing with it's meal he pounced upon the mini diver and sent it further out of control.

Quickly finishing his connections the Commander then regained control of the diver and shot up through the city at an amazing speed.

"Commander its gonna strike again!" Ensign Pertson yelled as she watched the sonar hologram while she clutched onto her chair.

"Not if I can help it!" See that building at 2:00? I'm gonna cruise through it and hopefully that thing will be stupid enough to follow me in, because I'm gonna try to blow it up around him."

"Sounds like a plan," Ensign Pertson nervously replied and said as she bit her upper lip, "Lets just hope it works because if it doesn't we're gonna be giant snake food."

"Oh no we're not," Commander Tomas replied as the serpent creature began to open it's mouth, "There's an opening right there in the center of the building and we're gonna swim right through it. Just hang on Joyce and we'll be there in a second."

Turning up the power and pouring on the speed, Commander Tomas then swiftly maneuvered the mini diver through the opening and sped into the building. Then as they made their way to the other side, the serpent creature violently slammed into the small opening and got stuck.

"Ha," Commander Tomas laughed as he found an opening on the other side of the building, "The stupid thing got himself stuck."

"Well that's what you wanted." Ensign Pertson said as she looked at the hologram of the now violently shaking serpent creature.

"Oh yeah," Commander Tomas replied and said as he maneuvered the diver through an opening, "that's exactly what I wanted. Now watch this."

Spinning the mini diver around, Commander Tomas then clenched his hands together and positioned the diver approximately 100 yards in front of the building. Mindfully aiming a holographic scope he then proceeded to fire all of the Mini diver's weapons at once. Then as they hit the building with one gigantic under water explosion, the brilliantly colored Hawk loudly screeched and spread his wings when he heard the loud, vicious roars of the struggling serpent creature. Lifting into flight with the speed of a jet and the awesome agility of a hungry leopard, the hawk then made his way high over the tree tops and flew feverously across the land.

"Commander, um we better get out of here before that shock wave tears us apart."

"My thoughts exactly." Commander Tomas replied as he turned the diver around and quickly out ran the blast that had instantly collapsed the building. "I fully agree!" He then yelled as Ensign Pertson hung on for dear life while she yelled back.

"Oh my god Commander! We've cleared the blast, I think you can slow down now!"

"You think so!" Commander Tomas yelled as they quickly cleared the city and he headed for the exit cave, "I think this is kind of fun!"

"Yeah okay Commander!"

"Just kidding Joyce."

"Good because you'll never be able to maneuver through the cave at this speed."

"Yeah I know," Commander Tomas replied and said as he slowed the mini diver down and prepared to enter into the cave, "I should also put this thing back on auto pilot. If my memory serves me right it was pretty narrow in there."

"Yeah it was," Ensign Pertson replied and said as she caught her breath, "and you'd better do it fast because our friend is on the move again."

"What, how?" Commander Tomas said as he looked at the holographic sonar image, "I can't believe that thing didn't die when the building blew up and fell in on it."

"Yeah no kidding," Ensign Pertson replied and said, "you know in a strange way it's kind of amazing that it didn't die. How it didn't is beyond me, but it didn't. Oh! And judging by the way it's moving commander! You must have made it really mad. Because its' moving fast . And boy does it look hungry!"

"Well it's not gonna eat us," Commander Tomas replied as he guided the diver into the cave and finished setting it back to auto pilot, "there's no way that thing can get us in here."

"Let's hope not," Ensign Pertson said as she stared at the sonar image, "Because we're history if it does."

"Why do you say that Joyce, you don't think we could out run it again?"

"Not in here we couldn't. Nuh uh no way, this cave is way to narrow. You'd crash for sure."

"Nah, I could do it Joyce. Maneuvering through tight spaces at high speeds is one of my specialties and besides I got us through that building without a scratch."

"Yeah you did," Ensign Pertson replied and said as she patted Commander Tomas on the shoulder, "and you deserve a. Woe what's going on, why are we stopping? Did the engines quit?"

"Yeah they did," Commander Tomas replied while he started checking the diver's systems, "and by the looks of it, the jets are closed as well. Hmm, do me a favor. Shut down all of the secondary systems while I run a diagnostic on the primary ones."

"Aye, Commander, I'm already on it."

"And Joyce, keep an eye on our power levels. If you see them running low start shutting some of the primary systems down as well."

"Aye, Commander, do you also want me to radio the Osdel and let them know of our situation?"

"Yeah but do it on a low power text frequency. The batteries aboard this thing don't store much power and until we get the magnetic engines up and running we're gonna have to conserve as much as possible, because when it comes to a computer glitch there's no telling how long it's gonna take to fix the problem."

"What makes you think it's a computer glitch?" Ensign Pertson asked as she finished sending a message to the Osdel, "I mean couldn't one of the engines magnets have just fallen out of alignment?"

"Yeah but according to this reading, those magnets are lined up perfectly. So it has to be a simple glitch and besides that wouldn't cause both of the engines to quit."

"No Commander I guess it wouldn't. But an over heated propulsion module would."

"You know what Joyce, your probably right," Commander Tomas replied and said as he got up and went to the back of the diver, "and that would also explain why the jet closed. The engines and impellers that feed water to the main jet drive all run off the same module. And if it over heated," Commander Tomas then said as he opened a panel and pulled a small see through chip from it's port, "Then the both of them would shut down simultaneously, and by the looks of this chip that's exactly what happened. Come here and look at it Joyce, the center point literally melted away."

"Wow Commander, you burned it up good."

"Me?"

"Yeah you, Mr. speed freak."

"Aw come on, you think I did this?"

"I know you did," Ensign Pertson laughed.

"How? If I was going to fast when we out ran that blast the computer should have given me some kind of warning before this thing burnt up."

"That's true Commander but for some reason it didn't and before you start passing blame on the computer, just let me say one thing."

"What's that?"

"Well," Ensign Pertson replied with a laugh and said as she moved towards Commander Tomas's face and acted like she was going to kiss him, "Its still your fault and if I was in charge I would write, you, up."

"Oh you would Hu." Commander Tomas replied with a snarl.

"Yeah I would. I would bust you so bad, that it would take you a week to realize what hit you."

"Well," Commander Tomas replied and said as he wrapped his arms around Ensign Pertson's waist while he pulled her body firmly against his, "you don't have to be in charge to bust this guy."

"Oh I don't Hu."

"No you don't." Commander Tomas replied as he slowly slid his hands down Ensign Pertson's back and carefully rubbed the soft out line of her cushiony behind.

"Then what do I have to be?" Ensign Pertson then asked while the Commander firmly squeezed the round cushions of her fruit shaped behind as he gently lifted her off from her feet.

"Just you" Commander Tomas replied as Ensign Pertson wrapped her legs around the Commander while she softly said, "Well then, I guess your busted."

Rubbing the center crease of Ensign Pertson's bottom while he stared into her eye's the Commander then replied, "yeah I guess I' am, so now you get to take me away. Right."

"Right," Ensign Pertson replied and said as she kissed Commander Tomas and felt her body fill with warm feelings of lustful pleasure, "Oh Mark, I've been waiting so long for this."

"So have I," Commander Tomas replied and said as he looked deep into Ensign Pertson's brown eyes while he lustfully squeezed harder on her behind, "I just hope when this over we'll be able to take this further."

"We can take it as far as you'd like Mark. I mean if that's what you want?"

"Oh yeah, that's exactly what I want." Commander Tomas whispered as he began to feverishly kiss Ensign Pertson's neck while he worked his hands closer to her warm throbbing rose petal, that had been painfully pressing so hard against his fully erect man hood, that it made Ensign Pertson quiver and tingle with such an overwhelming pulse of electric pleasure, that it caused her to jump with such force when she pressed her wet woman hood even harder against his throbbing man hood, that it made the both of them simultaneously fall to the floor with laugher.

Then while they began to fall into a deep, deep, kiss the already disgruntled serpent creature who'd been angrily swimming around the entrance to the cave. Abruptly stopped, grew twice it's size and viciously roared when it caught the scent of loving, erotic, pheromones that had been permeating through the water as they flowed from the inside of the mini diver.

"What was that, did you hear that?" Commander Tomas Asked as he pulled himself out of the deep kiss, "It sounded like a lions roar."

"Yeah it did," Ensign Pertson replied and said as she slid out from underneath Commander Tomas and then quickly rose to her feet, "I bet it's our snake friend."

"Yeah I bet it is too. Instead of fooling around, maybe we should think about getting out of here."

"My thoughts exactly Commander."

"Find me a piece of wire while I shut the binary propulsion modules down. I'd hate to burn the whole thing up when we restart it."

"Yeah no kidding Commander. But wasn't that chip the primary propulsion module?" Ensign Pertson asked while she hunted around for a piece of wire.

"No that was just a fuse."

"Oh really, I didn't know that. So what does it do Commander?"

"It regulates the power coming from the converter and sends it to the primary propulsion module. And it also acts between the two as a safe guard. Which is a really good idea because if there's some kind of surge or a malfunction from another system the fuse will burn up before the problem reaches the module and ruins it. The down fall is, no one ever puts an extra supply of them on these ships and when things like this happen we have to rig things up."

"Well Commander, I don't know what you planned on doing with a piece of wire, but I can tell you it's gonna have to change because I can't find any."

"Uh, that's not good," Commander Tomas sighed and said as he finished shutting the binary modules down, "we have to use. Oh wait a minute. Give me a couple of your hair pins."

"My hair pins?"

"Yeah your hair pins. All I have to do is wind them together and they'll make as good of a jumper as any piece of wire."

"Jumper," Ensign Pertson asked as she pulled the pins out of her tightly wound hair and handed them to Commander Tomas, "I don't understand, what do you do with a jumper?"

"Well you take these pins and wind them together like that and form them into a u like this. Then you plug the ends of it into your empty outlet like that. Then before you turn the power back on, you close your eyes and say please, please, please, work. Then you flip the power switch like this, and, Wa la." Commander Tomas said as the engines came back on line, "that's what you do with a jumper. Now lets just hope it holds up long enough to get us out of here. Because if it doesn't we're gonna have to swim back to the Osdel."

"Well lets just hope it does," Ensign Pertson replied and said as she started to turn the mini divers system's back on, "because that water looks cold and I'm not much of a swimmer, as a matter of fact I cant swim at all."

"Really, how did you manage to get on the Osdel? Being able to swim is a major requirement of her crew."

"I faked it."

"What do you, Woe. What was that? Did you feel that?" Commander Tomas Asked as the serpent creature spun around and swam full force into the entrance of the cave. Causing everything to violently shake,. He then backed up and rammed the cave again.

"That snake. Do you think it's trying to get in?"

"I don't know," Ensign Pertson replied while she feverously pressed some buttons, The holographic sonar won't work. For some reason the image processor decide to burn up."

"So there's no way to tell what it is." Commander Tomas said as he sat down and hooked himself up to the diver's systems, "And without the image processor this thing won't run on auto pilot. You'd better strap yourself in Joyce, I'm gonna have to do the driving. Also radio the Osdel and let them know we're up and running and we'll be back shortly."

"Aye, Commander, I'm already on it."

"Good now lets make this fish swim again."

Grabbing the controls Commander Tomas slowly raised the diver off from the floor of the cave, and as he started to maneuver it forward the serpent creature who'd been ramming head first into the entrance of the cave, turned around. And then with all of his power and strength he charged towards the cave at full speed.

Sensing what was taking place, the brilliant hawk flew faster then before. And as he made his way over the tree tops and out to the ocean the speeding serpent hit the entrance to the cave and ferociously roared while he opened his mouth and smashed through the opening. Biting down he then chewed up the rocks and roared again as he spit them out.

"Commander, did you hear that? I think that thing got in."

"You think," Commander Tomas replied and said as he looked back and saw the serpent barreling towards them, "Yep your right, it did and it's coming after us. Hang on while I try to out run it again."

Quickly turning up the power and pouring on the speed, Commander Tomas with the serpent creature slamming through the cave and hot on there tail, swiftly dodged falling rocks while he skillfully maneuvered the speeding diver through the twist and turns of the narrow cave.

"How ya doing Joyce!"

"Okay Commander, But I'll be a lot better when we clear this cave!"

"Me too," Commander Tomas replied as he squinted and said, "Well it's about to get better for the both of us, I can see a distant light and I bet it's coming from the Osdel!"

"Thank God!" Ensign Pertson yelled as she clutched onto her chair, "the Osdel is near and I can't wait to get out of here! You know Commander before we make it out you should try to kill that thing again."

"My thoughts exactly." Commander Tomas replied as he started dropping mines while he pushed the diver to go faster. "Now we're really moving!" Commander Tomas then yelled as they sped towards the opening while the mines began to blow up behind them. "Whew, this is how you do it! But if we're gonna out run those blast I'm gonna need more power."

"We can't possibly go any faster Commander!"

"Oh yes we can, watch this!"

Flipping a switch Commander Tomas then pushed the diver to it's maximum limit while the brilliant hawk who had began to circle above the water looked down at a large pack of blue, silvery, bottle nose dolphin's and called to them with a loud screech. Hearing his call the dolphins then one by one leapt from the water and majestically soared through the air like skilled figure skaters and answer him with the sound of chattering fish laughter before they softly splashed back into the water.

Quickly lining up like soldiers on a battle field, the dolphins then fell into a circle formation and began to swim at lightning speed. Picking up speed as they swam around and around, the dolphins then quickly relaye, d their sonar clicks to one another while they used them to create a electrified vortex of swirling water, that instantly lit the dark depths of the ocean with a warm, red, hue.

Calling out again, the brilliant hawk then dove head first into the vortex, then with a brilliant flash of blue light he slammed through it with the speed of a fighter jet and Quickly emerged from the bottom as an enormous black colored Diablo fish.

"Hang on Joyce, we're almost there! Just a little bit more!" Commander Tomas yelled as the opening grew closer, "I've got one more mine! I'm gonna drop it at the end and try to seal that thing in!"

"Good thinking!" Ensign Pertson replied as she looked back and saw the serpent barreling it's way through the blast, "Because your obviously not going to kill it!"

"Nope, Not with these things!" Commander Tomas yelled as he dropped the last mine while he accidentally slammed the diver into the side of the cave, "Ouch, That hurt!" Commander Tomas then yelled as the diver spun out of control, "Don't worry Joyce! We're going to get out of this!"

Frantically operating the controls and white knuckling the steering, Commander Tomas desperately tried to regain control of the mini diver but when he realized all of his attempts were futile, He gracefully let go of the steering and yelled, "Brace yourself, The last mine is gonna!"

"Blow!" Ensign Pertson interrupted in a scream as the mine blew up and instantly sent them violently spinning out of the cave. "Oh my god Commander, we're gonna die!"

"Not if I can help it!" Commander Tomas yelled as the serpent slammed through the explosion and came barreling towards them, "I still have a few tricks up my sleeve."

Flipping some switches, the Commander shut the divers engines down, and as he quickly restarted them the gigantic Diablo fish who'd been swimming through the water like a speeding freight train, swiftly moved in and right before the serpent got to the mini diver, the Diablo fish opened it's mouth and swiftly caught the serpent by the neck. But before the Diablo fish could bite down and sink it's large poisonous fangs into the serpents rough and slimy flesh. The serpent managed to shake with such a bruit force that it sent the both of them violently spinning towards the ocean floor. Then just like a bomb hitting it's target, they explosively slammed into the sandy bottom and emerged from their impact crater as two gigantic, glowing, warriors, that now fought in a majestic sword battle of power and strength.

"Mark, did you see that? Something just came out of nowhere and grabbed that big snake."

"No," Commander Tomas replied as he finally regained control of the spinning mini diver, "I didn't see it, but you know what they say. There's always gonna be a bigger fish."

"That's true," Ensign Pertson laughed and said as she felt the divers engines quit again, "Now what! Don't tell me that jumper thing burned up."

"Okay I won't," Commander Tomas replied as he answered a incoming, visual message from the Osdel.

"Mark! What's going on, are you two alright?"

"Yeah we're fine Sir. I take it you saw all of that?"

"Yeah we did, that last explosion blew you straight across our bow. What was that all about?"

"We were being chased by a giant snake Sir."

"Giant snake?"

"Yes Sir, a giant snake."

"Where did it, oh never mind. I'm sure I'll hear all about it when you make your report."

"You sure will Captain."

"Anyways what's your status?"

"Well right now we're a dead stick."

"How about your package, is that secure?"

"All safe and sound Sir."

"Okay then. You two sit tight and we'll come and get you, Flyer Men out. Helm swing us around and take this tub to the divers location. Once we have them and their package onboard set your course for the old St Lawrence sea way. We're going to be making port at station 23 in Oscoda Michigan."

"Aye, Captain."

"Oh and would someone get General Douglas on the horn and let him know we're on our way with the package?"

"Aye, Captain."

Adjusting the submarines controls as the Captain walked off the bridge, the helmsmen then carefully turned the large submarine around, and as he slowly piloted it to the mini diver's location, the serpent creature in hopes of catching the diver before the Osdel got to it, forcibly broke away from the sword fight with the Indian warrior and tried to morph back into the enormous snake. But when he did the giant Indian warrior swiftly swung his mighty sword through the light of the creatures morph and shattered him through the water like broken glass. Then with another swing and the loud clap of thunder, the Indian warrior sent the torn creature screaming back to it's bright white realm of soft, lustrous, satin.

Howling out in victory the giant Indian warrior then raised his sword, and with a flash of yellow light he quickly ascended to the surface while he shrunk back to normal size.

PART XXXII

The Fall of David

"David, are you ready?"

"Almost Beth, I'll be out in a minute."

Struggling to put on a shirt David then fell onto their bed and grunted from the pain that had been burning through his shoulder.

"I heard that, are you alright?"

"Yeah Beth I'm fine." David replied while he finished struggling with his shirt.

"Don't make me come in there!"

"I won't Mommy!"

"Smart ass."

"Thanks Beth," David replied and said as he grabbed his cane while he slowly got up, "I resemble that remark."

Making his way out of the bedroom and through the hall David then said, "okay I'm all set."

"Hey why aren't you using your walker?" Elizabeth sternly asked while David stood and smiled at her.

"I don't like it."

"Yeah and you also don't like to follow Doctors order's either. You know your not supposed to use that cane for a whole nother month. If You!"

"Don't worry," David interrupted, "I'll be fine."

"Yeah sure, I've heard you say that before."

"Really I will be. I promise," David said as he reached out and hugged Elizabeth, "I'll just take it as easy as I possibly can."

"You promise?"

"I promise," David replied as he ran his hands down to Elizabeth's stomach and proceeded to rub it, "Besides if I'm gonna walk her down the isle one of these days I'm gonna have to take it as easy as I possibly can. Because daddy doesn't want to do it from wheelchair."

"Oh your silly," Elizabeth laughed and then asked, "what makes you think it's a girl?"

Bending down and lifting Elizabeth's shirt up, David put his ear to her belly button and said, "Because she told me so, and right now she's saying. Tell mommy it's true, tell her I'm a girl and for my first birthday daddy's gonna build me a doll house."

"Or daddy's gonna have to build himself a big nut house to live in, because we're gonna be twins."

"Really," David asked as he pulled his head back, "did she tell you that?"

"Yeah David, right. And she also said we better stop screwing around because mommy's gonna be late for her eye appointment. Now common Mr. goofy, lets go." Elizabeth said as she pulled her shirt down and helped David stand up straight, "you really want a girl, don't yah?"

"Actually," David replied and said as they made there way out of the house and into the car, "as long as it's healthy I don't care what it is."

"Well I'm glad you feel that way. I was beginning to worry."

"About what?" David asked as Elizabeth maneuvered their car out of the drive way and then headed down the road.

"That you would be disappointed if we had a boy."

"No way not one bit. The only reason I keep saying girl is because in my spare time I've been designing a wooden dollhouse. You know, one with working lights and running water?"

"Mm hmm."

"Well anyways I kind of wanted to build it and give it to our daughter. You know for one of those family heir loom type of things. But now that you've made it clear that we're having twin's. Our girl will get the dollhouse and our boy will get the air bike, or vise verse' a."

"David that's so sweet of you and I adore you for it, but."

"Yeah I know." David interrupted and said, "It's way to early to tell what the sex is gonna be and we shouldn't be making any plans until we know."

"Well I wasn't gonna say it like that. As a matter of fact Mr. lets put words in his wife's mouth, I wasn't gonna say that at all. I was going to say, but if they both end up being boys, your dollhouse will have to be given to some other girl."

"Really, do you have one in mind?"

"Yeah me, I've always wanted one."

"Well I'll have to build two then. One for you and one for her, that's if it's a girl and you learn how to behave."

"Me behave? You're the one that needs to learn how to behave, all ready walking around with a cane. Your lucky you don't get spanked for it. Of course you'd probably like that."

"Not me, no way. I'm to fragile for that kind of thing," David laughed as he flipped the car's radio system off and said, "man I'm already tired of hearing about Montes Jura, I mean. I know it's a tragedy that the city got blown up and all of those people died. But do we have to hear it every ware we go and why does the media have to make such a spectacle out of every single detail, don't they have a life? Or those stupid conspiracy theorist with their stupid idea's of why this or why that. Someone need's to tell them all to shut the you know what up and make em realize, It happened and there's nothing we can do about it. So lets honor our dead and move on but no they."

"Mr. Leviticus," The cars computer generated voice interrupted, "You have an incoming call from Don Mayor. Do you accept or would you like me to take a message?"

"No I'll accept the call."

"Very Well Then."

"David."

"Yeah Don, what's up?"

"The sky, the clouds, the moon, you know all of the usual thing's."

"Okay," David slowly replied and asked while Elizabeth began to boil with anger. "what can I do for you?"

"You can come clean out your office and pick up your last pay stub. Your fired!"

"Fired!" David replied and asked, "for what, is this some kind of joke?"

"Nope! Your fired! I've had enough of you."

"Well, what does Carl have to say about this?"

"Nothing David, he turned the business over to me yesterday and now your out. So good by!"

"Call ended, vehicle one will now stand by."

"What was that all about?" David somberly asked as he looked over at Elizabeth and noticed anger in her posture while she said.

"I knew that creep was gonna pull something like this. I just didn't think he would sink that low."

"So," David said as he stared at Elizabeth while she carefully drove the car into her eye Doctor's parking lot, "do you care to share your clairvoyant view on how you knew this was gonna happen, or do I have to guess?"

"No David you don't have to guess, just let me park the car and calm down for a moment. I feel like my heart is gonna blow out of my chest." *Woe ok deep breaths*, Elizabeth then thought to herself as she scanned the lot for a place to park, *In through the nose out through the mouth. Okay here we are,* "engine off," *look in the mi*rror. *Uh oh, calm down your beet red.* "Okay," Elizabeth then said as she turned and looked David in the eye while he still stared at her with a puzzled look, "I beat him up, he came onto me after Big Jim's funeral, so I beat him up."

"In Jim and Diane's house?"

"Yeah as a matter of fact it all took place in the kitchen."

"Well how did he come onto you Beth, was it the sly approach or was it the grab on and try to take what you can approach?"

"Well, he pressed himself against my butt and gave me a speech on how he could take care of things while you were out of commission. So I guess it was a little bit of both. Then I."

"Beth," David interrupted with a laugh and said, "you should have just cut a fart on him, if he was that close a good loud one probably would have scarred him off."

"David, Stop it. Anyways just to make him think that he was gonna get what he wanted I turned around and pressed my monkey against his groin. Then after I led him on for about two seconds, I decided to beat his ass."

"Really?"

"Yep I sure did. With one swift, slam of my heal I stomped the top of his foot."

"Ouch!"

"Then I rammed my knee so hard into his sack that it sent him crying all the way to the floor."

"Wow!"

"Oh and that wasn't the end of it. He then had the nerve to threaten me. So I turned around, grabbed a dish cloth, slammed it in his face and mocked his threats while I gave him a couple of hard kicks in the gut."

"Why?"

"Shh, I also dumped a glass of cold water over his head and told him to cool off. Now before you say anything, I know I should have told you about this sooner and I'm sorry I got you fired. But I"

"Beth," David laughed and said as he interrupted her, "all I was gonna say is you probably should have let the fart. It would have been easier then kicking his butt."

"Yeah but kicking his sorry ass was a lot more fun."

"I bet it was. You know that guy has had something like that coming to him for a long time."

"So your not mad?"

"No Beth I'm not mad, Don Mayor's a jerk and he's also stupid. I can't work right now any way's, so what is firing me gonna do? Make me lose my birthday or something. I mean I'm getting paid by the architects union so all I have to do is heal and then find a different job." leaning over and kissing Elizabeth David then said, "I'm just glad you didn't take him up on his offer. The two of you wouldn't have made a very good couple."

"You don't think so?" Elizabeth asked as she kissed David back.

"No not at all. Now lets go in," David said as he looked at his watch and opened the car door, "your starting to run late."

"Are you sure you wouldn't rather stay here and make out?"

"Well yeah, I would love to," David replied and said as they got out of the car and made their way across the parking lot. "But first I'd like to know what's wrong with your eye's."

"So maybe later?" Elizabeth asked with a pouty and flirty look.

"Yeah most definitely," David replied and said as they entered the Doctor's office, "just don't beat me the way you beat poor Don."

Pulling a I.D. Card out of her purse Elizabeth then slid it into an automated registry machine and said as holographic nurse appeared and confirmed her appointment, "I'll beat you worse then I beat him if you keep it up."

"You promise."

"David," Elizabeth laughed and said, "go sit down, I'll be back in a minute."

Opening a door while David sat down and scowled at a holographic news broadcast, Elizabeth then went through the door way and closed the door behind her.

Making her way through a hall and into a small room, Elizabeth then dropped her purse to the floor and sat in front of a large optical machine while a holographic Doctor appeared in the room and said.

"Mrs. Leviticus, How are you?"

"I'm fine thanks."

"Good, It say's here that your having problems with blurred vision which is usually accompanied by mild dizzy spells."

"Yes that's correct."

"And your also pregnant."

"Yep I sure am."

"Congratulations, how far along are you?

"About a month, I think."

"Well your symptoms could be due to your pregnancy, but it never hurts to check other systems. Do you have any sinus problems or inner ear problems such as drainage, plugged ear's, stuffy runny nose, congested lungs?"

"Nope."

"Are you taking any medications?"

"Nope."

"Very well then. If you'll lean forward and look into the machines optical viewer we'll get started. The test only takes a few moment's."

"Thanks Doctor."

"You bet." the Holographic Doctor replied as is slowly dissolved.

Leaning forward Elizabeth then looked into the test machines optical sensors and sat real still as it began to flash brilliant colorful hues' into her deep green eye's. Stimulating Elizabeth's senses, the optical machine then sent pulse beams through the cornea of her eye's and slowly dilated both of her pupil's. The machine then sent a image of a summer field of green grass and pink flowers straight into the visual cortex of Elizabeth's brain.

Becoming entranced by the image, Elizabeth's body then filled with warmth as she stared at the green grass and imagined the life that she carried so proudly in her womb, freely toddling through the field of flower's that stood, softly, swaying before her.

Staring deeper, Elizabeth then saw her self running after the child she had been dreaming of.

"Mommy's gonna get cha," the vision of herself said as she scooped the child up into the air and blew on it's belly, "See Mommy got cha, now what cha gonna do," she said as the child filled with laughter from Elizabeth's tickling hand's, "Where's Daddy, you wanna go see what daddy's doing? Yeah I know you do," Elizabeth said while she rubbed her rosy cheek's against the child's soft face, "lets go and see him. Oh look there he is," the vision of her self then said to the child as they approached the warm image of David who happened to be standing under an apple tree.

Then as they made their way to him a large serpent slithered out from the darkness of the trees blossoming branches and started to verbally attack David while Elizabeth jumped back and said, "Woe." as the machine clicked the image off and a voice said.

"Exam over. Thank you for choosing Doctor Lee's automated, optical, diagnostic center. We are processing all of the information from your exam. For your convenience you may call our main frame systems for your results. Or punch *652 Doctor Lee to access them through the world, wide communications network. Thanks again and have a nice day."

Getting up and trying to shake the image of the serpent from her head, Elizabeth rubbed her stomach and said as she grabbed her purse and made her way out of the room, "Well that was easy, now lets go and see daddy for real."

Swinging her purse over her shoulder, Elizabeth then made her way through the hall and into the room where David had been waiting.

"Hey grumpy boy, are you ready to go?"

"Yeah," David replied and said as he grabbed his cane and stood up, "that was fast, I was expecting to be here for at least an hour."

"So was I." Elizabeth replied as the both of them made their way out of the office and to the car.

"Do they know what's wrong?"

"No," Elizabeth replied as they got into the car. "engine on. I have to call them for my results and I bet I can get them before we get home."

"Yeah you probably can," David said as Elizabeth maneuvered the car out of the parking lot and onto the road, "as fast as that exam went the diagnosis is probably gonna be even faster."

"Yeah no kidding grumpy boy."

"Why do you keep calling me grumpy boy."

"Because, ever since you sat down at the Doctor's office you've had a real nasty look on your face."

"Sorry, I just got a little annoyed when I had to watch more of the coverage on the Montes Jura tragedy."

"Yeah I understand. It is getting a little annoying. But you'd better stop frowning, because if you don't your face is gonna freeze that way and you'll never be able to smile again. Well at least that's what my grandmother would have told you. She used to tell me that all the time."

"Yeah," David replied with a laugh and said while Elizabeth gave him a funny look, "I used to have teacher's in school tell me the same thing."

"Vehicle one."

"Yes Elizabeth?"

"Please connect me to Doctor Lee's main frame system and ask them if my test results are in yet."

"Very well"

"Cross you finger's David."

"Oh I 'am."

"Elizabeth"

"Yes Vehicle one?"

"Your test results are in. Would you like to hear them?"

"Yes Please."

"Very well."

"Elizabeth Helen Leviticus. Born November 30th of 2004. Test results from Doctor Lee's Automated Optical diagnostic center. The exam we ran today turned up no abnormalities in your optical or visual cortex. Note, our records show that you are approximately one moth pregnant and the blurred vision followed by acute dizziness is more then likely being brought on by your pregnancy and they should subside within the next few week's. If they don't, we recommend that you contact your regular physician for a follow up. If you would like to hear this message again. Simply say repeat or if your done just hang up. Note, this recording will terminate in five business days. Thank."

"Vehicle one end call."

"Very well. Call ended. Do you require anymore assistance?"

"No thank you."

"Very well then. Vehicle one will now stand by."

"Wow that's great," David said as he smiled, "there's nothing wrong with your eye's and it sounds like your gonna be fine."

"Yeah it did." Elizabeth replied as her vision blurred while she tried to concentrate on the road.

"Beth what's wrong?" David asked as he looked at her and noticed that she was having trouble focusing, "are you alright?"

"Yeah I'm fine David. I just feel a little light headed."

"A little, It looks like your starting to float away."

"Maybe I' am." Elizabeth replied with such a slur that would have made the sloppiest drunk on the planet sound clean and sober. "and maybe," Elizabeth then tried to say as her vision all of a suddenly went black, "you should. Nan nun are you, where are, I can't."

"Beth!" David yelled as he watched her become frighteningly disoriented while she quickly lost control of the car. "are you?"

"No, I. David. I can't."

Oh no, not now. No way, David thought as the car began to veer and spin, "This isn't good." David then said as he swiftly leaned over and held Elizabeth's shaking head with one hand, put the car in low gear with the other, and then grabbed the steering wheel while he yelled, "Engine off."

Spinning off the road in a cloud of blue smoke and slamming sideways through a vacant field of mud, Elizabeth violently convulsed and passed out while David vigorously slowed the car and regained control of it.

"Okay just a little more, we're almost there, Ahh here we go." David then calmly said as the car finally came to a halt at the edge of the field. "Whew! That was close," David said as he took his hands off from the steering wheel and immediately checked Elizabeth's pulse, "ok her heart is still beating and she's still breathing."

"Mr. Leviticus. Are you in need of assistance? Vehicle one's sensors have indicated a sudden lose of control."

"No vehicle one everything's fine."

"Very Well then."

"Nice time to ask, ya piece of junk." David Mumbled as he softly laid Elizabeth's head back before he Painfully slid him self across the seat and out of the car.

Grabbing his cane from the floor board and making his way around to the drivers side of the car, David mocked the car's computer, then lifted the door open and said, "Beth wake up baby girl. I can't lift you to the other side of the car and I need to take you to the hospital."

"Mr. Leviticus, would you like me to call a medical transport?"

"No Vehicle one, Now shut up!"

"Very well."

"Common Baby girl," David then said as he leaned in and rubbed Elizabeth's face, "please wake up."

"David, Where am I?" Elizabeth then softly mumbled while she tried to sit up and open her eye's, "what happened?"

"You passed out and we almost had an accident."

"Really?"

"Oh yeah," David replied and said as he carefully removed Elizabeth's belt harness, "Now you have to do me a favor sweetheart. Try to scoot over. I'm gonna have to take you to the hospital, okay?"

"Okay." Elizabeth wearily replied as she slowly scooted to the other side of the car and passed out again.

"Alright David now how am I gonna do this? She's passed out and I can't drive with my right leg. Oh I know," David then said to himself as he got into the car and shut the door down, "I'll just sit in the middle and drive with my left foot."

Scooting to the center of the car, David then put his right arm around Elizabeth, Grabbed the steering wheel with his left had and said engine on. Then with a hard stomp of his left foot David put the car in gear and slammed the car's electronic accelerator switch while he painful spun the steering wheel and quickly maneuvered the car out of the field and back onto the road, where he with the loud sound of screeching and burning tire's vigorously spun the car into 180 degree turn before speeding off to the nearest hospital.

PART XXXIII

The Meeting Of The Six Stone Tablet's

"Doctor John, Marcy," Lieutenant Davis said and asked as he entered a small sitting room, "Are you ready? General Douglas is waiting and the meeting is about to begin."

"Yeah sure." Doctor John replied while him and Marcy gathered a couple of flash drives together and then immediately followed Lieutenant Davis into another room.

"Doctor John, Marcy. Please have a seat," General Douglas said as the two of them walked into the meeting room and sat at a large table, "Lieutenant if you would please."

"Yes General." Lieutenant Davis replied while he walked across the room and pressed his hand to a wall mounted touch screen.

"Very well," General Douglas then said as Lieutenant Davis removed his hand from the screen while two holographic men appeared and sat down at the table. "Marcy, Doctor John this Jeff Stalenbeck and Tuan Dockerson. They're president Conley's highest advisors. Gentlemen this is Doctor John Scott and his assistant Marcy Green.

"Pleased to meet you." The two men said as they looked around the table.

"Like wise." Doctor John replied while Marcy looked at the men and smiled.

"Doctor John," Tuan Dockerson then said, "the General has informed us that you and Ms Green have fully deciphered the six stone tablets that were brought back from the Mar's pyramid, and they are a schematic for some kind of power supply?"

"Yes That's correct," Doctor John replied and said, "well partially correct. One of the tablets tells us what the power supply is and how it works. It's the other five that show's how to build it. Would you like to see?" Doctor John then asked with a laugh while he pulled a flash drive from his pocket. Pausing and catching a dull stare from the two men, Doctor John then plugged the flash drive into a slot on the table and mumbled, "What am I thinking, of course you'd like to see. Marcy, um if you would please and thank you."

"Sure." Marcy replied while she leaned forward and typed a six digit number into a key pad that laid imbedded in the table before her.

"As you can see," Doctor John then said as he stood up while six vertical images appeared to float over the middle of the table, "the first tablet say's what it is and how it works, and like I said before it's the other five that are the actual blue prints. Or as you would say schematic. So yes they are a blue print to a power supply. A huge one at that and if built it would supply an endless stream of energy to everyone on the face of the planet."

"For how long?" Jeff Stalenbeck asked while everyone in the room stared at the images.

"Well if it doesn't break down and Earth's Em Field never collapses, Hmm I'd say probably until our sun burns out. That's if our species is around that long."

"I Don't understand Doctor?"

"Well the planet's Em field is what power's the Energy fountain."

"Energy fountain?"

"Yeah," Doctor John said as he pointed to a diagram on the first floating tablet, "These post collect some of the Em particle's that a planets core generates and then pushes them through the bottom end of this crystal which amazingly speeds the particles up to the speed of light before it shoots them out of the other end and slams them into another Em filed which is created by fixed super conducting magnets that are placed at the top of the power supply, thus creating an enormous fountain of negatively charged and positively charged electrons that are captured through these prongs as it circulates the electrons around these lower coils, until they are used or sent to a different place. Now," Doctor John said while he motioned to Marcy, "We've created a computer generated model and converted all of the language on the tablets to English and put it all on these files. Which Ms Green is now up loading to you. Um so while you wait for the files to get to your system's lets take a look at the working model. Marcy if you would please?"

"Sure Doctor." Marcy Replied while she leaned forward and pressed more digits on the keypad, which dissolved the image of the tablets and replaced them with a hologram of a working energy fountain, that filled the room with bright, red and blue streams of green flashing light as it appeared over the table.

"That's amazing," Tuan Dockerson blurted while the colorful hue's of the fountain mesmerized his visual senses, "how soon can we build it? Well I mean that's if the President approves."

"I assume as soon as the crystal gets here. Which will be?" Doctor John asked as he looked at General Douglas.

"The Osdel should be here with the crystal in a few hours. But we can't build it anyways Doctor. You said besides the crystal and the magnets that most of it was made from a material that's not available on earth."

"Your right General, I did and that's true, but we compared the molecular compounds that are listed on the second tablet to some usable materials here on earth and we found gold to be the closest match to the materials the species on Mars used to build their fountain."

"So we can use gold to build the parts that we don't have the right material for?" Jeff Stalenbeck asked.

"Yes that's correct," Doctor John replied and said, "that's also listed in the files I had Marcy upload to you."

"Well I'm truly amazed," Stalenbeck then said as he looked around the room and asked Doctor John, "what about the diary devise have you made any head way with that?"

"Yes and no. We got it to upload into our system's and as far as we can tell it's a child doing the talking. But what she's saying is still a mystery."

"Why's that Doctor?"

"Well I don't understand the language. I've never read it or heard it before and I don't think who ever used the diary came from Mars. But thanks to my wonderful assistant to whom I' am so grateful that the military was nice enough to assign to me. We've found a way to decipher the whole thing and we should have all of it fully deciphered in the next day or two.

"Very well," Stalenbeck replied and said, "we'll go over the uploaded files and report everything to the president. Our next move is going to be up to her. General, Ms Green, Doctor John. Keep up the good work and we'll be in touch."

Standing up and turning around, the two holograms of the Presidential advisors then slowly dissolved and disappeared as they walked away from the table.

"Well that was painless." Marcy said while she shut the hologram of the energy fountain down as Doctor John unplugged the flash drive from the table's port."

"Yeah it usually is with those two." General Douglas replied while he got up and moved away from the table.

"So, what do you think the President is gonna say General?" Doctor John asked while he walked over and handed the flash drive to Lieutenant Davis, "do you think she's gonna give the go ahead and have the fountain built?"

"Yeah I think so. with what just happened to Montes Jura, she'd be crazy not to have it built. Lets just hope if she say's yes that another war doesn't start over a shift in energy economics' again. Any way's we'll talk later. Lieutenant follow me and we'll put that flash drive in safe keeping."

"Okay General, as you wish."

"So. Marcy," Doctor John said and asked as he watched the General and the Lieutenant leave the room, "What now, we just sit and wait?"

"No we still have the diary to finish."

"Oh yeah that's right, for some reason I forgot about that thing."

"Wow you must be over worked Doctor. You yourself just got done talking about it."

"Yeah either that or I need a drink." Doctor John replied while Marcy laughed as she gather something's together and said while the two of them left the room.

"I tell you what. When this is over I'll bye the first round. Sound good?"

"Sounds great," Doctor John replied as he stopped at a water fountain and got himself a drink, "ahh but that's gonna have to do for now. What a lovely invention." Doctor John then said as he began to walk behind Marcy.

Following Marcy to their office, Doctor John then jumped in front her and shuffled his feet while he slid the door open and said, "ladies first."

"Why thank you," Marcy replied and said with a flirty smile, "I had no Idea that you could be such a gentlemen."

"I try." Doctor John said as he walked into the room and closed the door behind them.

Making his way to his desk, Doctor John then sat down and said as he flipped his holographic key pad on, "let's see what we have."

Pressing some letter's on the key pad, Doctor John then pulled up a view screen and read some files.

"Marcy. It worked your program put all of the diary's vocabulary into English."

"Really, that's great," Marcy replied and said as she walked over to Doctor John's desk and looked at the screen, "it also looks like it organized everyone of the child's entries into numerical order."

"Yeah I was thinking the same thing," Doctor John replied as he stared at the file numbers and asked, "shale we take a listen?"

"Sure but your gonna have to fill me in when I get back. I really have to use the bathroom."

"Are you sure you don't want me to wait until you get back?"

"No that's okay," Marcy quickly replied as she ran to the office door and opened it, "I'll be right back."

Slamming the door behind her, Marcy fumbled as she tried to pull a small robotic bug from a compartment in her wrist watch, "shoot, come on. Come on. Ah here we go," Marcy then said as she finally got the bug out of her watch and dropped it to the floor, "That fool really thinks I have to use the bathroom."

Hurrying off to the bathroom while the tiny bug crawled under their office door and silently made its way across the floor, Marcy barreled through another door that was marked ladies and made her way into a stall, where she firmly sat on a toilet while the tiny bug quickly hopped up like a jumping flea and fixed it self to the office ceiling.

Leaning back in his chair while Marcy adjusted a small speaker that was fixed in her left earring, Doctor John thought for a moment, *I really should wait for her*. "Nah," he then said as he leaned forward, "She said it was alright for me to listen without her."

"And besides John," Marcy whispered to herself as she sat and listened to the bug's short wave transmission, "there's always play back. Now play the stupid thing you idiotic buffoon."

"Okay," Doctor John then whispered to himself as he pressed his finger to the first file on the view screen and said, "Play audio one."

"Hello, my name is Sarah," a young girl's voice then clambered through the computer's digital audio system, "my father and I traveled to this world through the great gate of the second planet."

"Second planet?" Doctor John snapped as he leaned back and mindfully visualized the girl and her father, "that's Venus."

"He was contracted by the scientist of this world. It seems they found a crystal that they could use to create some sort of new energy and my father just happened to be the only one in the whole solar system brilliant enough to come up with a working plan for it, well at least they thought he was. I didn't want to come here but my father said it would be a great learning experience. Yeah learning experience alright more like a stuck experience. Am I ever going to get to see my true home again? I hope so. Father say's he feels responsible for what went wrong and we have to stay here in Cydonia until he can fix it. I just hope it's soon, because if it's not us and the people of this world are all gonna die within the next year. At least that's what I've heard father say. I don't get it, how can a stupid machine shut the core of a planet down and how does my father think he's gonna fix it before our star blows the atmosphere off from this planet. I keep asking myself because I don't know and I don't think he does either."

"Sarah."

"Yes Pa, pa.?"

"It's time to go honey."

"Okay I'll be out in a minute. If there is anyone listening? You will find a picture of my father and I imbedded at the end of this entry, Sarah out."

Quickly leaning forward and snapping out of his daydream Doctor John said, "Show image please. Oh my goodness," He then said as the picture of a young brunet girl and her brown haired, bearded father appeared on the view screen, "they look just like us."

"What did you think they were gonna look like you stupid idiot?" Marcy whispered to herself as she pulled the speaker earring from her ear while she stood up, "little green men. I don't think so," she then said allowed as she threw the earring into the toilet water and flushed it, "What a moron."

Turning and swinging the stall door open, Marcy then made her way out of the bathroom while Doctor John stared at the image and slowly fell into a trance as he had a deep vision of his mother telling him to let them succeed and how she would see him soon, *Let them succeed and I'll see you soon*, Doctor John thought, *the dream it was real this whole thing is*.

"Hey!" Marcy boasted out as she came bounding back into their office and startled Doctor John out of his trance, "Did I miss anything ?" she then asked as she walked over to a filing cabinet, opened a drawer and started to fumble through it.

"Um, No," Doctor John replied while he quickly shut the computer down behind Marcy's back, "I know you said it was okay to start without you, but I figured I would wait for you anyways."

What a liar, Marcy thought as she shut the drawer while she turned around and put on a fake smile and said, "well that was sweet of you but it's getting late and I don't really feel like listening to the diary right now, so why don't we go and have that drink?"

"Now?

"Yeah now," Marcy replied with a grin as she walked over and sat on Doctor John's desk and said, "everything is technically over, isn't it? I mean the tablet's are done and my program worked. So common we deserve it."

"Yeah I guess your right. Besides I haven't been off from this base in what seems like an eternity."

"So we have a date then?"

"Sure Marcy, why not."

"That's the spirit Doctor."

Sliding off from Doctor John's desk and landing on her feet, Marcy then asked as the bug silently dropped from the ceiling and ran to the back of her foot, "you don't mind if I stop at my place and change my clothes, do yah?"

"No I don't mind," Doctor John replied and said as he stood up, "just let me get my jacket."

Opening the compartment on her wrist watch while Doctor John had his back turned, Marcy replied as the bug ran up the back of her leg and hopped from her lower back to the top of her shoulder, "no problem." Then with a lighting, fast, flying leap, the bug jumped down and softly landed inside of her watch. Putting her right hand over her wrist Marcy then secretively closed the compartment while Doctor John turned around and said as he put his jacket on, "Okay I'm all set. I know it's been unusually warm, but I've heard the weather in this part of Michigan can go from warm to cold in a blink of an eye. So even though I can't stand to ware a coat."

"You decided it would be a good idea to ware one." Marcy interrupted while she grabbed her jacket from the back of a chair and put it on as they began to make their way to the office door.

"Yeah," Doctor John replied and said as he opened the door, "ladies first."

"What a gentle men." Marcy Flirtatiously replied while Doctor John followed her through and said as he closed the door behind them.

"Like I said earlier, I try."

"Well," Marcy replied as they made their way down a hallway and through a security door, "my mother once told me. The only reason a man, or in her own words a pig holds a door open for a lady and acts like a fake gentle men is so he can check out your butt when you walk through and step in front of him. Is that true Doctor, where you eye balling my butt?"

"No, that's not true and no I wasn't," Doctor John replied while they stepped through another security door as they made their way outside, "honestly I was just being polite." Coughing Doctor John then asked, "Did your mother really say that?"

"Yep, she sure did."

"Sounds like you believed her."

"No I didn't believe her, I just wanted to mess with you."

"Well Marcy, you messed well."

"I try," Marcy laughed and said as they walked up to her car and she pressed her right index finger to a print identifier which opened the car doors, "I'm not like my mother. I don't really care if someone looks."

"She must have." Doctor John mumbled while they got into the car and the door's automatically closed.

"Nah, she just liked to be negative towards the opposite sex."

"Why do you think that is?" Doctor John then asked while Marcy pressed her finger to another identification pad which powered up the car.

"Well," Marcy replied as she maneuvered the car out of it's parking spot, "she obviously had some bent up anger towards men and all of her negativity was just a sign of her own insecurity."

"Wow, that's a good analyses miss psychologist. Now what do you think happened to make her that way?" Doctor John asked while Marcy drove up to a security gate and said.

"Hang on. Driver shield open." Holding her thumb to a automated laser print scanner while the gate opened, Marcy then said, "shield closed," as she drove through the gate, "My father left her when I was very young."

"That made her bitter?"

"Yep," Marcy replied as she stopped at a stop sign and then turned as they took off, down the open road, "and later on I followed suit."

"Why, was she abusive or something?"

"No not abusive, she was just an over bearing control freak. No matter how hard my father worked or no matter what he did for her, she was never loving or satisfied. Then after he left it all turned towards me."

"Well that's abusive in itself isn't it?"

"Yeah I guess it is," Marcy somberly replied as she glanced into a mirror and faintly saw the image of the sinisterly, smiling, serpent creature who'd been riding in between the back ground, ever since they left the base, "So anyways," Marcy then said as she smiled and looked back at the road, "enough about me. How about you, do you have any deep family drama?"

"Oh yeah," Doctor John replied with a deep look of concentration on his face, "I sure do, but probably nothing you would care to hear about," Doctor John then said as he looked at Marcy and smiled, "My stories are to long, they'd probably make you fall asleep."

"I doubt it," Marcy replied as she stopped the car at a traffic light and then patiently waited to make a turn, "It takes a lot to bore me. I think somebody just doesn't want to share."

"Maybe." Doctor John said as Marcy maneuvered the car forward and made her turn.

"Well since you don't want to talk about your family. Maybe I can get you to tell me the answer to a question that I've been dying to ask."

"What's that?" Doctor John asked as Marcy maneuvered the car around a corner.

"How did you know where the diary came from and that it was an actual audio diary if you couldn't make out the language?"

"I guessed."

"You guessed?"

"Yep, don't tell the general, but I guessed. I mean the markings on the top obviously said where it came from. You know the ones with the large circle in the middle followed by the four smaller ones?"

"Mhm." Marcy replied as she slowed the car down and then turned into her drive way.

"So after I figured that out I thought it would be safe to assume the rest and wha lah, I was right. And that's a good thing because you know as well as I do if I wouldn't have made what I like to call an educated guess, the government would have never let us work on that thing."

"This is true," Marcy replied as she parked the car and shut it's power down, "and you and I would have never met."

"What's that supposed to mean?"

"Nothing," Marcy slyly replied and asked as she pressed a button that opened both car door's, "are you gonna come in?"

"Sure," Doctor John replied while the serpent creature peered through his colorful aura and secretively dissolved back into it's bright white, realm of soft, lustrous satin as Doctor John got out of the car and looked around while the door closed behind him. "Nice place." Doctor John then said as he followed Marcy to the front door of her pricy looking condo that sat perched along the sandy, golden shore of the mighty, baby blue, lake called Huron.

"Thanks," Marcy replied as they stepped to the porch and she opened the door, 'my grandfather left it to me when he passed."

"How long have you lived here?" Doctor John asked as he followed Marcy in and closed the door behind them.

"About four years," Marcy replied while she flipped on some lights and then made her way down a hall, "I moved in right after college. Luckily for me I bagged a job at the base, because I would have never been able to afford the taxes on this place if I didn't."

"Yeah no kidding," Doctor John whispered to himself as he walked around the condo and looked at extravagant artifacts that where nestled neatly about the room's, "what did your grandfather do?"

"He wrote children's books."

"No kidding, really?" Doctor John asked as Marcy made her way into the room where he stood.

"Yep, he was the famous author of what do I want to be when I grow up and Is the milk ready mom."

"Really, your actually Donald E Swaybuck's granddaughter?"

"Yep that's me, in the flesh," Marcy replied and said as she pointed to a picture on the wall, "and that's him with me on his lap."

"I would have never guessed. You know when I was a kid I could never get enough of his stories. I used to make my mother read them to me at least three times a day…that's until she," Doctor John then said and paused as he abruptly snapped into a flashing daydream of his mother's funeral.

"Until she what?" Marcy asked as Doctor John quickly snapped out of it and shook his head while he said.

"Oh nothing."

"Are you sure?"

"Yeah I'm positive."

"Okay then, I'm gonna go and change. Make yourself at home and I'll be right back."

"Alright." Doctor John replied as Marcy walked away and made her way down a hall and into a room while he stepped to a couch and thought to himself as he sat down and deeply stared at a porcelain statue of an Egyptian god that sat on a table in front of him, *how am I gonna hide what's going to happen if I allow the military to fire that thing up? Think John think.* "Mother is that you?" Doctor John then whispered while a blurred image of his mother said with a faint whisper as it seemed to appear inside of the porcelain statue.

"Let them succeed and I will see you soon."

"Mom I don't know what to do?"

"You will John, you will." The image then repeated as it slowly vanished from Doctor John's mind, "you will."

I hope so, Doctor John thought while Marcy snuck out of the room she was in and tiptoed down the hall as she slowly made her way into the room where Doctor John was sitting.

Being quiet and careful, Marcy then snuck behind the back of Doctor John's head and made her way to a desk where she quietly unzipped her pant's and slowly pulled them and her cotton flowered panties down to her ankles then called as she bent her half naked body over the edge of the desk while she wiggled the bobbling cushions of her rather voluptuous behind, "Oh John, you wanna do some serious celebrating lover boy?"

"Wow," Doctor John boasted with red burning excitement as he quickly turned his head and caught the luscious sight of Marcy's pale behind that bobbled like a bowl of jelly every time she wiggled it, "You really want to celebrate, don't Yah?"

"Mhmm," Marcy purred while Doctor John stood up and immediately tripped over the table as he tried to make his way to Marcy, *ok slow down*, Doctor John then though as he swiftly regained his footing, *you can do this*.

"Is everything okay back there?" Marcy giggled while she kept wiggling her pale wobbling tail.

"Yeah everything's fine," Doctor John replied with a cough as he finally made his way around the table and up to Marcy's bare behind, "this was just a little unexpected," Doctor John then said as his blood pressure began to rise from the close adoring sight of Marcy's smooth brown crevice which immediately filled Doctor John's senses with the lovely, musty aroma of feminine hormones that had began to drip from deep inside of the moist mound of soft woman hood that Doctor John had now began to softly, squeeze with his right hand while he asked, "Do you like that?"

"Oh yeah," Marcy moaned while her soft skin filled with blistering goose bump's, "do you?"

"Absolutely." Doctor John slurred as he all of a suddenly became mesmerized by the chemicals that his brain quickly released from its pulsating testosterone center.

"Good," Marcy then whimpered while Doctor John squeezed her moist mound hard, "cause your really gonna like this."

"What's that?" Doctor John slurred as he ran his hand up the front of Marcy's shirt and pulled her soft, round, medium, hanging, mammary from the silky, slot of her soft, pink, cotton, bra and playfully fondled it while he stopped squeezing her soft, moist, mound and ran the side of his right hand up through the center crease of Marcy's bobbling pale behind where he softy, rubbed her brown puckering rosebud before he firmly held each piece of her soft, bouncy, flesh apart and said, "another surprise?"

"Oh yeah," Marcy passionately moaned and said as she shook with excitement, "and when I hit you with it, it's gonna be unlike any experience you've ever had."

"Oh hit me with your best shot." Doctor John then slurred with emotional drunkenness while he continued to rub and squeeze all of Marcy's now fully exposed female zone's.

"Okay, here you go," Marcy then softly whispered while she slid her arm around and opened the compartment on her wrist watch, "Surprise!"

"What the fuck!" Doctor John yelled as the mechanical bug scrambled onto the desk and swiftly pounced into the air and landed on his neck where it like an attacking black widow, quickly drove it's poisonous, steal fang's into the hard pumping vein of Doctor John's main jugular, While Marcy boasted as she quickly turned around and shoved him.

"Ignorant fool! Did you really think you were gonna have your way with me?"

Looking confused and trying to say, "what's this all about," Doctor John then uncontrollably stumbled backwards, then fell over the back of the couch and slammed through the table head first while Marcy stood naked and laughed before she said.

"Um Duh, what's this all about you moron. It's about me saving the world from your crazy plan."

"What crazy Plan?" Doctor John wearily asked as he rolled through the pieces of the broken table.

"Oh you know what's gonna happen if you let the military build that thing."

"I don't know what your talking about." Doctor John mumbled as he held the back of his head and tried to get up from the floor while Marcy grabbed her clothes and said as she began to put them back on.

"Yeah right and I suppose you never spoke to a man with long blond hair or you never heard what happened to Mars when the people there fired that thing up. Well I spoke to him and I also heard what the girl in the diary had to say and I also know that your not gonna tell the military anything. It's just a shame they got to you before we did."

"You don't understand Marcy, that man or thing or what ever it is, is evil. It doesn't care about us all it cares about is it's ability to manipulate the human race. It's his plan always has been always will be. But I have a way to end it, all of it." Doctor John wearily exclaimed as he mindfully realized that Marcy had something to do with the group of people that tried to abduct him.

"Well there's no since in trying to convince me Doctor, because the strain six venom my little bug injected into your blood stream will soon kill you and I'll be the one to save the world," Marcy calmly explained and said as she turned around and grabbed her bra from the desk and then began to slowly put it back on, "so just shut your pie hole and die."

I've got to get out of this, Doctor John wearily thought as he rolled to his stomach and noticed the statue of the Egyptian god laying within arms reach, *Bingo*!

Quietly reaching out and grabbing the statue through blurred vision, Doctor John staggered to his feet, yelled, "Oh Marcy!" Then like a pitcher in a ball game throwing his fastest fastball, he whipped the statue across the room. And as Marcy turned around with a look of horrific surprise, the statue just like a ball cracking into a batter's swinging bat, slammed into her skull with such force and speed that it immediately sent her tumbling into the desk before she hit the floor and fell into the blackness of cosmic unconsciousness.

"Whew! Now that's how you do it!" Doctor John yelled as he stumbled into the couch while he sloppily made his way to Marcy's limp body and said, "Shake your flatulent smelling, methane ripper and try to have your little bug poison me. What were you thinking when you planned this, did you really think you were gonna pull it off? Not! Well Ms Green in your grand scam to kill me you forgot one important detail," Doctor John said while he stood over Marcy's face and pulled the bug from his neck, "anyone living in the Midwest that was born after world war three had the luxury of having their nervous system inoculated against your useless strain six venom. Oh and guess what?" Doctor John then asked as he squashed the bug in his hand and set it on Marcy's belly button, "I was one of those lucky people. So I guess you can have this back, you know since it didn't work in all. I'll tell you one thing though, you sure succeeded in giving me a heck of a bump on the back of my head. Hey," Doctor John then paused and said while he looked around and began to speak like a drug starved lunatic, "you wouldn't be able to tell me where I could find something cold to put on it would yah? Because it really hurts right now, no. Okay I guess I'm gonna have to find something myself. Don't go away I'll be right back."

Frantically walking around the condo with his left hand on his head, Doctor John quickly found the kitchen and made his way to a refrigerator where he opened the door to the freezer part and said, "what? No ice no frozen food. Well lets look in here," Doctor John then said as he opened the refrigerator part, "Ahh cold beer this will work." Reaching into the refrigerator, Doctor John grabbed a can and held it to the back of his head while he grabbed another one and looked at it and said, "light beer, who drinks this goat urine? Looks like I do," Doctor John then said as he cracked it open, guzzled it down and slammed the empty can to the floor while he belched and yelled, "there's the drink you owe me Marcy! Woe, now I have take a leak," Doctor John mumbled as he all of a suddenly swaye, d from a quick beer buzz. "Hey Marcy! Where's the bathroom? Oh never mind yah stupid bitch I'll find it."

Staggering around the condo with a painful head buzz while he held the cold can of light beer to the back of his head, Doctor John quickly found the bathroom, then flipped on a light switch and proceeded to relieve his throbbing bladder into an already open toilet.

"Ahh! That's better." Doctor John moaned as he ripped a Earth shattering fart before he finished relieving himself. "Now," he then mumbled as he shook his junk off and put it away while he flushed the toilet, "What am I gonna do with you?"

Staggering out of the bathroom and making his way back to Marcy's limp body Doctor John then blurted out in a belch as he stood over her head, "I know, I'll strip the rest of your clothes off and use them to tie your naked butt to the toilet. You know just incase you have to do a dirty when you wake up. Even though by the smell of this room, I think you already did. Anyways, does that sound good to you Marcy? Yeah ok then, but first thing's first. I'm gonna have to borrow your car after I tie you up. You wouldn't want me to have to walk back to the base would ya? No I didn't think so," Doctor John then said as he stepped to the desk and began to fumble through the drawers.

"Ahh, here we go!" Doctor John yelled as he spotted a bottle of quick dry glue in one of the drawers, "This! Will! Do!

Stepping back to Marcy, Doctor John removed the cold can of beer from the back of his head and sat it on the floor while he squatted down and opened the quick dry glue. He then lifted Marcy's left hand and poured the glue over her index finger and said as he waited for the glue to dry, "now what? Oh I know, now that my head feels a little better I'll put that cold can of light goat urine to another use."

Gently laying Marcy's hand down, Doctor John then grabbed the can of beer and cracked it open while he said, "Here's to the universe," he then leaned back and quickly guzzled it down, "ahh that was wet," Doctor John then slurred as he lowered the can from his mouth and wiped his lip's off, "and cold too. Well let's see if we're done."

Tossing the empty can across the room, Doctor John then looked at Marcy's index finger and said, "yep we're all done."

Grabbing Marcy's limp hand and carefully pealing the dried glue from her finger, Doctor John then slurred with heavy drunken eye's while he lifted the dry piece of fake skin to his face and said as he tried to focus on it, "I hope this works. Cause if it doesn't I'm walking back to the base."

Standing up and swaying for a moment, Doctor John then stepped to the desk and did a little drunken dance while he set the fake piece of skin down and said, "Ok Ms Green are you ready? No, well I 'am."

Stepping back to Marcy, Doctor John then staggered around her head as he bent down and slid his arms underneath her arm pits, while he straightened up and drug her half naked, still breathing, limp body through the hall and into the bathroom, where he drunkenly removed what clothes she still had on, before he lifted and propped her naked, pale body onto the open toilet. Then as he used her pant's, bra and her now soiled panties to tightly tie her to the toilet's water tank, Doctor John uncontrollably blurted out in a loud slurry sneer, "You know you and I would have made a great team, but no you had to try and kill. Oh wait a minute. We're all gonna die soon any way's just some of us are gonna go quicker then other's. I think. I don't know and I don't care. Hey maybe if there is some kind of after life I'll see you there. Yaw think you would stop by and say hi. Man I hope not," Doctor John then mumbled as he finished tying Marcy up.

Slurring Doctor John then said, "well there you go, all done. Now if you would excuse me I have a diary to erase and a planet to destroy. So enjoy your front row seat to the end of the world. I'll try not to catch you on the flip flop or see you on the other side. Ok? Ok." Doctor John then said with a smile as he staggered out of the bathroom, "and to prove to you what a nice guy I 'am, because right now your probably thinking to yourself. What a jerk, I'll leave the lights on for you. Alright. But! Only if you let me get a couple more cold, cans of that light goat urine you like to drink. You know so I can toss a couple down while I hit the open road and make my way back to the great global military base. Don't say no because I'll take em anyways," Doctor John then yelled with a laugh as he staggered into the kitchen and grabbed the rest of the beer from the refrigerator, "Otay! Otay," Doctor John then slurred out in baby talk before he gulped down two more cans of beer and then sloppily slurred out in even worse baby tongues as he tossed the empty cans over his shoulder's before he pocketed the rest of the beer.

"Ahh, dat wha gue! Me will have some moe on duh dwive home, Otay? Otay, but why not now? Betause we have to doe home and bowe up pwanet. Yeah you whitc. I fowc gah. Otay wcs doc dcn, mon!"

Staggering out of the kitchen, Doctor John then practically fell to the front door as he made his way across the room and slurred before he passed the desk, "Don't forget finer pwint. What you talk about? Finer pwint dupid you nea it to tart da car. Oh yeah I almost for dot."

Staring at the desk, Doctor John then drunkenly picked up the dried glue, and then with a stupid look of drunken concentration he stumbled and danced in place while he wrapped it around the tip of his right index finger and said as he stumbled and danced harder, "I dot it, I dot it now we can go bye byes. Otay wes doe den. Otay? Otay!" Doctor John then yelled as he fell to the door and managed to open it, "Bye, byes Marcy! You have a gue one. I know I gonna."

Falling through the door way with the handle in hand, Doctor John then yelled, "Wheeew!" as the door loudly slammed behind him while his hand slipped off the handle and gravity caused him to lose his balance and stager through the yard after he nearly fell off the porch.

"Man I messed up! it's a good thing I hardly ever dwink. Ok John get your head together and try to make it to the car, you have a job to do. You sure you don't wanna have another bew first? Maybe after I dit in da car, otay? Otay."

Standing still for a moment, Doctor John then looked around the yard and stumbled to the car where he slurred, "Okay lets see if this is gonna work," slowly pressing his right finger to the car's print identifier, Doctor John then yelled as the door's popped open, "Yea! good it worked."

Falling into the car, Doctor John then pressed the other identifier and slurred, "I'll drink to that," as the car powered up.

He then tried to slam the door shut and said as he realized it would shut on it's own, "oh yeah dat how it works."

Doctor John then pulled a beer out of his inside coat pocket and cracked it open. He then proceeded to quickly gulp it down while the door's clamped shut.

Tossing the empty can to the back seat while he belched, Doctor John then pressed the car's gear selector screen to drive as he belched again and said, "dis is gonna be fun."

Not realizing he had the car in the wrong gear Doctor John then mashed his foot to the accelerator switch and screeched towards the garage while he howled, "woe! Woe!" as he frantically spun the steering wheel and flung the car into the front yard, where he tore through it with a large rooster tail of flying grass and mud, before he ran over the mail box and bounced off the curb while the car skidded into the road with the loud sound of burning tires as he sped off in a cloud of stinking, blue smoke.

"Wow, I thought I had this thing in reverse," Doctor John then slurred loudly as he laughed like a cackling hyena while he recklessly drove back to the military base, "well now dat we under way wes have another bew, otay? Otay. But what we gonna do to dah diary and all da file's? Erase dem dupid. Oh yea that's a gue idea," Doctor John slurred after he guzzled another beer and then tossed the empy can to the floor, "Den what? I duno, we just gonna have to wing it. Sound's like a pwan to me. Good den sut up and dwive. Dat what I doin. Got any moe bew? Yea deers one weft. Well less dwink it. Otay." Doctor John then slobbered and slurred as he pulled the last can of beer out of another pocket and cracked it open before he immediately guzzled it down and said as he threw the empty can to the back seat while he kept driving, "ahh dat was good. Now les just hope we don't get pulled over. Don't worry bout it, you not going to. Just keep duh car on duh woed and don't peed otay. Otay, you wanna here some music? Yeah! Radio on."

"What would you like to hear driver?" The cars automated voice then asked while Doctor John tried to think and then said with a slur.

"A goog metal station, and I wanna here it loud."

"Very well then."

"Hello, this is Demur Blasphemy and your listening to satellite metal 29. You just heard an old song from social waste's first LP called dog shit. You go boy's keep it heavy, I guess, Any way's now that our brains our severely fried I'd like to play you a new single from one of the planet's first, new, up and rising to the top heavy metal band's. Can you guess who they are?"

"City of the ram fire!" Doctor John yelled out and over the rather loud Dj's voice.

"That's right listeners it's the new single from city of the ram fire, and even though it may seem like a bad time to play this. Lets hear it any ways, common and blow up the moon!"

"Yeah!" Doctor John then roared while his ear's tuned into a loud electrified guitar that immediately hammered out a low, aggressive arpeggio when it blasted through the car's audio system, which rapidly shook from the thundering sound of fast pounding base drum's, that nailed Doctor John's chest with every slamming triplet.

"Whew! This is what it's about," Doctor John yelled as the singer's voice finally came screeching in with the bashing sound of a electrified bass guitar, "It's just to bad it's gonna all end soon. Well maybe some other civilization is playing this kind of stuff, yah think? I don't know but it's possible. Very possible." Doctor John yelled while the song blasted into his eardrum's as he drove and bashed the steering wheel with his fist, "If they are I'll never hear it. And I highly doubt I'll hear it in the after life. That's if there is one. Hey we almost deer. Yeah we are. Shh better be quiet otay, otay."

Saying radio off when the song stopped and the Dj started to speak again, Doctor John carefully maneuvered the car around a corner and turned into the main drive of military base. He then slowly crept up to the closed security gate while he slurred, "Driver shield open." and then sloppily held his thumb up to the automated, laser, print scanner which quickly read his thumb print and opened the gate.

Driving through the open gate while he sloppily pulled his hand into the car, Doctor John slurred, "driver shield closed." As he found a parking spot and parked the car.

Laughing Doctor John then slurred while he powered the car down and fell out as he pressed the door open button, "that must have been airplane beer because I have to take another leak. You know drink one p49. Oop's I hope no one saw that," Doctor John then mumbled while he staggered to his feet and instantly fell along side of the car as the door closed, "Cause I'll be in big twouble if someone did. No you all white, now mon wes go in. Otay."

Staggering across the parking lot, Doctor John tried his hardest to act sober while he went through the main entrance and passed through a couple of security door's as he made his way through the hall's and to his office, where he opened the door and slammed it shut as he stumbled to his desk and brought his computer on line, while the serpent creature hid with a look of anguished, disgust and watched Doctor John through the back side of a foggy looking glass that hung on the office wall.

"Okay here we go," Doctor John slurred while he hooked the diary up to the computer and touched some file's that were on the display screen, "Delete all information on the diary down load and send a reversal signal back to the diary, then terminate all hard drive information. Except the tablet file's for main hard drive info while I plug in a new user port. Understood computer?"

"Yes Doctor John, understood. The computer's automated voice replied while Doctor John pulled the computer's user port from it's position and smashed it before he plugged in a new one. "Doctor."

"Yes."

"All transfers and reversal deleting are now complete. The stone tablet file's are now your main hard drive file's. I will now delete all back up one's as well."

"Good," Doctor John replied while he sat down and slobbered as he threw the pieces of the smashed user port into the trash, "I almost for dot about dat. It's a good think you didn't." Doctor John then said while he drunkenly stared at the screen as the computer's automated voice said.

"All task complete. Do you need anything else Doctor?"

"No thank you."

"Very well then."

"Very well then," Doctor John slurred and said while he powered the computer down, "why does every piece of technology with this stupid voice command control always have to say? Very well then. The designers couldn't think of anything else or what?"

"I Guess not," the serpent creature them mumbled while he snapped from the looking glass and said as he appeared in his bright white, realm of soft, lustrous satin, "Oh Johnny boy didn't come through for us, so I guess it's time for plan b. Yes plan b a whole nother world for you and me, oh but I've got one more human to trip up. Yes, yes," the serpent creature then gleefully said as a smooth, romantic, 1930's style, jazz tune began to play through out the room's of his realm, 'Ah the lovely Elizabeth," the creature then said as he danced about, "who has appeared laid out before me all dressed in a white cotton gown with her hair so soft and gold. Will you rise from your warm bed of silvery satin and come dance with me? Oh yes, oh yes," the creature said as she awoke in a trance and began to dance. "Ah that's it my dear won't you please come here, come here and lend me your ear because I've got something to say that you might like to hear. That's it that's right," the creature said as Elizabeth danced to him and he held her tight, "I promise it won't take all night. So lean your head back and hear what I say. Your husband David is gonna stray and oh yes," The creature then said while he dipped Elizabeth and whispered in her ear as she vanished into thin air, "the time is near."

"The time is near," Elizabeth whispered as she blindly woke up in a hospital bed and began to toss and scream while she opened her eyes, "David, David, where are you? Where am I, I can't see anything!"

"Beth, calm down," David said as he stood by Elizabeth's side and grabbed her right hand, "Shh I'm right here, lay back and be still before you hurt yourself and stress the baby out."

"No!" Elizabeth kicked and screamed, "let me out of here! Grandma where are you? I can't see, I can't see!"

"Nurse, I need some help in here!" David yelled as he desperately tried to comfort Elizabeth.

"Mr. Leviticus, your gonna have to move," a lady Doctor then said as she and a team of nurses came rushing into the room and began to hold Elizabeth's now violently convulsing body down to the bed, "Elizabeth can you hear me? Your having a massive panic attack."

"Doctor her heart rate is way to High, she could go into cardiac arrest at any moment."

"Administer a hypo gas sedative into her airway."

"A gas sedative Doctor?"

"Yes Ms Beard a gas sedative. This woman is with child, a regular spray injection could abort the pregnancy."

"Understood." Nurse Beard replied while David stood back and thought as he helplessly watched the team hold his wife down and administer a gas sedative into the lung's of her convulsing body.

"Why is this happening? Everything besides my best friend getting killed was going so good and now this. "Please stay with me," David then whispered as Elizabeth stopped convulsing and her heart rate began to slowly come down, "I don't think I could go on without you."

"Doctor, her pulse is returning to normal."

"Good I think we can let go now," The Doctor replied and said as she turned to David while the team of Nurses let go of Elizabeth and then began to leave the room, "She's heavily sedated now and she'll probably sleep for at least 24 hour's."

"Why did this happen Doctor?"

"We don't know, I can't run any test until she's fully awake and the panic attack's subside."

"Panic attack's, that's the only one she's had."

"Yeah and there could be more."

"More, why?"

"Well when a person wakes up with the loss of one of their major sense's gone, such as the case of your wife's inability to see. The consequences of that and being pregnant can put an enormous amount of stress on the human psyche, which can lead to violent panic attacks."

"Could you give her something when she wakes up? So she doesn't have another one."

"No I wouldn't advise it. The mildest dose of the drug she needs could seriously complicate her pregnancy. So what I'm strongly advising is for you to stay with her and talk to her while she's out. Hopefully that alone will help hold her mind together and this won't happen the next time she wakes up."

"Okay I'll give it a try." David calmly replied as he looked at Elizabeth's soft, sleeping face.

"Good and remember," The Doctor said before she left the room, "don't forget to also take sometime to heal yourself. Because if your unhealthy it's only gonna make matters worse for the three of you."

"The three of us?"

"Yeah, the child within her needs your support as well. So good luck and I'll see you when she wakes up."

"Thanks Doctor."

"You bet."

Taking a deep breath, David then stepped back to Elizabeth's bed side and sighed while he reached over and held her hand, "hey baby girl, it's me David. How yah doin? Yeah I know not to good, but don't dwell on it because thing's are gonna get better and your gonna be a mother soon."

"David," Diane's voice interrupted as she came bounding into the room, "I got here as soon as I could. What happened?"

"Oh it's a long story."

"Yeah I bet, and looks like you've had a long day."

"Oh trust me I have, but hers has been longer and a lot more difficult."

"Well what?" Diane paused and then said, "oh never mind you can tell me later. Right now you should go and take a load off. Go get something to eat, I'll stay with her."

"Are you sure Diane?"

"Yeah David I'm positive."

"Okay, I really appreciate this," David replied and said as he leaned down and kissed Elizabeth's cheek, "Ill be back soon baby girl."

"Eh hem," Diane then grunted while David started to leave the room, "take your cane."

"Oh yeah," David replied while he turned and grabbed his cane, "I almost forgot it."

"Sure you did," Diane said as David walked out of the room While she turned to Elizabeth and said with a smile, "I just don't know what your gonna do with that man."

Leaning over and gently pushing Elizabeth's gold hair away from her warm for head, Diane then said, "he's so stubborn sometimes. Anyways enough about him, you wanna tell me about your day? Or Maybe," Diane said as she held Elizabeth's hand as her lip's twitched into a smile while her mind fell into a deep dream, "you wanna tell me how the baby is doing. I bet she's doing real good."

"Real good." Elizabeth barely mumbled back as her unconscious mind heard Diane's voice while she began to fully dream about the child that laid ever so softly in her womb.

"That's wonderful sweetheart. Now you have to do me a big favor, you have to get well so we can have a big party for you when she arrives. Sound good to you? Yeah I know it does," Diane then said as she began to rub Elizabeth's stomach as she dreamed deeper while, Doctor John finally passed out at his desk and woke up the next day with his head down in a pile of drool.

"Oh I feel terrible," Doctor John mumbled as he sat up and noticed that he had severely pissed himself while he slept, "oh man! This is bad. I knew I should have used the bathroom before I sat down."

"Doctor John," an automated voice called through the office view screen, "you have an incoming call from General Douglas."

"Oh boy this isn't gonna look good. Um power up and put it through to the main viewer."

"Very well."

"General, what can I do for you on this bright and early day?"

"Well Doctor, I have some good news. The President has given the go ahead. She wants the energy fountain built and she also wants you and Ms green to over see it's construction."

"Really General, wow that's great. But there's one problem. Marcy had to leave, she had some kind of emergency. Her mom is sick or something. Can she do that? You know up and leave during a time like this."

"Well she's not military Doctor. She's only on our payroll so I guess she can leave anytime she wants."

"Well who's her supervisor So I can let them know."

"Don't worry about that John, I'll take care of it. You have more important things to do."

"Yeah I guess I do."

"John are you feeling okay?"

"Yeah General, I feel fine."

"Well you don't look fine, as a matter of fact you look like you haven't slept in a while."

"I haven't. I was up most of the night trying to figure out the diary's files."

"Well did you come up with anything?"

"Other then it was a young girl's audio diary, no. To my dismay all of it's data was corrupt and only a few seconds of it's internal hard drive would play. I'm sorry General but given the diary's age and the atmosphere that it sat in for all of those centuries it's really no surprise to me that it didn't work."

"Yeah that's true. Thanks for trying though. I'll let the President and the W.S.A. know what you found. Now that we know it's not some kind of weapon they'll probably want to put it in the Mars museum. In the mean time while you get some well deserved rest, I'll have Lieutenant Davis pick the diary up from your office and put it in safe keeping."

"Well I can do that."

"No I want you well rested. An air chopper is scheduled to fly you and the crystal to southern Nevada tomorrow."

"Southern Nevada?"

"Yep the energy fountain is going to be built inside of the gates of the old area 51 and your team as we speak is being assembled. That's if you want to go Doctor?"

"Well Yeah I wanna go. It'll be an honor."

"Well then god speed and good luck to you. Oh and one more thing, when this is over I would like to by you a beer."

"Um I just recently swore off alcohol General. So how does a soda sound?"

"Sounds good to me." General Douglas laughed and said, "Douglas out."

"Oh my head hurts," Doctor John then mumbled as he stood up and said, "see John that wasn't so bad. As a matter of fact it was to easy. Hmm, now that my little white lie has been told it's time for a shower and a change of clothes."

PART XXXIV

The Fall of David

"David."

"Yeah Beth, I'm here."

"Where am I, What happened?"

"Your at the hospital and you passed out behind the wheel yesterday."

"Really?" Elizabeth wearily asked while she slowly opened her eyes as she tried to focus on David's blurry image.

"Oh Yeah, you sure did."

"Well how did I get here?"

"I drove you."

"You drove me."

"Yes I drove you."

"David you silly ohff, you know your not supposed to be driving."

"I had no choice Beth."

"There's always a choice, you could have called a medical transport."

"Yeah I know, but I thought I could get you here allot faster then they could of."

"Well did you?"

"Yeah Beth I did, I think. What does it matter any way's, I got you here without harming myself or anyone else."

"Yeah I know, I just wanna give you a hard time."

"A hard time. You know young lady," David giggled and said as he leaned down and kissed Elizabeth while he rubbed her stomach, "I don't think your in any kind of position to give me or anyone else a hard time."

"Oh really." Elizabeth softly snickered as David kissed her again and said while a lady Doctor stepped into the room and stood unnoticed.

"Oh really, so you better behave or else."

"Or else what?" Elizabeth asked before they kissed again, "you gonna spank me or something?"

"Only if you want me to."

"Of course I want you to."

"Oh so that's why your being a brat."

"Maybe."

"Well Beth I got some bad news for you. It's gonna have to wait."

"Oh and why's that?"

"Because I think we should get you better first. Don't you?"

"Yeah but that's no fun."

"I know it isn't but."

"Ehm," The lady Doctor interrupted as she slowly stepped to the edge of Elizabeth's bed, "would you two like a few more minutes?"

"No I think we're good." David replied as he stood up straight and smiled while he stepped back and sat on a chair.

"Very well. Mrs. Leviticus I'm Doctor Nichole Alenour. How are you feeling?"

"I'm groggy but functional."

"Good, and how's the eye sight?" Doctor Nichole then asked as she stepped around the bed and looked at a heart monitor while she checked Elizabeth's pulse."

"Very, very blurry."

"Can you describe how blurry, is it like a groggy morning blur or is it like looking at an out of focus photograph?"

"It's neither. Um have you ever looked at bright lights through a kaleidoscope?"

"Em hm. I sure have." Doctor Nichole replied while she finished taking Elizabeth's pulse.

"Well it's more like that. But only without the colors."

"Okay then," Doctor Nichole said and asked as she reached over and turned the lights off, "what do you see now?"

"Darkness, did someone turn the lights off?"

"I can see we can't fool you."

"No you can't."

"Well that's a good thing."

"What's that?" David calmly asked while Doctor Nichole pulled a pen light from her pocket and asked Elizabeth to close her eye's, "That she can make out the difference between night and day, How's that good?"

"Well it's good because it means there's probably no to damage to your wife's visual cortex."

"Oh." David replied while Doctor Nichole turned the pen light on she asked Elizabeth to open her right eye.

Swiftly flashing the light into Elizabeth's open eye while she watched her pupil quickly dilate, Doctor Nichole said, "good. Now close and open the left one. Good, good." Doctor Nichole then said as she watched Elizabeth's left pupil also dilate, "ok if you wanna close your eye's again I'll turn the lights back on."

"Alright," Elizabeth laughed and said in sarcasm, "I'd hate to be blinded by it."

"That's not funny." David snapped while Doctor Nichole put the pen light back in her pocket while she flipped the light's back on.

"Don't get snippy with me Mr. grouchy head," Elizabeth snapped back while she opened her eye's and blankly stared at the ceiling, "I'm just trying to lighten the mood David."

"Nice way to lighten it Beth."

"David would you behave please?"

"I."

"So Mrs. Leviticus, can you."

"Doctor I don't mean to sound rude, but will you call me by my first name please. The whole Mr. Mrs. thing just sounds. I don't know, blah. Like we're in some kind of ancient school room or something."

"Yep!" David blurted out while he interrupted Elizabeth and said as Doctor Nichole almost jumped out of her shoe's, "She definitely feels better!"

Laughing and holding her now pounding chest while Elizabeth laughed as well, Doctor Nichole chuckled, "woe you almost gave me a heart attack."

"Your in the right place for it." David then mumbled.

"I heard that David."

"Heard what Beth?"

"You know what."

"Okay, Elizabeth it is." Doctor Nichole interrupted and said, "now that's all out of the way, tell me what you can remember before you passed out."

"Well I remember everything up until. No wait a minute, I'm trying to think. What happened before I passed out. Oh I know, shortly after we called the eye doctor and I got my results I started having problems seeing again."

"Again?"

"Yeah it's been happening on and off for a couple of weeks and it's usually followed by a quick dizzy spell. But only this time everything phased from light to dark. You know it was like someone was flipping a light switch on and off. Then I woke up here."

"Who did the eye exam?"

"Doctor lee's automated eye examination center."

"Oh yeah I've been there myself. Pretty high tech stuff."

"Yeah no kidding." Elizabeth replied while Doctor Nichole pulled some small ear phones from her coat pocket and put them to her ear's and said as she plugged the end of them into a small digital stethoscope, "I'm gonna have to look over their results."

"They said my eye's were fine."

"Yeah I bet they also said your dizzy spell's were brought on by your pregnancy and they should subside in a week or two."

"That's almost exactly what they said. But in light of everything that's just happened I doubt that's the case."

"Hmm maybe," Doctor Nichole replied and said, "Now with your permission I'd like to take a listen to the little one."

"Oh be my guest." Elizabeth replied while she sat up and pulled her blankets down to her feet and then laid back down as she pulled her hospital gown to the top of her belly button.

Gently placing the digital stethoscope along the top edge of Elizabeth's swollen pubic mound, Doctor Nichole politely said as she began to slowly slide it around Elizabeth's lower abdominal region, "excuse me if my hand's are cold."

"Oh your fine," Elizabeth replied while David tried not to watch.

"What have you been eating, are there any foods that you might be allergic to?" Doctor Nichole then asked while she continued to slid the stethoscope around.

"Nothing out of the ordinary. Just the normal foods. Meats, fruits, pastas and a lot of deserts. Actually I've been making a pig of myself. Ha, Ha, Ha, I got pregnant and I've been filling my face ever since. But as far as having an allergy to certain foods. No, at least none that I'm aware of."

"Good," Doctor Nichole replied as she finished the exam and put the stethoscope back into her coat pocket, "you may cover back up."

Pulling her gown back down and her blankets back over her Body, Elizabeth then said, "whew good," while she shivered, "it's cold in here. David will you raise the head of this bed up please?"

"Sure."

Getting up from his chair while Doctor Nichole grabbed a clipboard and filled out some paper work, David then pressed a button on the edge of the bed and raised the head end up and asked.

"How did the baby sound Doctor?"

"Good," Doctor Nichole replied and said as she finished the paper work and hung it to The end of Elizabeth's bed, "the blood circulation inside of the placenta sounds normal and the heart beats are just a ticking away."

"Heart beats, they're twins?"

"No David they're not twins. What I met by two heart beats and what I should have said is. The baby's heart beat along with Elizabeth's are beating together like two finely tuned base drums."

"Ah, ha, ha, ha, ha," Elizabeth laughed and said, "she got you."

"Hey that wasn't funny, I almost ended up in bed with you."

"Why don't you get in any way's?"

"G Beth don't you know when to quit?"

"Well I'm cold, I thought maybe you could warm me up."

"Here." Doctor Nichole said as she paged the nurse's station.

"Yes."

"Hi Karen. Would you have someone bring a couple of extra blankets to room 213?"

"Right away Doctor."

"Thank you. Ok Elizabeth, I'm gonna take a little bit of your blood. Is that ok?"

"Yeah that's fine, just don't hurt me."

"I won't, I promise. David if you'll excuse me."

"Yeah sure." David replied as he stepped away from the bed and sat down.

Pulling a electronic blood drawing device from her coat pocket, Doctor Nichole then tapped the backside of Elizabeth's forearm with her finger's. She then pressed the end of the devise to Elizabeth's arm while she squeezed it and said, "now hold still."

Softly humming, the device then kicked on and with out piercing Elizabeth's skin, it quickly drew two MLS of her blood into it's see through vile.

"See that didn't hurt a bit, did it?"

"Not at all." Elizabeth replied while Doctor Nichole removed the blood filled vile from the device and then labeled it.

"Here are the blankets you asked for Doctor." A lady Nurse then said as she stepped into the room.

"Thank you," Doctor Nichole replied and said as she patted the end of the bed, "you can set them here."

"Okay, do you need anything else Doctor?"

"Yeah so don't go any ware," Doctor Nichole replied and said as she got a small glass vile from a medicine cabinet, "we need one more thing. Well actually two."

"What's that?" Elizabeth asked while David sat frowning.

"A hair sample," Doctor Nichole replied while she put on a pair of sterilized gloves "that's if you'll consent to a back ground genetic test?"

"Yeah that's fine." Elizabeth said as David immediately sat forward and sternly asked,

"A back ground genetic test, for what?"

"So we can rule out any history of preexisting abnormalities that might have been preventable."

"Like I said. For what?"

"For insurance purposes," Doctor Nichole replied while she pulled a pair of steel tweezers from her shirt pocket, "They usually request it."

"It figures." David mumbled while Doctor Nichole plucked a small piece of hair from Elizabeth's head and said as she dropped it into the vile.

"Alright Elizabeth, One more thing. We're gonna need a urine sample."

"Oh boy," Elizabeth replied as Doctor Nichole capped the vile off and then labeled it while she said.

"All of the sample containers are in the bathroom cabinet. If you need anything Nurse Beard will assist you. Ms Beard when she's done I need you to label the sample, bag it up with these samples, then have them sent to the lab. I'm gonna call down there and order a full screening. Understood?"

"Understood Doctor."

"Elizabeth, David. I'll see you when we get your results, good day, Oh yeah, one more thing," Doctor Nichole said before she walked out of the room, "Mrs. Leviticus prefers to be called Elizabeth."

"Oh okay." Nurse Beard laughed as Doctor Nichole then turned and walked out of the room while, Elizabeth slowly sat up and scooted to the edge of the bed.

"Well are you ready to do this?" Nurse Beard then asked while she stepped to Elizabeth's side.

"As ready as I'll ever be."

"Alright, lets just role your Iv cart out first. Here we go you can use it and my shoulder to help you keep your balance."

"Okay." Elizabeth replied while she slowly stood up and felt around for the IV cart, "Got it." she then said as Nurse Beard stepped to her side.

"Beth your moons hanging out." David then deviously said as Elizabeth began to feel out the floor with the bottoms of her feet.

"Stop it David, your embarrassing me."

"Well it is."

"Oh you just never mind him Ms Elizabeth and don't be embarrassed," Nurse Beard then said as she reached around Elizabeth and tied her open gown shut, "we all gonna have our moon slip out sometime and I know he has too."

"Oh quiet a few times." David laughed.

"There you see and if god didn't want it to slip out once in a while, he probably wouldn't have made em look so good. Ha, ha, ha, ha you know what I'm saying."

"I suppose." Elizabeth giggled as she put her hand on Nurse Beard's shoulder and they along with the Iv cart carefully stepped to small bathroom.

"You doing good."

"Yeah it's not as hard as I thought it would be." Elizabeth replied as Nurse Beard opened the door and they stepped inside.

"Well if you think positive it's only gonna get easier."

"I sure hope so." Elizabeth replied while Nurse Beard got a sample container from a cabinet

"It will you just have to believe it, cause if you don't it won't. Sometimes thing's can only be as hard as we wanna make em. God makes it easy, it's people that make it difficult."

"You know I've always felt that way." Elizabeth replied while she felt her way to the toilet and lifted her gown before she sat down.

"Well you just keep on feeling that way. Don't let this obstacle bring you down, you be you and you let the lord take care of the rest, and while you take care of this business I'll step out side and give you some privacy," Nurse Beard said as she put the sample container in Elizabeth's hand and then stepped out of the room while she said, "just knock on the wall when your done. Yep she's gonna be just fine, you both are gonna do real good." Nurse Beard then passionately exclaimed as she started to softly hum a religious gospel song while David sat across the room and stared eerily into Nurse Beard's deep brown eye's which made him tingle with warm goose bumps as she hummed him into a waking daydream.

"David Tall Tree, Come lets take a walk."

"Where to?"

"Just come," The Indian man in his daydream said, "We have much to do and times running out. You have to complete your journey, so come."

"What journey?" David asked as he abruptly snapped out of the day dream and then saw Elizabeth and Nurse Beard making there way back to the bed, *What's going on*? David then thought to himself, *am I losing it or something*? *Naw I cant be. It's gotta be the stress I'm under*, "Maybe." David then mumbled while he watched Elizabeth get back into bed.

"Here we go. I'll just put these extra blankets on you before I go. That's if you still want them?"

"Oh yeah," Elizabeth replied, I'm freezing."

"Ok, gots to keep you and the baby warm."

Grabbing the extra blankets and unfolding them, Nurse Beard then carefully covered Elizabeth up while she mysteriously stared David in the eye and hummed the gospel song again. only to pause and say, "there Ms Elizabeth. How's that.?"

"Good thank you."

"Alright and your welcome. Is there anything else you need?" Nurse Beard then asked before she started to hum the song again.

"No I'm good, I think I'm gonna sleep for a while."

"Alright then you all take care."

Turning and walking to the bathroom while she kept humming, Nurse Beard then collected Elizabeth's urine sample and labeled it. She then packed it up with the other samples and looked David dead in the eye and said without a sound as she hummed from her mind to his while she grabbed the samples together and walked out of the room, *Toetana knekwa, I'll see you soon kid.*

What Was that all about? David thought as hc shook thc voicc from his head and snottily remarked, "That woman was weird."

"Oh hush David, I thought she was nice."

"Nice doesn't cancel out weird Beth."

"Oh your just saying she's weird because she was humming."

"Yeah that and what she said to me before she left, I mean you did hear it didn't you?"

"David, all I heard was the sound of a lovely gospel song that was being hummed through the lips of a wonderful woman that was only doing her job."

"Man! I really must be losing it. I swear she said something to me in a language that I've never heard."

"Oh David you've been here to long."

"Yeah your right maybe I have."

"So why don't you do your wife and child a big favor."

"What's that, jump out the window?"

"No you fool!"

"Go take a walk or something. Maybe step outside, get a breath of fresh air. You know take your time and pick me up a soda before you come back."

"There's always a catch, isn't there?" David asked as he stood up and stepped to the side of Elizabeth's bed.

"No," Elizabeth replied and said as David leaned over and kissed her warm lips. "I just thought you'd be nice and get us one while your gone."

"Who said I'm gonna go." David Chuckled as he kissed Elizabeth again.

"I did, now you better get moving before you get your butt kicked or I die from thirst."

"Alright," David laughed and said, "But you told the Nurse you were gonna go to sleep and are you sure you can drink anything, you know you do have an Iv stuck in your hand."

"Oh I have the ability to drink."

"I didn't ask you if you did."

"Oh yes you did. You asked are you sure you can? Well yes I can." Elizabeth laughed while David frowned and said.

"Okay Miss grammar teacher. Are you sure you should be consuming carbonated beverages while you have this thing stuck in you?"

"No I'm not Mr. Leviticus. But if you unstick it, I'll let you stick me with something else while I consume the cold, carbonated beverage that I know your gonna get for your blond, blind, sexy, pregnant wife that likes to walk around the room with her wiggling moon sticking out from the back of her ever so soft, white, cottony, hospital gown as she."

"Okay, okay," David laughed and interrupted while he kissed Elizabeth's lips and said, "I'll get you the soda."

"Thank you David, and I love you."

"I love you Too."

"Oh Yeah one more thing," Elizabeth sternly said as David stood up straight while he stopped kissing her, "use your cane when you go."

"Yeah, yeah, yeah," David sarcastically replied while he stepped away from the bed and grabbed his cane as he began to walk out of the room, "I'll see you in a little bit mother."

"You're a brat!"

"Yeah I know." David replied as he stepped into the hall and thought as he made his way to an elevator, *she's the one in bed and I have to use this cane to get around. What's the big deal if I don't I can move just fine without it. Oh she's just looking out for you David. Yeah I know so just to make mama happy I'll use it.*

"That's the spirit." David's inner voice then whispered as he stepped into an elevator and said.

"Level one." while the door closed behind him and he quickly road to the first floor and thought, *fresh air that does sound good. I think I'll step outside before I go and find Beth a soda. Yeah that's what I'll do*, David thought as the elevator slowed and stopped.

Stepping out of the elevator when the doors opened and an automated voice said, "level one," David then made his way through the building and to the main entrance, where he stepped outside and looked up at the blue sky as he slowly moseyed around the side walk before he sat on a bench and gazed even further into the light blue, heavenly sky, which like a majestic portrait of true celestial beauty, hung in his concentrated mood of deep blue, emotional passion of inner frustration while he thought, *what are we gonna do*? *Why is this happening*? *Did I do something wrong*, *did she*? David asked himself while a few fluffy white clouds, hung against the background of late October's crispy, color's of fallen leaves that twitched and glistened with the cool breeze, "I just don't get it."

"Neither do I."

"What?"

"I said neither do I," a long haired man in a wheelchair said as he rolled up while David turned his attention from the sky to him, "You know, this, that. Why me? Why him why us? The Man in the wheelchair then said as he lit up a cigarette and toked on it, "you got that look in your eye kid."

"Pardon me." David replied with a puzzled look.

"You heard me, that look every man gets in his eye's when he looks to the sky and ask why did things that were once so good have to go so wrong. I've looked at the sky and asked the same thing. Ever since my wife was killed and I was crippled in that dispute our government called the rise to world peace."

"You fought in world war three?"

"Yep I sure did, the whole five months it lasted."

"Wow it's an honor to meet you. I've never met anyone that was in that war."

"That's because most of us died," the man replied while he puffed his cigarette and then laughed, "anyways what I'm getting at is, when you look to the sky. Don't ask why, ask how to accept what man kind has dealt you so you can move onto what the universe will give you. Because this little small spec of sand that we call life can drag us into perpetual madness if we let it. And if, I say if there's some kind of divine creature that forged the cosmos into existence then let him take care of it."

"Take care of what?"

"The madness your feeling. Because if you don't, It will drive it's way into your soul in ways that you could have never fathomed."

"I'll try and keep that in mind." David mumbled while he stood up and the man in the wheelchair quickly grabbed him by the forearm and said with a cackling mad laugh while David's eye's opened wide as his heart began to thump with the rush of adrenaline.

"Your gonna make it kid, trust me your gonna make it."

"What, are you mad?" David then sternly asked as he shook his arm away from the man's strong grip while he quickly took off and made his way back to the hospital's main entrance and the man then yelled and laughed.

"Think about me when you get there."

What's with all of the weirdo's today, David then thought as he stopped walking and looked around the hospital lobby, *does someone know something I don't? Was that man my? No way I never knew him, how could? Ok David get your head together Beth needs you. Okay lets go. Wait you forgetting something. What, what am I forgetting? Oh man this isn't good! Oh I know a soda, Beth wants a soda. Vending machine or cafeteria? Wait a minute this place has a fast food joint in it, Beth likes a lot of ice. I'll get her a fountain soda and me a cup of water.*

Slowing his thoughts and his pounding heart rate down, David then made his way across the lobby and into a food service center where he ordered Elizabeth's soda with extra ice and himself a cup of water, which he stood and drank before he made his way back to Elizabeth's room.

"Ah that was good, ok lets go." David then said to himself as he crumbled the empty water cup while he dropped it into a recycle container as he walked back to the main elevators, where he stepped through open doors and said, "Level six," as they closed behind him.

Who was that guy? He seemed so familiar like I met him before. Hmm maybe I have? Your losing it David. Perhaps but I still say I knew him from somewhere. Maybe he was? Naw he couldn't have been. But it's possible. Anyways lets try and think about something else, David then thought as the elevator slowed and stopped while an automated voice said

"level six." as the doors opened and David stepped into the hallway, only to be stopped by Doctor Irvan before he made his way to Elizabeth's room.

"David Leviticus, what brings you here?"

"My wife had a little mishap and the hospital is running some test."

"Well I hope everything's okay."

"Yeah me too."

"Speaking of okay, How's the hip and shoulder doing? I couldn't help but notice your already using a cane."

"Well besides a little stiffness, they actually feel pretty good."

"Good I'm glad to hear it, but you do know you're supposed to be walking with a walker for the first month or so?"

"Yeah that's what everyone keeps telling me, and I know there's probably a good reason why, but I just couldn't get the hang of that stupid walker."

"Well I guess if you take it easy there shouldn't be any problem."

"Oh trust me Doctor I've been taking it as easy as I possibly can, I think. Anyways why are you here, don't you work at the hospital across town?"

"Yeah normally I do but one of my patients got transferred to this facility and I was close by so I thought I should, Yeah you know, stop by and see how she's doing and stuff."

"Oh Doctor Irvan you ol softy you."

"Yeah well you know, what can I say she's kind of cute."

"Doctor Irvan shame on you."

"Well yeah you know, what cha gonna do tell my mother?"

"Ah ha, ha, ha, ha, ha," David replied with a laugh and said, "speaking of mothers I better get back to my wife."

"Shame on me, shame on you David."

"Um no not that kind of a mother," David laughed and said, "my wife's pregnant so I call her mom, mother or ma ma."

"Well as long as it's not the big mother you know what," Doctor Irvan replied as he patted David on the shoulder while they shook hands and David laughed and said as they broke away from their hand shake.

"Oh no. not that one, no way. Never. You take care."

"You too and I'll see you in three weeks for your first check up."

"You bet."

Man what a character, David thought as Doctor Irvan walked away while he made his way to Elizabeth's room, where she peacefully laid and waited for the arrival of her undoubtedly loving, devoted husband, who then stepped to her beside and kissed here on the forehead and said while he handed her, her soda, “here you go.”

“Thanks David.”

“Your welcome.”

“This is gonna be so good.”

Lifting the straw to her mouth and sucking out a large portion of the cold soda, Elizabeth then let out a long thunderous belch as she pulled the straw from her mouth and said while David laughed.

“Ahh! Now that hit the spot.”

“G Beth I guess. You think you could bring that up again so we could vote on it?”

“Sure,” Elizabeth replied before she slurped the rest of the soda down and belched a belch that was twice as long and loud as the first one, “Ahh. How was that?”

“Good,” David laughed and said, “real good, but I think you probably woke the morgue.”

“You think.” Elizabeth laughed while Doctor Nichole came walking into the room and clapped her hands as she said.

“Bravo Elizabeth bravo. The lady in the room below you, Mrs. Kliene, well she’s been in a coma for about three months. But now thanks to you and your one woman band of stomach reverberation, she’s gonna make a speedy recovery.”

“Oh your joking.” Elizabeth said as she handed David the empty soda container.

“Oh no I’m not Joking, as soon as your burp came crashing through the ceiling and into her room like pounding thunder. She woke up and became fully alert.”

“Wow! Beth you should be proud of that.”

“David I highly doubt my burp had anything to do with her recovery.”

“Well you never know.” David replied as he set the empty container onto a night stand.

Reading over an electronic filer that she brought with her, Doctor Nichole then said, “Yeah Elizabeth you never know. I’ve seen stranger thing's happen. Especially when a person consumes a liquid while they're hooked to an Iv."

"See Beth, I told you."

"Hush David, I'll be fine."

"Yeah you will be fine and so will the baby, but I wouldn't recommend that you do it again. You could over hydrate yourself which wouldn't do much to you, but it could seriously injure the little one."

"Really Doctor, how's that? David asked, "would it be like drowning in alcohol or something?"

"Yeah something like that. But don't worry about it because we're gonna take her off the Iv, as a matter of fact I'll do that right now."

Stepping to the side of the bed, Doctor Nichole then grabbed Elizabeth's left hand and said, "Unless you wanna stay hooked to it?"

"No that's okay."

"Some how I knew you were gonna say that."

Carefully removing the Iv cord from the top of Elizabeth's hand, Doctor Nichole then removed the IV's flow needle from her main blood vein and quickly covered the puncture wound with a band aid, "Okay there you go." Doctor Nichole then said as she stepped away from the bed and tossed the used needle tube into a biohazard container, "all done. Now we can discuss our next move."

"Our next move?" Elizabeth asked while David began to look worried.

"Yes our next move," Doctor Nichole said as she stepped to the foot end of the bed, "all of the test we ran came back negative. Well all but one."

"Which one?" David asked while Elizabeth laid back and listened.

"The back ground genetic test that we ran on the sample of hair we took turned up some abnormalities."

"What kind of abnormalities?"

"Well the information on the deoxyribo nuclea showed a significant higher level of nucleo cytoplasm which means Elizabeth could have a tumor somewhere and it's more then likely located along her visual path way. But in order to know for sure we would like to run what is called and F.L.S. scan."

"An FLS?" Elizabeth said, "sound's easy."

"It is," Doctor Nichole replied and said, "It's a machine that allows us to look at and into every colorful laye, r of the human anatomy and the easy part is, all you have to do is stand inside the machine while we watch and look into you from a view screen in another room."

"Alright Doctor, there has to be a hard part."

"There is but not really."

"Well what?"

"You'll have to stand inside of the machine naked and you're not allowed to eat at least five hours before the test or two hours afterwards."

"Hm. Standing inside of a machine naked isn't a big deal. As long as my husband gets to watch."

"I'm sure we can arrange that." Doctor Nichole replied as she smiled and giggled.

"But waiting five hours to eat is gonna be hard because I'm starving now."

"Well would you prefer to eat and then wait to take the test five hours from now or would you like us to run it a.s.a.p. so you can eat in two?"

"A.s.a.p. ." Elizabeth replied while Doctor Nichole grabbed the electronic file keeper and said, "good, a Nurse will come and fetch you when we're ready and until then drink a little water it'll help you not feel so hungry."

"Okay thanks Doctor."

"You bet and I'll see you two in a little bit."

"A full laye, r scan," David then said allowed, "why didn't they just do that in the first place? It would have saved a lot of time."

"Oh hush," Elizabeth replied and said, "you don't have anything better to do. And how did you know what F.L.S. stood for?"

"I saw it on one of those late night medical shows that you like to watch."

"Really, you actually watched one?"

"No not really. I just stopped channel surfing when I saw a nude woman climb into a scanning machine. The machine looked interesting so I sat and watched the show for a while, but as soon as they stopped showing the machine I went back to channel surfing."

"Yeah you went back to channel surfing when you realized you weren't gonna see anymore t.p&a."

"Oh common," David replied while Elizabeth laughed, "That's not fair, it really is an interesting machine and besides," David said as he stood up and stepped to Elizabet's bed side, You know I only have eyes for you."

"Even though I'm lying half blind and pregnant in a rather musty smelling hospital bed?"

"Yes," David replied as his deep dark eye's passionately stared into Elizabeth's unfocused, emerald green, look of desperate concern, "Even though your lying here in the shape your in, I only have eyes for you and I love you the same way as yesterday and if things get worse, I know in my heart I would love you more tomorrow. Even if the day brings us more sorrow."

"That's so sweet David."

"Well it's true. I didn't fall in love with you and decide to get married just to fall out when thing's get tough. I love you for what and who you are and right now if this is you, well I love that too."

"You mean it?"

"Oh yeah," David replied as he leaned down and feverously French kissed Elizabeth, "I really mean it."

"I'm so scared David. What are we gonna do if I have a tumor somewhere in my head, I'm probably gonna die aint I?"

"Oh no, your not gonna die. You're too tough for that. Nope your gonna pull through this and the three of us are gonna live a full and productive life."

"You think?"

"Oh Yeah I know," David replied as he kissed Elizabeth again and said, "just hold on tight this ride will end sometime."

"Yeah I know. All rides do come to an end but this one feels like it's gonna be a long one. Perhaps the longest one I've ever been on."

"Perhaps," David replied and said as he kept staring into Elizabeth's unfocused eye's, "But on this ride your gonna have me on your side and even if it doesn't feel like it. I'll be here riding with you."

"Till the end David?"

"Yes Beth, all the way to the end and probably beyond."

"How far beyond?"

"Infinity," David replied as he kissed Elizabeth again and asked, "you know what infinity is don't yah?"

"Duh yes David, I know what infinity is."

"Good then you know we'll be together forever."

"I sure hope so," Elizabeth replied with a shiney, bright white smile, "because I'd be lost without you."

"And I without you, my blond haired, green eyed, girl, who's stomach is growling so loud that it can probably be heard all the way across town. Man that's loud. Are you sure your gonna make it until your test?"

"Yeah I'll make it, well as long as you get me a glass of water."

"Coming right up."

Stepping away from Elizabeth's bedside, David then made his way across the room and into the bathroom where he got a cardboard cup from a cabinet and then filled it with tap water. He then returned to Elizabeth's bed side and said, "Here you go."

"Thank you."

Reaching for the cup while David held it to her hand, Elizabeth then grabbed it as David began to think about the man in the wheelchair, *who was he? man this is going to drive me nuts. Why can't I,* "Place him?"

"Place Who?" Elizabeth asked after she finished her water.

"Oh this weirdo I had a run in with earlier."

"Well tell me about him."

"He was older, like in his mid forty's. he had long grey hair and he was in a wheelchair."

"So why was he a weirdo?"

"Well when I was sitting outside and thinking to myself, he rolled up out of no where and just started talking to me."

"That doesn't make someone a weirdo David."

"Yeah I know it doesn't but when you get up to leave and that someone grabs you by the arm and starts spouting off crazy thing's like, your gonna make it kid. I Have a feeling about you. Well that makes someone a weirdo."

"That really happened?"

"Oh yeah, right out front."

"That's creepy."

"Tell me about it. But you wanna know what's even creepier?"

"What's that?"

"I knew that man from somewhere, I just couldn't. Wait a minute," David said as he looked up and closed his eyes, "That's it, that's him. That's the guy."

"Who?"

"The man that found me wandering," David replied as he opened his eye's and asked, "Remember how I told you I have no memory of my parent's and the earliest childhood memory I have is the one of myself wondering lost and scared through a wheat field at the age of three or four?"

"Yeah"

"And when I finally made it to the road a local farmer found me sitting in a ditch covered in mud and crying?"

"Yeah"

"Well that man was the man in the wheelchair."

"Are you sure David?"

"Oh yeah I'm positive. Because when he picked me up and put me into his truck, he calmed me down and said, shh don't worry kid your gonna make it. I have a feeling about you. Wow I wonder if he somehow knew that the child he saved was me?"

"That's amazing. Do you remember what happened after he put you into his truck?"

"No not really it's all to fuzzy. I do know this though, for some reason I wasn't scared anymore."

"Well if you run into him again you can ask him if he was the man that saved you and if he was you can thank him."

"Maybe," David replied and said as a Nurse rolled a wheelchair into the room, "But that will have to wait because it look's like your ride is here."

"Mrs Leviticus, I'm Nurse Drake. I'll be taking you down to the F.L.S. room. Do you need anything or have any questions before we go?"

"Yeah will you get me a house coat or something? I don't wanna be drug though this place in just a gown."

"Sure thing, I'll be right back."

"My luck my monkey would fall out this time and no one would tell me."

"Ah ha ha ha ha," David laughed and said, "you're funny Beth."

"Well it's true."

"No it's not I would tell you, well after I stared at it for a while. A long while actually."

"Yeah and by the time you would have said something, everyone here including there old perverted uncle bill would have gotten a sneak peak of my bush."

"Naw I wouldn't have let it gone that far," David replied with a laugh, "it probably would have scared everyone away anyways."

"G thank's," Elizabeth giggled as David tried to stop laughing and say.

"I was just kidding Beth."

"Sure you were." Elizabeth replied with a laugh and said as the both of them began to hysterically laugh, "look at my stomach, it obviously never scared you away."

"Naw just in." David then said with a laugh as the Nurse walked back into the room and gave them a strange look before he said.

"Okay Mrs. Leviticus I have a house coat for you. Would you like some help putting it on?"

"No I think I can managc, just sct it on thc closcst night stand plcasc."

"As you wish." Nurse Drake replied while Elizabeth flung her blanket's off and said as she slid to the edge of the bed and held her hand out.

"Better yet, I'll take it right here."

"Alright." Nurse Drake said as he stepped around and put the house coat in Elizabeth's hand.

Slowly standing up and balancing the back of her leg's against the bed while David watched, Nurse Drake stepped away and readied the wheelchair as Elizabeth carefully put the house coat on and slowly tied the front of it shut and said, "Wah Lah, Now if you'll roll the chair over here, I'll plop my butt in it and we can shove off."

"As you wish." Nurse Drake replied as he rolled the wheelchair up to the front of Elizabeth's knees.

Feeling her way onto the chair, Elizabeth then slowly turned around and sat down while David watched Nurse Drake firmly hold the chair in place.

"Beth your gonna have to put your feet on the foot rest."

"Yes David I know, I was getting to that. I have to find them first, ah and here they are. Am I covered good, I don't have any private parts hanging out do I?"

"Nope," Nurse Drake replied and said as he rolled Elizabeth away from the bed, "you're all covered up."

"For now," Elizabeth then mumbled, "I was told I have to stand inside of the machine naked."

"You do but don't worry the Doctor's are the only ones that'll be able see you."

"Good." Elizabeth sighed as they began to make their way out of the room while David followed and said.

"Don't sound so disappointed Beth."

"I'm not."

"It sure sounds like you are."

"Well I'm not and by the way Mr. Do you have your cane?"

"I was."

"Oh yeah that's right," Nurse Drake interrupted and said as he stopped rolling the wheelchair, "I knew I forgot something. On my way in today I ran into a Doctor Irvan and he told me if I saw you that I should remind you to use your cane."

"Is this some kind of joke!" David replied as he grabbed his cane and said, "you really ran into Doctor Irvan and he said that?"

"Yeah he sure did." Nurse Drake said as the three of them made their way out of the room and into the hall, where they strolled to an elevator.

"See David, someone's trying to look out for you."

"Yeah right Beth, a Doctor looking out for someone, that'll be the day. That is weird though, I did just recently run into him."

"Really, when?"

"When I came back with your soda. I stepped out of the elevator and there he was."

"Well you should be glad you have a Doctor that's that concerned with one of his patients. Now days that's a hard thing to come by."

"That's true," Nurse Drake said as they stepped into an elevator and the door then closed behind them, "level three."

"I guess, but I still don't get why everyone is on my back about the cane. I really don't think I need it. I didn't need the walker."

"Yeah," Elizabeth said, "and as soon as you fall and re injure your hip from not using your cane your gonna go. Oh I should have listened to everyone and used the stupid cane until the Doctor told me I didn't have to."

"Maybe," David replied as the elevator slowed then stopped, "But I doubt I'm gonna fall and re-injure it."

"Okay confident boy." Elizabeth snickered as an automated voice said,

"Level three." and the elevator doors opened.

"If you say so."

"I know so." David said as they stepped out of the elevator and made their way down a hall and into a small room.

"David come hear and let me pop that big head of yours."

"Nope I'll pass on that Beth. I think I'm gonna need it." David replied and then looked at a tall silver cylinder while Doctor Nichole stepped into the room with another Doctor and said.

"Elizabeth, David. This is Doctor Harold Hechow."

“Pleased to meet you.” David replied as he reached out and shook Doctor Hechows’ hand.

“Like wise.”

“He will be assisting me with Elizabeth’s test. So Elizabeth if your ready we’ll get started. Nurse.”

“Yes?”

“Your excused. I’ll page you if I need anything.”

“Alright then, good day Doctor.”

“You Too. Elizabeth after David finishes helping you undress all you have to do is step inside the cylinder, don’t worry about closing the door it’ll shut by itself. Once it closes the machine will start automatically. You’ll feel some heat and a little bit of tingling, if it gets to bad for you just let us know and we’ll abort the test.’

“I’ll be able to communicate with you?” Elizabeth interrupted.

“Oh Yeah, we’ll be able to hear everything and you’ll be able to hear us as well. David if you’d like, you may stay in here, wait outside or step into the observation room with us.”

“I think I’ll step into the observation room with you guy’s. It’s not everyday one gets to see the inner workings of their spouse, if you know what I mean.”

“Oh Yeah I sure do. Now you’ll finally be able to see what makes her tick.”

“Very funny.” Elizabeth remarked while David Laughed and Doctor Nichole locked the wheelchair’s wheels into place and said as she pointed to a door.

“We’ll be in there.”

“Okay.” David replied as Doctor Nochole and Doctor Hechow then made their way into the observation room, where they closed the door and prepared the F.L.S. for its scan of Elizabeths body.

“Alright Beth, are you ready to do this?”

“As ready as I’ll ever be.” Elizabeth replied as she stood up and leaned against David.

“You know Beth if circumstances were different, this could turn out to be a lot of fun.”

"No kidding," Elizabeth replied while David began to remove her house coat, "but unfortunately there not, so if you can't handle it close your eyes."

"Oh no, no way," David said as he laid Elizabeth's house coat over the back of the wheelchair before he untied and removed her gown, "if I did that I wouldn't be able to see your beautiful birthday suit."

"Please David, it's not like you've never seen it before." Elizabeth replied as David then laid her gown over the back of the wheel chair and said.

"Yeah I know I have but there's nothing like seeing it again and again and again and again."

"Okay David. I get your point." Elizabeth interrupted while she kicked her sox's off and shivered with hard tingling goose bumps as David picked them up and laid them in the wheelchair, "man it's freezing in here. Why are hospitals always so cold?"

"I have no idea," David replied and said as he began to feverously rub the sides of Elizabeth's arms with the palm's of his strong hands, "come on it should be warmer inside of the cylinder."

"I hope so," Elizabeth said as David stopped rubbing her and hung his cane over his shoulder, "I'd hate to catch pneumonia as well."

"Yeah that wouldn't be good." David replied while Elizabeth balanced her self against his body and they made their way across the room and into the cylinder, where David kissed her cheek as he put his cane in her hand and said, "use this, it'll help you keep your balance. Okay baby girl?"

"Okay," Elizabeth replied and said with a soft smile, "I love you."

"I love you too," David said as he kissed Elizabeth, "good luck and I'll see you soon."

"Thanks David."

"Your welcome."

Stepping out of the cylinder and watching Elizabeth carefully balance herself as the cylinder door's slowly closed her inside and hid her from David's look of loving concern, Elizabeth while David then turned away and made his way to the observation room, patently stood in the shivery darkness of the cold, closed cylinder and calmly waited for the test to start.

"Elizabeth."

"Yes?"

"How are you doing?" Doctor Nichole asked as David stepped into the room and sat down.

"Fine, but it's freezing in here."

"Alright well just hang on tight. It'll warm up when the f.l.s. sensor's kick on."

"I sure hope so."

"Trust me it will and once they do we're gonna need you to stand as still as you possibly can. Alright?"

"Alright I'll try."

"And if you at any moment start to feel dizzy or get to hot you let us know okay."

"Okay." Elizabeth replied as the cylinder started to hum with the sound of fast moving electrons, which quickly built up power and picked up lightning speed while they swiftly, swirled around the cylinder and filled the inside with warm, colorful light.

Then when the machine reached full power it's thousands of tiny serigraphic sensors kicked on and silently clicked as they passed low frequency dolphin echoes through Elizabeth's soft feminine skin.

"Woe, that felt weird."

"Is everything okay Elizabeth?"

"Yeah Doctor everything's fine. My ear's just popped is all. Is that normal?"

"Yes," Doctor Nichole replied and said as a wide, wall mounted view screen powered up and displaye, d a real time three d image of Elizabeth, "It's perfectly normal."

"So my brains not gonna explode or anything is it?"

"No your brains not gonna explode. Your ear's popped because the barometric pressure inside of the cylinder slightly rises when the f.l.s. sensors come on line."

"Oh, okay."

"Doctor Hechow, if your ready we can begin."

"Yes okay. Computer please scan skin laye, r one and note any abnormalities."

"One moment." the computers automated voice replied then said while the realtime image of Elizabeth spun from front to back and top to bottom, "Commencing scan of skin laye, r one."

"That's amazing." David muttered as he sat and stared at Elizabeth's spinning image.

"Yeah it is." Doctor Nichole replied as the automated voice said.

"Scan complete Doctor Hechow, no abnormalities detected."

"Alright remove skin laye, r one and scan muscular laye, r two."

"Very well. Commencing scan of muscular laye, r two."

"Woe," that's wild looking," David then blurted out as him and the Doctor's watched the computer digitally remove Elizabeth's skin and display a Three D Image of her muscular system while it ran it's scan, "I really will get to see what makes her tick."

"Elizabeth."

"Yes Doctor?"

"How are you doing, is it still cold in there?"

"No it's actually quite warm now."

"Good, I'll take it your okay then?"

"Yeah I'm fine."

"Excellent." Doctor Nichole replied while the computer completed its scan and Doctor Hechow said.

"Now remove muscular laye, r two and combine circulatory laye, r three with endocrine laye, r four. Run scan and note all abnormalities."

"Very well, now removing muscular laye, r two and combining circulatory three with endocrine four. Commencing scan."

"Doctor Nichole."

"Yes Elizabeth?"

"My legs are starting to feel a little tingly."

"Can you describe tingly.?"

"Yeah it feels like there falling asleep."

"Okay just hang on, after the computer finishes its scan we'll have you move around before we run the last one."

"Alright sounds good." Elizabeth replied.

Sitting in silence while the computer finished its scan, David then gazzed at the amazing sight of his wife's internal organs which were all pumping and pulsating to the mystical, rhythmic timing of the known universe and thought, *that is truly amazing*.

"Okay Elizabeth feel free to move around, take your time and let us know when you're done. Alright?"

"Okay," Elizabeth replied as she moved around and shook the tingling stiffness from her legs, "Alright I'm good now."

"Are you sure?"

"Yeah, now that I can feel my legs I'm good."

"Okay then, hold on tight and we'll be done in a few."

I hope so, Elizabeth thought as she stood in place while Doctor Nichole said.

"Computer scan lower abdominal pubic region and magnify the internal structure of subjects uterus to the fifth power and note any abnormalities."

"Very well. Commencing scan of lower abdominal pubic region and magnifying the internal structure of subjects uterus."

"Um Doctor Nichole. If you don't mind me asking, why are you running a internal uterus scan?"

"Because Doctor Hehcow, I think it would be wise to check on the little one, especially since it's now a working part of Elizabeth's primary systems. Don't you think?"

"Good point." Doctor Hechow replied as the computer finished the scan and said.

"Uterus scan complete Doctor Nichole. No abnormalities detected."

"Good lock on and hold position."

"Very well, locking on and holding position."

"Now magnify fifth power to the third and increase by one."

"Very well, magnifying fifth power to the third and increasing by one."

"Now focus on the fetus please."

"Don't you mean fetuses? It looks like there's two."

"You know what Doctor Hechow? You're right." Doctor Nichole replied as the image of two tiny babies that floated inside of Elizabeth's warm, nurturing womb of loving, embryonic, genetic perfection became crystal clear.

"Um so," David blurted out and said as he leaned forward and stared at the real time image of his two offspring, that laid nestled before his eyes of fatherly love, "you really wasn't kidding when you said there was two heartbeats where yah?"

"Actually I wasn't sure. So if I made it sound like a joke I'm sorry."

"That's alright."

"Now if you'd like to continue?"

"Oh be my guest Doctor."

"Very well then, computer create a snapshot of the twins and add it to subjects file."

"As you wish. Creating snapshot and adding it to subjects file. Doctor."

"Yes."

"Would you like to know the sex of the twins?"

"Um Elizabeth, David, that's your call."

"Oh yes I definitely wanna know. How about you Beth?"

"Come on David that's a silly question of course I wanna know."

"I knew she was gonna say that."

"Okay then, computer you may state the twins sex."

"Very well Doctor Nichole, both twins are of the female gender."

"Girls! There both girls?"

"Yes David," Doctor Nichole replied and said as Elizabeth shed a small tear while David's body filled with warm emotion, "they're both girls and gorgeous ones at that."

"You hear that Beth, They're both girls?" Now I get to build two dollhouses."

"Only if you let me name them."

"That work's for me."

"Okay Doctor Hechow lets continuc."

"As you wish Doctor. Computer remove laye, rs three and four. Scan nervous system five, note all abnormalities."

"Very well Doctor Hechow. Removing laye, rs three and four. Commencing scan of nervous system five."

"Doctor Nichole, are we almost done? I'm starting to feel real hungry."

"Yes Elizabeth we're almost done. The computer is doing its final scan."

"Good," Elizabeth mumbled while her stomach growled real loud, "I'm so hungry I could eat a house."

"Scan of nervous system five complete Doctor Hechow. One abnormality detected."

"Alright, list place of origin and create a full snapshot of the abnormality then place it in subjects file and power down when you're done."

"Very well. Listing place of origin, creating snapshot and adding it to subjects file. Good day Doctors. F.l.s. is now off line."

"Well that's it," Doctor Nichole said as she and Doctor Hechow turned from the View screen and looked at David, "That wasn't so bad was it."

"Nope not at all," David Replied as he stood up and began to step out of the observation room, "A little bizarre but not to bad."

"Bizarre, whys that?"

"Well now I can say I've seen my wife in a totally different light and now I don't know if I'll ever look at her the same."

"Oh you will," Doctor Nichole replied and said with a laugh, "trust me you will. Isn't that right Doctor Hechow?"

"Oh yeah," Doctor Hechow said as the three of them stepped out of the room, "the first time can be a little shocking. Ha ha ha ha ha ha ha, the first time I just saw my wife naked is still shocking me if you know what I mean, ha ha ha ha ha ha. So I can understand why seeing everything else would boggle ones mind a little. Ha ha ha ha ha h ha ha, anyways I will have a full analysis of Elizabeth's test done with in the hour and I'll be back with you. Doctor Nichole I'll see you when you're done here."

"Oh yeah you bet." Doctor Nichole replied as Doctor Hechow then smiled at David and said.

"Don't worry Elizabeth's gonna be just fine, we gonna take good care of her and dah little ones okay."

"Okay." David replied as Doctor Hechow swiftly shook his hand and said.

"Very good I'll see you soon. I'm off and away. Oh and don't forget you use your cane when you wife's done with it."

"Don't worry I will," David replied with a puzzled look and said as Doctor Hechow then turned and quickly left, "what is it with everyone and that cane."

"I don't know David."

"Beth, how did you?"

"I helped her." Doctor Nichole interrupted as she wheeled Elizabeth to David's side and then handed him his cane.

"When?"

"While you were speaking with Doctor Hechow."

"Nuh uh, no way."

"Yeah way," Elizabeth Laughed and then asked, "is someone having a little trouble with paying attention to what's going on around them?"

"I must be." David replied as he bent down and kissed Elizabeth's forehead while she asked.

"Doctor, do I really have to wait two hours to fill my face? Cause I don't think I can."

"Um no not really. We just suggest that you don't."

"Why's that?"

"Well some people tend to get a little nausea's if they eat before their two hours are up. But if you wanna take the risk of throwing up perfectly good food then yeah you can eat as much as you want, and if you'd like I'll even have a nurse take you to our cafeteria."

"Um if you don't mind I would like to do that?"

"David are you sure? You know you're not supposed to be."

"Yeah Beth I know, pushing a lot of weight or walking with out my cane. I promise I'll take it easy and besides you don't weigh that much, plus we're in a hospital if something goes wrong help won't be that far away. Right Doctor?"

"Maybe but I'm not gonna be the one to tell you yes or no."

"Beth?"

"Alright David. Just be careful you know your fragile."

"Please me fragile, it took two bullets to take me down."

"Is that all?" Doctor Nichole asked with sarcasm as David handed Elizabeth his cane and then stepped to the back of the wheelchair while Doctor Nichole stepped away and said before she left the room.

"Okay then. Now that's settled, Elizabeth you enjoy your food."

"Oh I will."

"And I will see you two in a little while."

"Thanks Doctor."

"You bet."

Grabbing the handles to the wheelchair, David then casually rolled Elizabeth out of the room and down the hall, where he followed arrows that pointed the way to the cafeteria.

"Well that's good."

"What's that David?" Elizabeth asked as they rolled along

"The cafeteria is on this floor. Which means we're not gonna have to go very far."

"That is good," Elizabeth replied while her stomach let out a loud thundering growl., "because if we did have a ways to go I might actually try to eat this wheelchair or your cane. No wait a minute you need it."

"Oh here we go with the cane bit again."

"Ah ha ha ha ha, I said that on purpose David. Well the eating it part anyways."

"You know what Beth?"

"What?"

"When my hip is fully healed and everyone does not care whether I use the stupid thing or not. You know what I'm gonna do?"

"What Poop head, what cha gonna do?"

"Wow! You just called the person that's pushing your wheelchair a poop head, that took a lot of nerve. Anyways I'm gonna grind it into little tiny pieces and serve it as steak seasoning at our next cookout. You know one of those warm summer day cookouts when everyone comes over with side dishes like you know. Potato salad, cole slaw, pink salad and they all drink ice cold beer as they gather around and converse while they wait for the nice juicy steak that has been marinating in sauce and seasonings for 24hours to get."

"Okay David stop! your driving me, mmm I smell food."

"Yeah and it aint no barbeque either."

"I don't care what it is as long as it's food."

"Are you sure about that? Because I."

"You know what I mean David."

"Yeah I know just checking," David replied and asked as they rolled into the cafeteria, "you're gonna want to eat here right?"

"Oh yeah, most definitely."

"Alright let's find a place to sit."

Scanning around for an open table, David then quickly found one and rolled Elizabeth to it and said, "here we go. Do you know what you want?"

"Yeah a big heaping plate of goulash and a large soda with a lot of ice."

"How do you know they have goulash Beth?"

"Because I can smell it."

"Well what if your nose is wrong, what'll you want then?"

"Oh trust me my nose isn't wrong, I know the smell of goulash."

"Okay," David Laughed and said I'll be right back.

"Ehhem, your cane Mr."

"Yeah, yeah, yeah," David replied as he grabbed his cane from Elizabeth's lap, "I can't forget the mighty cane."

"Oh David stop."

"I'll try."

"You better."

"I will, maybe. I think. You know I'm gonna go and get your food now."

"Hurry back."

"I will."

"Promise."

"I promise," David replied and said as he began to walk to the food line, "don't go anywhere."

"Oh trust me David I wont, I'll be right here when you get back."

"Ok you better be or else."

"Or else what?"

"I don't know I'll think of something."

I bet you will, Elizabeth thought to herself as David finally walked off, *or maybe not. What do you two think, you think daddy could think of something? Yes, no, maybe.*

Mommy.

Yes.

Don't be scared. Everything is gonna be ok, *don't believe him.*

Believe who?

He can't hurt you.

Okay little ones your confusing mommy. Elizabeth your going crazy you really can't hear the girls. Hm maybe I can.

You eat now mommy.

Mommys gonna because her comes daddy whom I can hardly make out.

You'll see normal again and everything is gonna be ok.

I hope so little ones, I hope so.

"Well Beth your nose was right." David said as he walked up to her and set a big plate of goulash on the table."

"I told you my nose knows what it smells and man does it smell good."

"Nose knows."

"Huh yep, nose knows." Elizabeth replied while David slid the goulash in front of her and asked as he put a fork in her hand.

"Does your nose know soda too?"

"David stop." Elizabeth replied as she began to eat while David set her soda next to her plate and said.

"Uh oh, I forgot napkins. I'll be right back."

Peacefully eating while David went to fetch her some napkins, Elizabeth shoveled the goulash into her mouth and thought as she ate like she hadn't eaten in a week, *mm this is so good. I can't believe people say hospital food if the worst. Oh you better slow down you don't want to make yourself sick. Yeah I know but I can't help it.*

"Here we go got you some napkins."

"Thanks David." Elizabeth replied as he walked up and handed them to her before he sat down and noticed her plate of food was almost gone.

"G Beth, you wasn't kidding when you said you were starving."

"Nope." Elizabeth replied before she took a big drink of her soda and went ahh as she shoveled another fork of goulash to her mouth and mumbled while she chewed it up, "you have to remember I'm eating for two more people."

"What did you say? I can't understand you when you talk with your mouth full."

"I said," Elizabeth replied before she took another drink, "you have to remember I'm eating for two more people."

"That's what I thought you said."

"And they're probably just as hungry as I am."

"This is true," David replied and said while Elizabeth kept eating, "speaking of two more people. Have you thought of any names yet?"

"Why were you serious when you said I could name them?"

"Yeah a deals a deal, right."

"Okay yeah since you put it that way actually I have."

"Well?"

"Hang on."

Shoveling more food into her mouth and chewing it up before she washed it down with a big drink, Elizabeth then silently let out a long belch and said, "woe excuse me. I think I'm starting to get full. Anyways I think Shaylee Rose and Kilee Reese sounds nice. What do you think?"

"I think those names sound beautiful."

"Really?"

"Really," David replied and said as Elizabeth finished up her last bite, "I think there as beautiful as the woman who thought of them and if that's what you wanna name our girls it's fine with me."

"Aw," Elizabeth said then asked while her body filled with warm emotional love, "why do you always have to be so sweet?"

"It's my nature and besides I'm not trying to be sweet, I'm telling you the truth."

"I know you are but your way with words sometimes makes me melt and I think it's sweet."

"Well I'm glad you appreciate it."

"Oh trust me I do." Elizabeth replied before she gulped down the rest of her soda and said after she finished it, "I don't think words could ever express how much I appreciate you."

"Hmm now your making me melt." David said as he wiped Elizabeth's face off.

"Well like you said I'm only telling the truth so don't melt away on me okay."

"Okay." David replied in a laugh as he stood up and said, "it looks like your finished. Are you full?"

"Oh yeah."

"Do you want anything else?"

"Yeah will you see if you can find me some breath mints? I know my breath has to be kicking and it'll probably be a while before I can brush my teeth."

"I sure will." David replied and said as he collected the empty plate and soda container from the table, "just let me toss this junk into a recycle can and I'll be right back with some mints. Until then don't go anywhere."

"I won't." Elizabeth replied while David leaned over, kissed her on the head and then walked to a nearby recycle bin, where he tossed the used plate, fork and soda container in and said to himself as he looked around the room, "breath mints where can I get some? Ahh that's where. Some nice person left a whole bowl of them sitting on that table and look there's a sign that says complimentary please take one. Ok no problem."

Making his way to the table, David then thought, *something free*, as he stopped at the bowl of mints and quickly grabbed a couple of them then mumbled as he turned and made his way back to Elizabeth, "Can't beat that. Something free in this world is hard to come by. Isn't that right Beth?"

"What?"

"Nothing." David replied as he stepped to Elizabeth's side and put the mints in her hand, "I just wanted to see if you were paying attention."

"Yeah right," Elizabeth said as she opened the mints and then handed David the wrapper's while she put them in her mouth, "I know you, your brain was up to something."

"Nope not this time." David replied and said as he folded the mint wrappers up and put them in his pocket, "scouts honor. I cannot tell a lie."

"Sure you can't," Elizabeth said while David hung his cane from the back of the wheelchair and then proceeded to roll her away from the table.

"Really I can't."

"And like I said sure you can't"

"Honestly I can't."

"David," Elizabeth said as they began to stroll there way out of the cafeteria, "my grandmother always told me when someone says they don't lie or can't lie."

"Yeah I know that's the biggest lie they have ever told."

"Yep that's right, so stop trying to fib me."

"I'm not trying to fib you baby girl."

"It sure sounded like it." Elizabeth replied as they made their way into the hall and strolled along while David looked for an elevator and asked.

"Do you remember what level we need to go to."

"Yeah level six. Why did you forget?"

"No I just wanted to see if you remembered."

"Ahh see David there you go with them fibs again."

"Nuh uh, that wasn't a fib."

"Okay, then what was it?" Elizabeth asked in a laugh as David spotted an elevator and said while they strolled to it and patiently waited for the doors to open.

"A test."

"A test?"

"Yeah a test," David replied as the doors opened and he rolled Elizabeth inside.

"What kind of a test?" Teacher boy."

"A test to see if you remembered." David replied while he spun Elizabeth around as the doors closed and she said.

"Level six please. David I may have lost most of my sight but I haven't lost my memory."

"I know baby girl. I'm just picking at you."

"Picking at me huh?"

"Yep that's right." David replied in a laugh before he leaned down and kissed Elizabeth on the head as the elevator slowed and then stopped, "now don't get all up set on me."

"Oh I'm not." Elizabeth replied while an automated voice said.

"Level six" and the doors opened.

"Then what's wrong? You got awfully quiet on me."

"Oh nothing," Elizabeth replied and said as they strolled through the open doors and into the hallway where they casually moseyed along while they made their way to Elizabeth's room, "I'm just planning a payback."

"Oh are we planning a big attack?"

"Yes I am, plus I really have to use the bathroom!"

"That bad huh?"

"Oh yeah I really gotta go."

"Well hold your britches on because we're almost there." David replied while Elizabeth franticly shook her legs and said.

"Oooooohh I hope so, cause I've gotta go go go go go go go go go."

"Hey Beth."

"Oh what!"

"What ever you do try not to think about running water."

"Oh David that's not funny."

"Sorry I couldn't help it." David said with a laugh as they turned a corner and then quickly strolled into Elizabeth's room, where David rolled Elizabeth up to the bathroom and said as they stopped in front of the door, "here you go, we're here. The bathroom is right in front of you."

"Good give me your cane."

"You want some help?"

"No. I mean yeah," Elizabeth replied while David put his cane in her hand as she stood up, "Just open the door and turn on the light. Oh and hurry up."

"Okay." David said as he stepped around the wheelchair and opened the door then flipped on the light while Elizabeth balanced her weight on the cane before she stepped into the bathroom and said.

"Alright David out!"

"Are you sure?"

"Yeah now out!"

"Alright." David replied and said as he stepped out and shut the door, "just yell if you need anything."

"Oh I will." Elizabeth replied while David looked at the wheelchair and thought.

I've got an idea.

Turning around and sitting in the wheelchair David then frantically rolled himself around the room and hysterically laughed when he heard the sound of a rather long and loud echoing fart that sounded like an un oiled door hinge, as it whipped it's way around a damp bowl of cool, hard porcelain before it blasted through the walls and smashed into his ear drums.

"Grow up David."

"Why Beth what did I do?"

"You know what you did."

"No Beth I think you did it." David replied while he stopped rolling around and kept laughing, "are you all right?"

"Yes David I'm fine." Elizabeth replied as she slowly opened the bathroom door and began to carefully make her way to her bed.

"Here Beth, let me help you." David then said as he stood up and stepped to her side.

"No let me do it."

"Are you sure?"

"Yeah I'm sure. I'm gonna have to do it sometime, might as well be now."

"That's true. David replied as he then stepped into the bathroom and flipped the light switch off and said while he stepped back out, "I'll leave the door open for you okay."

"Okay," Elizabeth replied and said as she carefully sat on the edge of her bed, "see I found it."

"Good job."

"Why thank you, thank you. I guess you can have this back now."

"G thanks," David replied and asked as Elizabeth Handed him his cane, "Are you sure you don't wanna hang onto it for a while?"

"Yep I'm sure."

"Are you positive?"

"Yes David I'm positive, now will you take the stupid thing before I beat you with it."

"Okay, Okay," David laughed as he pulled his cane from Elizabeth's hands and said, "seriously though, it probably would be a good idea if we got you one."

"Maybe."

"Maybe?" David asked as he walked around the bed and stepped to a chair where he sat down, "why maybe?"

"Because the Doctor's might be able to fix me, so until I find out if they can or not I'm not gonna worry about getting a cane. I'll just keep harassing you to use yours."

"Oh that's your plan huh, you think it's gonna be that easy?"

"Em hm I sure do."

"Well what if I don't make it easy?"

"Well besides beating you with your own cane I'll beat you twice as hard with my mine. That's if I end up needing one. Actually no I wouldn't."

"Why not?"

"Because you'd probably like it."

"Nuh uh not me, that sounds like it would hurt."

"Well in that case, maybe I will beat you. Naw I'll just stop beating something else, yeah that's what I'll do that'll be my payback."

"Stop beating something else. What are you talking about Beth?"

"You know what I'm talking about."

"No. Oh man, okay I get it, very funny. Is your mind ever not in the gutter?"

"Honestly?"

"Yeah honestly."

"Okay you want a percentage?"

"Sure Beth why not?"

"Alright 95 percent of the time my mind is in the gutter and the other 5 it isn't."

"Man Beth that's bad."

"Well you asked."

"Yeah I did didn't I? So when Don came onto you. What were you in then 5 percent mode or 95 percent mode?"

"5 percent yah doe, doe head, and even if I wasn't I surley would have been. Aw especially when I got a whiff of his breath. You know that man has to be the most disgusting man on the planet. I could never, no way. I can't even fathom how his wife does. Oh that poor woman."

"Maybe she doesn't and maybe that's why he came onto you?"

"G thanks David. It had nothing to do with me huh?"

"I'm sure it had everything to do with you. Ah ha ha ha ha ha and I'm also sure that he might have put you in 95 percent mode."

"Oh yuk yuk yuk yuk that's not funny David. Are you trying to make me barf or something?"

"No I'm just kidding, I know better."

"I hope so."

"Trust me I do."

"Good cause like I said before I could never nuh uh no way, not with him or any other man at that."

"Knock knock."

"Yeah?"

"Oh it's just me." Doctor Nichole said as she entered the room and handed David a photograph before she stepped to the foot end of the bed.

"Wow," David said as he stared at the picture, "this is so cool."

"What is it?"

"It's a photo of the twins Beth. And it's so clear looking. Thanks Doctor I'll have to hang it in my home office."

"Boy I wish I could see it."

"Well Elizabeth," Doctor Nichole said as she pulled a electronic file keeper from her pocket, "there's a good chance that in time you'll be able to."

"Really?"

"Yep." and that's what I'm hear to talk about. Doctor Hechow and I have finished analyzing your f.l.s. scan. Now I know your both aware that the scanner's did turn up an abnormality."

"Oh yeah we heard that part." Elizabeth interrupted while David sat and stared at Doctor Nichole as he carefully listened to what she had to say.

"And as I originally suspected Elizabeth does have a small tumor. The good thing is it's benign."

"Benign, what does that mean?" David asked while he set the picture down and his heart began to sink with agonizing emotion.

"It means it won't spread like cancer," Elizabeth replied and then asked, "right Doctor?"

"Right it won't spread. Well it shouldn't spread. Now the bad part is it's located on the part of the visual pathway that we call the lateral geniculate body and due to Elizabeth's condition it would be impossible to remove it without aborting the pregnancy first, but."

"Are you kidding me?" Elizabeth blurted out and said while David's heart sank even further, "I'm not killing my children! I can't believe that kind of shit even exist. You know the global military police post signs along our highways that say buckle up we need you but we'll still fucken let you kill your kids!"

"Beth Calm down."

"No David I won't calm down that's bullshit I can't believe!"

"Beth! Calm down and let Doctor Nichole finish what she was saying!"

"Sorry Doctor I thought you were done."

"No I wasn't, but that's okay because I agree with you. Anyways as I was saying. But since the tumor is benign, if you don't mind staying in the hospital for the duration of your pregnancy we can easily perform the surgery after you give birth."

"Yes" Elizabeth replied and asked as David's falling heart some what leveled off, "how long after I give birth?"

"Probably with in a week or two. Or." Doctor Nichole then said as she paused and punched some things into the electronic filer.

"Or what?" David asked.

"Or," Doctor Nichole said as she finished and put the filer back into her pocket, "there's a new treatment we can try. It's along shot and you'll still be required to stay here so we can monitor your progress."

"Well what's the treatment?" David asked while Elizabeth's pulse began to race.

"It's called a S.I.P. treatment, Subsonic, Ion, Pulse. A small mechanical chip attaches itself to the scalp, usually above the tumor's point of origin. Then it slowly releases a low frequency ion pulse beam into the tumor which biochemically commands Elizabeth's white blood cell's to basically eat the tumor and the surrounding tissue that caused it's growth."

"Sound's easy."

"It is Elizabeth, well that's if you don't mind losing some of your hair."

"How much is some?"

"A three by three inch sqaure will have to be shaved off."

"I can live with that. How about you David can you live with me having a bald spot for a while?"

"Bald spot beats being half blind doesn't it? So yes I can live with it. Now what's the catch Doctor?"

"There's actually three catches," Doctor Nichole replied while David's emotion's quickly turned from ones of fear and panic to ones of anger and frustration, "one is through out the treatment Elizabeth could sustain some short term memory loss. Two because of the tumors position Elizabeth is gonna experience a heck of a light show when the beam kicks on and off. Three is your insurance might not cover any of it, but."

"I was waiting for that." David interrupted Doctor Nichole while Elizabeth spewed out and interrupted David.

"What! We've paid them people good money why would they not cover any of it? Oh let me guess it's because the genetic test turned up some abnormalities and there some how calling this thing in my head an avoidable preexisting condition! I can't believe them fucken cocksuckers that call themselves the civil servants of humanity would do something like that. Next thing you know they'll some how call hemorrhoids a preexisting condition. You know Mrs. Leviticus we found out you ate uncooked corn last year and when you shit it out 24hours later, it preexisting caused veins to fall out of your asshole a whole year later. So we're sorry that even though you've paid us more money then a whale could possibly shit in a year, we're not gonna pay for the treatment you need. Them mother fucker's I wi."

"Elizabeth! Shh!"

"They all"

"Elizabeth!" Doctor Nichole yelled and laughed at the same time, "Shh calm down your gonna implode the whole hospital."

"Well I'm sorry I just can't fu."

"Elizabeth Shh. Zip it, let me talk. Doctor Nichole said again as she stepped away from Elizabeth's bed and carefully closed the door to the hall, while David watched her and wondered to himself.

Okay what's going on?

"Alright are we calm now?"

"Yeah I guess, sort of but not really."

"Well try to calm down."

"I'll try."

"And don't interrupt me this time. David you neither. First of all I agree with everything you said. Second of all I never said they wouldn't cover, I said they might not cover. Third of all if they don't know what the background test turned up then they couldn't call the tumor a preexisting preventable condition. Now could they?"

"But aren't you supposed to." David started to ask before Doctor Nichole stared him in the eye and sternly said while she interrupted him.

"If they don't know what the back ground test turned up then they couldn't call the tumor a preexisting condition! Right?"

"Right." David somberly replied as Doctor Nichole then turned to Elizabeth and asked with a smile.

"So what do you wanna do Elizabeth?"

"I'll do the S.I.P. treatment. That's only if I don't have to stay here when their done."

"Nope you won't have to but you will be here for at least a month."

"Well that beats nine."

"This is so true," Doctor Nichole replied and said with a smile, "good then I'll inform the staff on level five and I'll schedule you to start the treatments first thing in the morning. Sound good?"

"Sounds great." Elizabeth replied as Doctor Nichole then turned and made her way out of the room while David said.

"Thanks Doctor."

"You bet."

"So Beth," David then said as he stood up, put the photo of the twins in his shirt pocket and stepped around the bed, where he sat on the edge and put his arm around Elizabeth, "What's up with the filthy language, do we have to put soap in your mouth?"

"No you don't have to put soap in my mouth. I only cussed because I got a little frustrated."

"A little," David said as he rubbed and kissed Elizabeth's head, "that sounded like a lot of frustration."

"Yeah I guess it did didn't it."

"It sure did but I don't blame you and I highly doubt you're the only one to ever go off like that. Especially when it comes to those people. I do it all the time."

"David you do not, you never say anything about them or anything else."

"Oh yeah I do, I just do it in my head."

"Why?"

"Because I've always felt that stupidity and flat out ignorance just isn't worthy of my precious energy in take. So I usually focus my anger and frustration on the things that I feel are worthy of my attention."

"You make it sound so easy."

"Trust me it's not. Besides why should I spiel off about the morons on this planct. that's what I got you for, right?"

"If you say so."

"I know so, now come on," David said as he stood up, "your looking a little tired. So why don't you lay back and rest for a while, you've had a long day and tomorrow is probably gonna be just as long."

"Yeah you're right," Elizabeth replied as she swung her legs into bed, "I am feeling a little tired. Speaking of tired," Elizabeth then asked while David pulled some blankets over her, "when's the last time you slept or had anything to eat?"

"I don't know I haven't been keeping track. Why?"

"Because," Elizabeth said as David rubbed her stomach, "I know you you're probably exhausted and you won't admit it."

"No not exhausted, but I'am starting to feel a little hungry."

"Well will you do your wife a favor?"

"What's that?"

"Go home, relax and get yourself something to eat."

"I can eat here Beth."

"Yeah but you can't relax here and I think you need to."

"Beth I'm fine."

"Sure you are. Now are you gonna do that for me?"

"I suppose." David replied as he leaned down and kissed Elizabeth on the lips

"Good then. Oh I'm also gonna need you to do me two more favors."

"Ok what?"

"Have a courtesy shuttle take you home and call Diane, let her know what's going on."

"I'll call Diane but do I really have to ride home in one of those stupid shuttles?"

"Please David you know you're not supposed to drive yet."

"Aw come on Beth, I can do it."

"No."

"Come on please."

"Nope."

"Pretty please."

"No."

"Fine then," David replied and said as he leaned down and put his ear to Elizabeth's stomach, "I'll just see what Shaylee and Kilee have to say. What do you think girls can daddy drive home? Yeah he can. Are you sure? See Beth," David then said while she laughed, "they said it was alright."

"No they said you could, they didn't say it was alright."

"Aw you always have to find a technicality don't you."

"Yep I sure do. But if my little boy who's obviously not gonna stop begging promises to be careful his mommy will let him take the car home."

"I promise." David replied as he leaned down and kissed Elizabeth, "I love you."

"I love you too, now go home get something to eat, relax and I'll see you in the morning."

"Ok but I think I'm gonna stop some place to eat. I really don't feel like cooking."

"Where you gonna stop?"

"I don't know, maybe Buckingham's bar and grill. Their food is usually pretty good."

"Yeah it is," Elizabeth replied, "and so is their big selection of exotic beer. Speaking of beer you better not be planning on having one."

"Why not?"

"Cause you remember what happened the last time you drank. don't yah?"

"Ha ha ha ha ha Yeah how could I forget."

"I mean it David we don't need a repeat of Big Jim's birthday party."

"Ah ha ha ha ha no we sure don't," David replied as he leaned down and kissed Elizabeth and held her tight while he said, "Don't worry Beth I'll behave."

"You better you big ofe."

"I will."

"Good now get your cute little butt moving before I change my mind."

"Change your mind about what?"

"About letting you take the car."

"Oh you wouldn't do that to me. Now would yah?"

"I might." Elizabeth replied while David then kissed her on the forhead before he stood up straight and held her hand and said.

"I better go then. I love you and I'll see you in the mor, oh wait. Are you going to want anything from the house?"

"Yeah but I'll figure that out after they start my treatments."

"Are you sure?"

"I'm positive, just do me one more favor."

"Another favor?"

"Yeah but you'll like this one."

"Hmm okay what?"

"Will you get here early so I can have you help me take a shower before they stick that thing to my head?"

"Sure Beth that'll be my pleasure."

"I knew it would be. Hey and if your gentle with me I might even give you a little before I'm done."

"Done what?"

"Showering you brat."

"I knew what you meant Beth. But yeah I'll be here around seven am. Sound good?"

"Sounds great, now give me another kiss before you go."

"Well if you insist."

"Yes David I insist."

Leaning down and passionately kissing Elizabeth, David then put his arm around her and squeezed her tight while a tear trickled from his eye as he said, "good by. I love you so, so much and I'll see you bright and early. Okay baby girl?"

"Okay David, now go and relax."

"You too, sweet dreams and keep our girls warm."

"I will. Oh and David," Elizabeth Said as he started to leave the room, "try not to worry to much. I have a feeling that all of the hard road is now behind us, alright?"

"Alright," David replied and thought as he walked out of the room and into the hall, while Elizabeth stared at the ceiling and slowly dozed off with her hands gently placed her stomach, *god I sure hope so.*

PART XXXV

The Fall of David

Sitting in the car with the motor running, David pulled the picture of the twins from his pocket and quietly wept as he tearfully fastened it to the edge of the dashboard, *first my best friend gets killed. I get busted up in the process. My former boss comes onto Elizabeth and when he doesn't get to have his way with her, he just like a child throws a fit and decides to fire me and now Beth's not only pregnant but she has a tumor some where in her head and it's causing her to go blind. Boy it doesn't get any better then this does it. Could anything else go wrong*? "How about it, what do you two think?" David then said as he wiped away his tears and sat staring at the photograph, "could things get worse, or was Beth right when she said she had a feeling that the hard road is over? I sure hope so because if it's not and something happens that causes me to lose the three of you I don't know if I could go on. Man what would I do? I'd probably lose myself. Maybe I already have? No, no I haven't. be strong David be strong for Beth and the twins, she's gonna pull through and your going to have a heck of a story to tell. Now come on lets get going."

"If you only knew," The Indian man said as he stood in the hidden distance and mindfully watched David carefully maneuver the car around the hospital parking lot, "if you only knew."

"Radio please."

"What would you like to hear?" The cars automated voice asked as David maneuvered the car out of the parking lot and onto the open road.

"Oh I don't know, something mellow."

"Please be more specific."

"Yeah yeah yeah you stupid computer. I forgot I have to state the station. Um hmm, satellite 3600."

"Very well."

"Hello this is Sestina Awn and your listening to Heavy mellow satellite 3600. that's right Heavy mellow and for you listeners that might have just tuned in and you have no idea what heavy mellow is."

"Oh shut up and play some music!" David yelled while the Dj carried on.

"So now that we have that out of the way, I'd like to play an old classic heavy mellow group that just recently after playing together for almost 37 years. Well they've decided to retire. I personally whish they wouldn't, but hey whishes don't always come true. Hmm I don't know, maybe the guys in Sacred Circle will change their mind and keep going. Would you all like that? I know I would. Well anyways here's Sacred Circles heavy mellow single from their album Sacred Doors which was released way back in 2015. I don't wanna ride on. That's right its Sacred Circles Misery Train."

"It's about time." David Mumbled as the hard and heavy mellow song began to sound it's way through his ears and into the temporal lobe of his brain, where the song playe, d on the left while his frontal lob concentrated on the road and he thought of happier times on the right.

"Felt a lot of pain." *David Tyler Leviticus, do you take Elizabeth Helen Parable*

"Seen a lot of sorrow." *For you lawfully wedded wife? I do.*

"No hope today." *David, I'm pregnant.*

"No hope tomorrow." *You may kiss the bride.*

Attention everyone, I'd like to make a toast. Here's to

David and Elizabeth. The two whitest friends a man like

"Felt a lot of love." *me could ever have. If it wasn't for you two, heck I don't*

"Seen a lot of hate." *think I would have any friends at all. Let alone white ones*

"No time today." *at that. No seriously though, Congratulations and I really*

"No time tomorrow." *mean it when I say you two were made to be and I hope*

Your love takes you all the way through

This world and onto the next. I love

"I don't wanna ride on your misery train." *you guy's.*

"I don't wanna ride on your misery train." *Here's to Big Jim, Happy birthday*

"I don't wanna ride on you misery train." *and I hope you have many more.*

I'm being promoted.

Why being an orphan wasn't so bad.

"Love me today." *Elizabeth.*

"Hate me tomorrow." *What?*

"No time today." *I love you*

"No time tomorrow." *I love you too and guess what? Now your Stuck with me.*

Well I wouldn't have it any other way.

You wouldn't?

"Had a lot of hopes." *No I wouldn't?*

"Had a lot of dreams" *There both girls*

"Can't ever sleep." *Shaylee and Kilee, does that sound good to*

"Can't ever wake." *you?*

Oh Beth I think those names sound great

Really you mean it?

"I don't wanna ride on your misery train." *Yeah I think they are as beautiful*

"I don't wanna ride on your misery train." *as the woman who came up with them*

"I don't wanna ride on your misery train."

"and if that's what you want," David then mumbled as the song stopped and the Dj began to talk again, "that's what you'll get. Radio off."

"Very well."

"Pay good money for satellite radio and all you get is a rambling Dj. If I wanted that I might as well go back to Fm, that's if it still exists. Hmm I wonder? I heard a few years ago that someone. Oh what now?" David then yelled as his thoughts quickly changed when he glanced at the vehicles rear monitor and he realized he was being stopped by the G.M.P. "this is all I need, another firkin dilema!"

Slowing the car and swiftly maneuvering it to the side of the road, David then switched the vehicle to park while he said, "engine off, driver window down. I wonder what this jerk off's problem is? I know I wasn't speeding, hmm this stupid car generally won't let you. Remember to by pass that later." *Uh oh be cool here he comes now get your license chip out so Mr. boy scout can run it.*

Unplugging a small chip from the cars console and then leaning back against the door, David held the chip out of the window and as his blood began to boil with rage he sat in place and waited for the G.M.C. to walk up to his car, *I hope this don't take to long I'd like to get home before it gets dark.*

"Hi how are yah doing?"

"I was fine." David replied as the g.m.c. stepped to his window and said while he took David's license chip from his hand.

"Well I guess I don't have to ask you if you have one of these."

"Nope." David replied while the g.m.c. pulled a small electronic filer from his shirt pocket and said.

"Nice day." as he plugged the chip into it.

"Yep sure was." David replied while the g.m.c. read the filer's holographic information and said as he finished.

"David Leviticus."

"Yep that's me."

"And this is your wife's car?"

"Yep sure is."

"Okay, well do you know why I stopped you?"

"Nope I sure don't. But let me guess your gonna tell me right?"

"Yeah," the g.m.c. replied and said with a puzzled look, "we're conducting seatbelt and harness checks today and our spotter radioed me and said you didn't have yours on."

"Well as you can see," David quickly snapped back and said, "I have it on and it's been on since I left the hospital."

"Mr. Leviticus, I'm not here to argue that. I'm only telling you what our spotter said."

"Well your spotter's wrong!"

"Perhaps but I."

"Yeah yeah yeah," David rudely interrupted and said, "you still have to file a citation."

"Well I'm only doing."

"What your job?"

"Yes Sir."

"You know what!" David then yelled as he interrupted the g.m.c. again, "do us both a big favor! Don't speak to me! File your ridicules citation and then after I'm on my way go bye your asinied spotter a pair of glasses! Alright? Oh and do yourself a favor," David then said as he snatched his license chip back and plugged it into the cars console, "go home and think about the phrase I'm only doing my job. Think about what that means and what's been done by people like you that use it to hide their ridiculous actions. Good day and I hope you drive careful. Window up. Not. Engine on, jerk off." *Man what next, can this week get any worse*? David then thought as he put the car in gear and Maneuvered it back onto the road, where he thought as he drove, *poverty, war, starvation, pain, suffering, hopelessness and homelessness can still exist but drive your car on roads that you've paid for without your belt harness on and we're gonna nail your ass. Heck drive with it on and we'll still nail your ass. What a system of morons. Oh and dam it. Now in between helping Elizabeth and getting myself to the Doctor, just because of that jerk I'm gonna have to make time to dispute that stupid citation. Why do people think they have to always make other peoples lifes so difficult? Man sometimes I wish I could move to a planet where humans and their petty ideals didn't exist, maybe start a new race of higher thinking individuals. Maybe yah think*? "Yeah right." David then said allowed as he slowed the car and made a swift turn into the parking lot of Buckinghams bar and grill, where he slowly maneuvered the car around as he scanned the lot for a parking spot, *Man this place is packed I hope I can find a*, "ah here we go," David then said allowed as he found a place to park, I didn't think I was gonna find one now I hope I'll be able to find an empty seat."

Carefully maneuvering the car into the empty spot and coming to a complete stop, David then put the cars transmission into park and clicked his belt harness off while he said, "engine off, driver door open." *Here we go.*

Grabbing his cane, David then slowly stepped out of the car and carefully stretched the stiffness from his rather sore wound's, *aww that feels better. I think I'm gonna land myself a hot bath when I get home.* "That's if I get home." David then mumbled as he stopped stretching and began to walk across the parking lot while the car door closed and the Indian man said with eyes of concentrated destination as he watched David from a darkened, hidden distance.

"Oh you'll make it home David Tall Tree, trust me you're gonna make it home and beyond."

Stepping into the crowded and smoky bar, David then scanned around for a place to sit, "bingo. There we go." he then mumbled as he spotted a small table and made his way to it, *better get it before someone else does*, "excuse me, excuse me, pardon me," *man I wonder what's going on why's this place so pact? Oh that must be why*, David then thought as he sat down and took notice to a group of people hauling band equipment to the bars small stage, *they all must be here to see some lousy local band, probably a cover band at that. Boy and I thought my day was gonna get better.*

"David," a female called and asked as she walked up to his side, "what's the scowl all about? You usually have a smile on your face. You having a bad day or something?"

"Oh Paula my favorite waitress. Yeah bad day, wow more like a bad week or two or three. I don't know something like that. Everythings a bit fuzzy."

"Ok David your losing me."

"I'm sorry Paula, it's all just one big jumbled up mess right now and I don't know where to start."

"That bad huh?"

"Yeah and to top it all off I just had a run in with the global military's police, you know we're here for you and the people of Earth."

"Oh and let me guess, they said you were driving without your belt harness?"

"Yeah, how did you know?"

"Several other customers have told me the same story."

"Really? That's crazy."

"Tell me about it David. It almost makes you not wanna drive anywhere."

"Yeah no kidding."

"So where's Elizabeth?"

"Oh that's a whole nother story."

"Well is she sick or something?"

"Yeah kind of, lets just say she's gonna be in the hospital for a while."

"Oh I'm sorry. Is she gonna be okay?"

"I hope so."

"You don't wanna go into it, do you?"

"No not really, not right now."

"Well if you change your mind you let me know alright."

"Yeah I will and thanks Paula."

"Your welcome. Now what can I get cha?"

"Um just a burger with everything and a tall, dark, draft of Buckinghams amber al."

"You really want me to bring you a beer?"

"Yeah, why?"

"Well because, you remember what happened the last time you had one don't yah?"

"Yeah I do but trust me I'll be fine."

"Are you sure David?"

"Yeah Paula I'm positive."

"Okay I'm not your mom, I just don't wanna see you do something you'll regret."

"Hm the way I feel right now, I don't think I could do anything regretful."

"Okay then. I'll be back in a minute. Oh wait, do you want me to bring your drink now or do you want it when I bring your burger?"

"You can bring it with my burger."

"Okay I'll be back in a few then."

"Thanks Paula."

"No problem."

"Check, check. It works."

"Try mics two and three."

"Check, check. Hello, hey. They work."

"Good."

This is gonna be a long meal, David then thought as he sat and scowled at the people setting the stage up.

"Check the base drum."

I'll just have to eat fast.

"Base drums good and the vocal monitors are all powered up and ready to go."

"Good I'll go and let the band know that everything's all set."

That's if my food gets here before they start, "man I hope so," David then said allowed as he looked around and frowned at the crowd of people, "I'm not in the mood for this type of shit. If I knew it was gonna be this crowded I would have just stopped and gotten a pizza or something." *Oh well I'd better stop whining because if I really wanna leave I could always cancel my order. Oh no I can't because here it comes*. "Man Paula that was fast. It isn't gonna moo when I bite into it, is it?"

"No David," Paula replied and said as she set the beer and burger on the table, "it's not gonna moo."

"Are you sure?" David asked as he pulled the burger towards him.

"Yes, I'm positive."

"Well if you don't mind me asking, how did the cook prepare this so fast?"

"He's just that good." Paula laughed as David replied and laughed as well.

"Oh its like that hu?"

"Yeah it sure is, now do you need anything else?"

"No I'm good."

"Alright, enjoy your food and I'll be back in a while to check on you."

"Sounds good." David replied as Paula walked away and he began to eat, "wow this is good. Hey and its not mooing. Mm I should have ordered two." *Well,* David then thought as he took another bite and set the burger down while he grabbed the tall glass of beer, *here's to a lousy month. I sure hope the next one's better.*

Rasing the glass to his mouth, David then said before he quickly guzzled half of it down, "Beth's gonna kill me. Ahh that's good." *maybe I should have gotten two of these too, two too. Now I'm thinking and acting like my wife. Too two, uh oh I can see up your tu, to. Woe no David the beer's already hitting you. You'd better behave Mr.* "I'll try." David mumbled as his vision slowly blurred while he finished up his burger, *man why am I such a lite weight.*

"Hey how's everyone doin tonight?"

"Oh boy," David said as he started to feel really drunk, "it's time for the big rock show. Oh and it's gonna be so exciting." David then said as he watched a small crowd gather around the stage.

"People of Buckinghams bar and grill. I'd like to introduce to you a little ol band that's traveled all the way from the southern province of Texas just to play for you tonight at Buckinghams bar and grill. Do you know who they are? Yeah, no well okay then. Let's have a loud cheer and a round applause for that little ol band from the south that ironically calls themselves the Deep South."

"Oh boy!" David then drunkenly yelled as the band walked on stage and started playing while the crowd of people danced and cheerd, "it's time for some boot scooten, Burp! Oh excuse me. Bullshit! Whew! Yeah! Lets do it you fucken rednecks! Yeah haw, come on! Threew!" David then sarcastically whistled threw his teeth before he guzzled down the rest of his beer and knocked his empty plate of food to the floor, "ahh now that was wet. I wonder," David then said while the band kept playing as he drunkenly stood up and accidentally knocked over the table which caused the empty glass of beer to smash against the floor, "uh, oh that wasn't good. Oh well. Hmm I wonder if someone would bum me a smoke?" *lets go see.*

Grabbing his cane, David then drunkenly pushed his way through the crowd while the band finished up their song.

"Yeah how's everyone doin tonight, is everyone feeling alright? Aw common," the bands singer said as the crowd howled while David Bummed a smoke from someone and drunkenly yelled.

"You suck!" before he lit it up.

"You can do better then that. I said how's everyone doing to night are ya'll doin alright? Yeah that's better." the singer then screamed while the crowd howled back and David yelled as he stumbled around and continued to push his way through the crowd.

"You suck!"

"You suck too!"

"Yeah your mama."

"It looks like it's gonna be one of those night's." The singer then said as he stepped to the drums and grabbed a confederate flag before he stepped back to the microphone and said as he draped the flag over his shoulder, "and since it's gonna be one of those nights I think it's time to do our next song. What cha all think, is it time?"

"No! David yelled while the crowd yelled

"Yeah!"

"Good because I believe it's time. I say it's time," the singer yelled as he threw the flag into the crowd while the drummer did a drum roll, "it's time for the south to rise again. One! Two! Three!"

"I can't believe people still believe in this. Shit!" David yelled as the band began to play their next song, "you suck! Boo, loser's the south is gonna rise again! Ah h ah ha ha ha hah."

"Hey Paula!" A bouncer then yelled as he watched David drunkenly shove his way through the crowd.

"Yeah, what's up?" Paula replied as she stepped to the bouncer while he pointed at David and asked.

"How much has that dude had to drink?"

"Just a beer."

"Are you sure?"

"Yeah I'm positive, why?"

"Because look at him, he's awfully messed up for someone that's only had one. Don't you think?"

"Yeah maybe a little," Paula replied with a smirk and said as they watched David make his way out of the crowd, "maybe it's because he's using a cane?"

"Maybe," the bouncer replied while they then watched David slowly stagger to the corner of a small horse shoe counter where he stood and tried to relight a bent up cigarette, "do me a favor, don't give him anymore booze. Alright?"

"Yeah okay." Paula replied as she walked away and Bill the bouncer kept a close eye on David.

"Man walk off with a lighter and it won't work," David yelled while the band kept playing in the back ground, "this sucks!"

"Here man use mine. As a matter of fact," a man that sat at the counter said with a raspy voice as he handed David a cigarette and a lighter, "toss that one out and have a fresh one it's on me."

"Thanks!" David yelled as he dropped the bent up cigarette to the floor and then lit up the fresh one, "Thanks a lot."

"No problem." the man replied while the man next to him screamed,

"Whew!" as the band playe, d on.

"Yeah whew!" David then screamed before he toked on the cigarette, "you suck!"

"Ha ha ha ha hah ha your right man they do suck, he he he hee."

"You suck!" David then screamed again.

"Whew!" The man on the other side of the man with raspy voice yelled and said while the man with the raspy voice laughed Harder, "I think their great!"

"Well!" David yelled as he accidentally knocked an ashtray to the floor, "I think they suck!"

"He he he he he, no their great. Mon lets rock!"

"Ah ha ha ha ha," the man with the raspy voice laughed and said, "man you guys the bouncers are watching us, you two need to calm down man."

"Man Doug they aint gonna do nothing."

"Doug your names Doug?" David asked.

"Yeah man and this bearded old school hippy is Sonny."

"Well Doug, sonny I'm David and I'm with Sonny," David yelled while he dropped his lit cigarette and staggered against the counter, "the band sucks! He he he he he ha ha and Fuck! The bouncers! They aint gonna do nothing!"

"Oh boy," Doug then laughed and said as Sonny went

"He he he he he he he he he."

"Now you did it."

"Did what?"

"You got there attention."

"Who's?"

"The bouncers man, here they come."

"Spshh, big deal." David slurred as bouncer Bill and his side kick Rick the stick walked up from behind and tapped him on the shoulder, "Hey. What?" David then blurted out as he spun around and said, "Woe uh oh, look everyone it's vroom, vroom two old school bikers."

"He he he he he." Sonny laughed while David then pointed at each man and asked.

"So let me guess your har and your lee right? Seriously dudes, my brother's or what ever you call yourselfs. Did you know the whole outlaw born to be wild image died out or should have died out what about 200 years ago?"

"He he he he he," Sonny laughed again and yelled, "that's great!"

"Alright!" Bouncer Bill yelled back while his side kick Rick the stick stood and looked dumb founded, "you gotta go."

"Go where?" David asked as he went a little cross eyed and thought he saw the Indian man moving around and watching him from the other side of the smoky room.

"Home, you wanna leave peacefully or do we have to throw you out ?"

"Fight!" Sonny yelled while Doug laughed and David stood still and drunkenly stared at the two men and said as he squeezed out a loud and rather watery sounding fart, that immediately smacked the four men in the nose as it fumed around and stunk the whole area up, "may I use the bathroom first?"

"Man!" the two bouncers then yelled as they jumped back and fanned their hands around, "it smells like you already did."

"Nuh uh." David replied while Doug laughed and said,

"Man I think this guy shit his pants."

"Whew!" Sonny yelled while David saw the Indian man again., "that's ripe!"

"You know what," David then yelled as he watched the Indian man watch him, "I'll leave. Just remember, your all gonna die someday and you know aint none of this gonna matter. Sonny, Doug, Doug, Sonny, you guys take care and maybe I'll see you again. Oh and don't forget," David then said as he began to leave, "don't let the vroom, vroom bikers get yah."

"He he he ha ha ha ha ha, The vroom vroom bikers." The two men laughed as David then brushed past the bouncers and mad his way outside, where he under an orange street light stumbled around as he looked up at the starry night sky and moaned out in a drunken cry.

"Why, why is this happening? Answer me yah prick. Why? Yeah." David then said as he became dizzy and fell over, "you can't answer me because your not real. You don't exsist, if you do why don't you answer me? Cause you can't or because you won't" David then said while the Indian man watched from a hidden distance, "because you won't and you don't care. Well," David said as he laye, d his head down on the ground and began to pass out, "I don't care either so I'll just lay here and die. How's that sound, good to you ?"

"No," the Indian man replied as he stepped out of the hidden distance and said while David finally passed out, "that doesn't sound good at all."

Clapping his hands together, the parking lot then filled with mystical smoke while the Indian man chanted, "whoa cha ne ete yaw." He then walked up to David's sleeping body and said, "Its time David Tall Tree, it's time to begin your journey."

Firmly clapping his hands together while he stood over David, the mystical smoke then began to swirl, and as it created a vortex around the two men, the Indian man then looked high into the top of the swirling smoke and loudly whistled while a bright interdenominational door way began to open at the top. He then swung his hands up and yelled, "Wo ma chi," as a brilliant, brown eagle came screeching out of the shimmering door way, then like a fast moving fighter jet, the eagle slammed down through the center of the vortex and ripped David's yellow soul from it's unconscious body, before it with David's sleeping soul firmly clamped in between it's sharp silvery claws, swiftly proceeded up and back through the closing interdenominational doorway, that briskly carried the both of them through the colorful tunnels of the ever changing fabric of space time.

"Good," The Indian man then said as the doorway fully closed and he looked down at David's sleeping body while the mystical smoke swirled high into the air and quickly disappeared, "now lets get your other half home."

PART XXXVI

Consultation I

Lying in the fetal position on a hard floor in the center of a round dimensional room, while the Indian man carefully laye, d his empty, unconscious body onto his soft and comfortable bed, David's sleeping soul is abruptly woken.

"Hey wake up the universal clock is ticking."

"Huh what, where am I?" David's soul asked as it stood up and looked around the room, "What's going on, who are you and why?" David then paused and asked while he looked around and watched the colorful, circular walls flutter and mystically change themselves into a warm serene scene of a green earthly spring, "Am I here? Is this a dream or did that drink send me over the edge, or am I dead.?"

"No your not dead and your not dreaming."

"Well then what's going on?" David's soul carefully asked as it approached the backside of a tall slender, dark haired man that had been working out mathematical formulas on a illusionary whiteboard.

"Well?"

"Shh, hang on," the man replied and said as he quickly worked out a problem while the rooms spring scene changed to one of a wintery white, "a hah ha ha. See right on time. That's so amazing. Isn't it?"

"What that your formula predicted the change in this room or the fact that the room changed?"

"Both," the slender man replied and asked as he turned to David's soul, "Don't you think?"

"I guess." David replied as he looked around and watched the room then change to a crispy brown fall.

"You guess huh?"

"Yep," David said as he stopped looking around the room, "I guess if you say so."

"Boy we sure have an attitude don't we. Hm your defiantly not what I expected."

"What you expected?"

"Yeah the David Leviticus I expected would have shown a little more enthusiasm."

"Well would you show enthusiasm if you unwarily found yourself in a place such as this and you where told to shush when you asked what was going on?"

"I didn't say shush. I said shh."

"What ever, same difference."

"And besides I partially answered you when I said, no you're not dead and your not dreaming. Didn't I?"

"Okay I'll give you that." David replied while the rooms walls then changed from a crispy brown scene of earthly fall to a circling close up of Earth's star system. "But like I said if you were me would you be enthused?"

"No probably not and if I was human like you, well the other part of you I would probably be filling my pants right now."

"The other part of me?"

"Yeah the other part of you. The human part that's safely sleeping in your bed while this part is here in the in between universe talking to me."

Hmm that must be why I can't feel my injuries, David thought before he said, "the in between universe huh? Okay what ever you say. Um if your not human why do you look human?"

"Well I was human once."

"Ah did you have a name?"

"Yeah everyone called me Scott."

"Really, what are you called now?"

"Scott, why did you think it would change or something?"

"Yeah the thought did cross my mind. So again if your not human why do you look like a human?"

"Common David an intelligent being such as yourself should be able to answer that question."

"Um Scott if I could I wouldn't have asked now would of I?"

"No," Scott laughed and said, "I guess you wouldn't have. Um well to answer you lets just say that for the sake of your undeveloped, neurons that keep you tethered to your human body. This is the form I have to take."

"Really," David said and then asked, "so what your saying is your true form would basically overload my primitive wiring?"

"Yep that's right."

"Wow it's nice to know that I'm to primitive for something."

"Well you asked and besides it's only for a while."

"What's only for a while my primitive wiring?"

"Yep, some place, some time and probably in another laye, r it'll expand just enough to give you a bigger peak."

"Another laye, r, a bigger peak, what are you talking about? You know what never mind, I don't wanna know."

"Are you sure?"

"Yeah I'm positive."

"Okay suit yourself but I guarantee later on your gonna want to know."

"Maybe." David replied as he watched the rooms walls then change into a clear, blue sky before they blinked into a dark and starry image of the known cosmos, "now that was cool."

"Yeah it was wasn't it." Scott replied as he turned to the whiteboard and quickly began to write out a rather long formula.

"But let me guess," David asked as the room then blinked back to a clear blue sky, "you knew that was gonna happen right?"

"Ehh, nope wrong!" Scott replied while he finished writing out the formula, "not that time."

"Why not?"

"Because I wasn't working out the problem before it happened."

"Okay now I get it. If this isn't a dream and I'm not dead and my body's really laying in my bed while I'm here in some kind of in between universe. Oh and you were expecting me. Then your some kind of mathematician angel that my some what saturated with alcohol brain has made up for some strange reason, and when I wake up or sober up I'll realize that all of this was really brought on by the booze. Right?"

"Eeeh. Wrong again. Well sort of. Like I said no your not dreaming, your not dead, yes your body is in bed sleeping while this half is here but still tethered to the other half. No it's not the booze, yes I was expecting you and no I'm not an angel, angels don't exist. But yes I am a mathematician."

"Ok why am I?"

"Dat, dat, dat," Scot said as he interrupted David before he took his glasses off and wiped the lenses on his shirt, "let me finish." putting his glasses back on Scott then looked around and said, "okay that's better. Now you see these equations?"

"Yeah?"

"Do they look familiar?"

"Sort of. I mean they kind of look like the Fibonacci sequence."

"Very good. So you also know what it means."

"Yeah so what?"

"So what. G how did I know you were gonna say that? Anyways you're here because it's my job to partially consult you about the path that you by no means should stray from."

"Partially consult?"

"Yes Partially, search your thoughts there's already been another."

"The Indian man."

"Yeah the Indian man. By the way his name is Stalking Crow."

"Okay I'll try to remember that. That's if I see him again."

"Oh trust me your gonna see him again and he'll finish consulting you."

"On what and how do you know?"

"You see I told you, you'd wanna know. Okay I know because everything from the beginning to the very end is all written in these numbers and Stalking Crow is gonna finish consulting you about the journey that you, Elizabeth, Shaylee and Kilee are gonna embark on."

"Journey, I've heard that before."

"Of course you have." Scott replied as the room began to change while David asked.

"How do you know what we named our girls?"

"I told you," Scott then said as the image of two embryonic twins began to float around the circular walls of the round dimensional room, "it's all in the numbers, aww and look aren't they cute."

"Are those my?" David asked as he stared at the image.

"Yep they sure are."

"Wow that's amazing."

"Yes it is," Scott replied and said as the walls then changed back to the clear blue sky, "the human life is something else, its just to bad that every time it comes close to reaching its full potential this," Scott then said as he pointed to a entergel number on the whiteboard, "anomaly has to get in the way. But we think we've solved the problem and found away to remove it. And guess what?" Scott asked as he pointed to another number and then looked at David, "tag your it, you're the one that's gonna remove the anomaly. But you have to take the journey first."

"Man what journey? I think that's the tenth time I've heard the word or words, the journey. Now are you gonna tell me or."

"Duh David! Calm down, yeah I'm gonna tell you. Are you ready?"

"Sure why not."

"Alright. Earth the nine planets and all of their moons in your solar system, plus the star that holds them in their gravitational place are soon and I say soon, gonna be gone. Your species, your civilization is gonna be sucked right out of it's very existence. Well except you, Elizabeth and your two girls. The four of you are gonna be just fine. That's if you like we hope and the numbers say, erase the negative anomaly."

"Me why me and why is my family gonna be okay?"

"Well it's you, because that's how the formula works out and you and your family are gonna be fine because, when your star starts to go super nova. You and your family are gonna be on a ship traveling outside of your stars Heliosphere otherwise known to the scientist of your planet as the Heliospause, and right before your star explodes, the fuel in its core is gonna dramatically fuse together and cause it to collapse into a black hole. Where you'll fly the ship through the center of the event horizon and emerge on the other side of the universe. And fly your family to this." Scott then said as a planet and its twin stars appeared on the walls of the room.

"That's impossible." David replied as he looked at the planet as it revolved around its two stars.

"What's impossible?" Scott asked while David then looked at the formula on the whiteboard and said.

"Um flying a ship through a black hole. I mean if the intense gravity doesn't stretch you into spaghetti and kill you the singularity at the end will certainly crush you. Right?"

"This black hole isn't gonna have a singularity."

"It isn't?"

"Nope all the information is gonna be crushed and recycled on the accretion disk before its slammed through the other side as a streaming fountain of transferred energy. As far as you being spaghetti filed, don't worry about it. You're gonna be moving so fast the gravity won't be able to take hold. Well as long as you stay in the center of the hole."

"Wow so my family is gonna be the ones to move to another planet and start humanity all over again. That's almost like the story of Noah and the ark."

"Some what." Scott replied as David then looked around and asked.

"Um so what's gonna cause the sun to collapse and why can't we stop it?"

"Well lets just say your fellow, man is gonna cause your stars collapse and no it can't be stopped."

"Why?"

"Because," Scott replied and said as he pointed to a negative interger, "in order to erase this, That," Scott said as he then pointed to a quadradee paroplex, "has to happen."

"Can't you change the formula?"

"No David you can't. The formula was created when he created the universe it only goes one way."

"He, do you mean god?"

“Well you call him god. Some humans call him edoya. Some species call him yahwe, other people call him Jehovah.”

“Well what is he or she or it and why does he, she or it need me to solve a problem, why can’t you all just do it yourself? And if there are other species in the universe, why do you and your superiors care about moving a couple of primitive humans to another planet? Oh and if your all so powerful why do I have to fly a ship all the way across the universe to resettle my family, can’t you just wave your divine hand and send us there?”

“Boy you don’t miss anything do you?” The third council told me this was gonna happen.”

“What ?” David started to ask as Scott went.

“Shh!” Okay one last time for the cheep seats. It doesn’t work that way. Not because the formula says so or because your god says so, its because the rules of universal energy transferal says so. This formula was applied when it all began. You know you strike a cue ball on a pool table a certain way and the balls only go one way. Well that’s how it began and that’s how it works. If you want deeper answers, like I said earlier you’re gonna have to wait until you reach the next laye, r of existence. But in order to reach it you have to finish your path on this one first. Get it?”

“Yeah I guess, but you still haven’t said why you need us.”

“Yes I have.”

“No you haven’t. You’ve some what explained some simple physics of the universe and this laye, r thing that I kind of get but you haven’t said why you and whatever eles there is needs us so bad. Why don’t you just let us die, I mean what’s so special about humans. Oh wait. You need us for more then what you’re telling me,” David then said as he turned and stared at the formula, “ah and now I see. I have to erase this negative anomaly, which is fine with me. But what your not telling me is that the anomaly only exist amongst humans and if a human doesn’t erase it before we contact other Intelegent species that live within our laye, r that it, which I now know to be the serpent creature that stalking crow showed me in a dream, could move onto subconsciously influence and control other forms of intelligence.”

"Yeah." Scott staretd to say as David then pointed to a perplex quadraplex and said.

"Shh!" While he interrupted Scott, "and this part of the formula apparently says if the negative anomaly moves outside of the human race that it, by obtaining this higher value would increase its strength to the sixth power and then poses the ability to move through out the seven laye, rs of the universe, where it could possibly destroy all of the divine creation that was made possible by this once combined singularity."

"Yes! Very good your smarter then I thought."

"Yeah maybe," David said as he looked away from the board and watched the rooms walls change to thousands of small red doors, "but it still doesn't make sense to me because it seems like if humans just went extinct, well the anomaly's value would decrease as well. I mean since it only exist amongst humans."

"David, David, David, do we have to go through it all over again?"

"Yeah I know," David replied and said, "it's all already been written and there's no way to change things, and I'll get more answers when I complete my path and move onto the next laye, r, right?"

"Right," Scott replied while David then turned and watched a single red door appear on the far wall of the room as he said.

"Um there might be one little problem."

"What's that?" Scott asked while David turned his back to the image of the red door and said as he looked at the whiteboard formula again.

"I have no idea how to build a ship that'll take Elizabeth, myself and the twins into space, let alone one that will go through a black hole."

"You do now." Scott hastily replied as the image of the red door swung open and he swiftly smashed the palm of his hand into the forehead of David's soul while a colorful interdenominational port hole opened inside of the red doorway and briskly sucked David's soul out of the room and then closed as it transported him through the fabric of space time, before it opened up over his bed and quickly slammed him back into his sleeping body.

PART XXXVII

Consultation Confrontation
A Peaceful Find

Sitting up in bed while Doctor John along with the crystal and the plans to the energy fountain where being flown to southern Nevada's largest military installation, David then scooted to the edge and said as he put both of his hands onto his throbbing forehead.

"Aw man I feel terrible. How did I get home?" David then said as he pulled his hands from his head, "G's and what a nightmare, man I swear I'm never gonna touch alcohol again"

Slowly standing up and grabbing his cane, David then looked at his watch and mumbled, "man and I'm late for Beth's appointment, she's gonna kill me. Huh whew I'm gonna kill me if I don't wash this smell off. I'd better take a shower before I go and explain myself to Elizabeth. You know I don't think I paid for my food last night either. Hmm I better stop on my way and see if I did."

Stepping out of the bedroom and slowly walking down the hall David then thought, *I'd better look and see if Beth's car is in the driveway first.*

Walking to the front door of their house, David squinted and said as the bright sun light shined it's way through the windows and slammed into his eyes, "man that's so bright it makes my hair hurt. I wish someone would turn it down." David then said as he stepped to a door and slid a small curtain open while he looked through the window and mumbled, "good its there, I don't know how but its there."

Sliding the curtain shut he then turned around and dropped his cane as the sight of Stalking Crow, who then mysteriously stood in the room before him, startled his nervous system so violently that David's heart almost pounded out of his chest while he stood still and said, "you," as he stared into Stalking Crow's deep, dark eye's, "How? Please tell me last night was really a dream and if I close my eyes and open em real quick you'll disappear. Right?"

"Nope," Stalking Crow replied while he bent down and picked up David's cane, "last night wasn't a dream and no I won't disappear if you close your eyes. Now come," Stalking Crow then said as he stood up straight and handed David his cane, "lets take a walk, we have a lot to do."

"Do I have to?" David Asked as his heart rate slowed while he balanced his weight onto his cane.

"No you don't have to but I think it would be wise if you did. Don't you?"

"I suppose," David replied as he shook his head and said while he looked around the room, "I can't believe this is happening."

"Well you better believe it, because this is as real as it gets. Now come," Stalking Crow said as he turned to leave the room, "let's go times wasting."

"Alright," David mumbled and said as he began to follow Stalking Crow out of the room, "just let me grab a jacket first, it looks a little chilly."

"You won't need it." Stalking Crow replied as he stepped to the back door.

"Are you sure?"

"Yes David Tall Tree," Stalking Crow explained as he opened the door and stepped through the doorway, "I'm positive now come."

Standing still for a moment, David shook his head and said as he then stepped to the door and closed it behind him, while he walked out side and began to follow Stalking Crow across a rather large yard, "if you don't mind me asking?"

"No I don't mind." Stalking Crow replied and laughed while they moved through the grass.

"Very funny."

"Well you asked."

"Yeah," David replied while the scenery around them slowly changed, "I did but you didn't let me finish."

"I know. So finish David Tall Tree."

"Okay, where are we going?"

"We're going to one of the deepest places in this laye, r of the universe."

"Why?"

"Because," Stalking Crow replied as they stopped at the edge of a field and he stared into a large wooded area, "there's something you're gonna need for your journey and in order to get it we have to go deep."

"Well that says a lot."

"Shh, in time you'll understand. Now common let's go." Stalking Crow said as he stepped into the woods and began to slowly walk down a path while David looked around and said as he followed him in.

"Okay, how long is it gonna take though?"

"A while. Why?"

"Because I'm starting to get hungry. That and maybe if I ate I would lose this hangover."

"Maybe." Stalking Crow replied as he stopped walking and stood still while he looked up and gazed at a tall Oak Tree, "this one will do."

"Do what?"

"Recharge you."

"Recharge me?"

"Yes recharge you."

"Now," Stalking Crow said as he motioned David to the tree, "step to the TLu GII."

"TLu GII, what does that mean?"

"It means tree. Now come step to it and place both of your hands on the trunk."

"Why?"

"Because you said you were starting to feel hungry. The TLu GII will feed you, well that's if you nicely ask it to."

"Ask nicely. Um okay." David said as he handed Stalking Crow his cane before he stepped to the tree and placed the palm of his hands upon it's rough and barky trunk.

"Now David Tall Tree close your eyes and try to feel the energy coming from the TLu GII. Can you feel it?"

"Yeah I can," David replied and said as he began to feel the tree's invisible ode tic energy field, "and it feels amazing."

"Good now go deep into your mind and ask the TLu GII to feed you some of it."

"Okay here it goes." David Replied while he dove into the deepest part of is mind and silently whispered as the energy flowed from his body and through his hands, before it penetrated deep into the spirit of the tree, where it kindly asked, "Will you feed me?"

"Achi." David then heard and felt as the trees ode tic electrical energy field quickly built up and became so strong that as it traveled up from the trees roots and down through its high branches like an atom collider, that it caused the ground below David's feet to abruptly shake while the tree released the energy from it's core and filled David's body with electrical warmth as it passed through his hands and satisfied his hunger, "Woe. That felt weird."

"Are you okay David Tall Tree?"

"Yeah I'm fine." David replied while he slowly removed his hands from the tree and stepped back.

"Good. Now how do you feel, do you still feel hungry?"

"No," David replied and said as he looked up at the high branches of the Oak Tree, "and I feel, well I can't explain how I feel. I know I sure don't feel hungry anymore."

"Good." Stalking Crow said as he raised his hand to the tree, "you shouldn't feel hungry for a while, so WA do ya Ho TLu GII. Now come David Tall Tree lets go."

"Alright but what did you just say?"

"I told the tree you said thank you."

"Shouldn't I have said that?"

"Maybe." Stalking Crow replied while David stepped to him and said as he grabbed his cane.

"Maybe?"

"Yeah maybe you can thank it later, right now we must go the serpent creature is close bye."

"How do you know?" David asked as they began to walk down the path again.

"Because the breeze that was blowing just stopped and the energy here just became real still. You don't feel it?"

"Yeah actually I do and you know what's weird?"

"What's that?"

"Well the energy feels exactly the same as it did when Jim and I got shot."

"That's because the creature was there."

"Really, why?"

"Because," Stalking Crow replied while the creature stood in the hidden shadows of the forest and silently watched David and Stalking Crow talk as they walked, "like I told you in your dream, it doesn't want you to complete your journey."

"Yeah I forgot that part," David mumbled and asked, "so I was the one that was supposed to get killed, not Jim. Right?"

"Hmm maybe," Stalking Crow replied and said as the two of them came to the end of the path and stood still while they stared into the opening of a large and dark cave, "it's hard to say."

"Whats hard to say?"

"It's hard to say what the creature had in mind." Stalking Crow replied while the serpent creature silently morphed into the shadows of the forest and stopped watching them as it slithered back into its realm where it, while David and Stalking Crow stepped into the cave, watched Elizabeths confusion through his laye, red looking glass of social, sexual contempt.

Where the heck is David, Elizabeth thought as she pulled herself out of bed and blindly fumbled for her walking cane, *it's not like him to be late, let alone not show up at all. Something must have happened*, Elizabeth then thought as she found her cane, *I'm gonna go and find a phone*.

"You do that." the creature hissed while he lustfully watched Elizabeth make her way out of the room and into the hall, where she found her way to a Nurses station.

"Excuse me."

"Yes, hey wait a minute. What are you doing up? You're not supposed."

"Yeah I know." Elizabeth said as she interrupted the male nurse, "I'm supposed to stay in bed for the first 24hours of my treatment because my head has to get used to this stupid chip and if I'm up to soon it's waves or whatever they are might not work."

"Very good, so since you already knew all of that I'm gonna ask you again. What are you doing up?"

"Well I need a favor, my hand phone isn't on yet and I need to call my husband. He didn't show up for my appointment this morning and I'm kind of worried about him, um so do you think you could let me use an audio phone or something, I really, really, really, really need to see if he's okay."

"Yeah I suppose, but. You have to promise me that you'll go back to bed when your done."

"I promise."

"Okay then, follow me. We'll step into the hn's office, you can use her audio phone."

"Thanks," Elizabeth replied and said as she followed the Nurse to a small office, "I really appreciate this."

"Your welcome," the Nurse said as they stepped into the office, "but like I said you better go back to bed when you're done."

"I will." Elizabeth replied while she carefully sat on a chair and blankly stared at an illuminated touch screen while the nurse pressed his finger to a phone icon and said.

"Here you go all set. Just tell the server what you want and if you need anything else," the Nurse then said as he turned away from the touch screen and stepped to the door, "just let me know"

"Alright I will and thanks again."

"You bet." the Nurse replied and smiled as he stepped out of the office and closed the door.

Sitting and blankly staring for a moment, Elizabeth then said, "server please dial pound, star, star, polly tone 21. David and Elizabeth

Leviticus, alert all phones and net accesses."

"Please state carrier code for net access and all web messaging."

"Oh yeah. Um hm, Helen 216. I think."

"Very well, one moment while we connect."

Please answer, Elizabeth then thought while the server made its connection and said.

"Mrs. Leviticus."

"Yes."

"Your call has gone straight to your automated answering service. Would you like to leave a message?"

"Yes and make sure it also goes to all of David's web alerts. Oh and also send this message to B.D. Huges, star, star, five. Jim and Diane."

"Very well you may state message when your ready."

"David this is Elizabeth. Where are you, why didn't you show up this morning? I'm starting to worry. Will you please call the hospital when you get this? Diane will you drive by my house and see if David's there? Mr goofy didn't show up today. Oh and please contact me if you don't find him? Or contact me if you do. Either way please let me know something because you know as well as I do it's not like him to be late. Thank you, oh and David when I see you I'm gonna beat your butt. Server."

"Yes."

"End call message complete."

"Very well call ended. Do you need anything else?"

"Nope."

"Very well then, thank you for using world wide lunar net corporation. Have a nice day."

"Yeah, yeah, yeah." Elizabeth mumbled as she stood up with her walking cane and carefully made her way out of the office while the serpent creature snarled and said as he watched and felt Elizabeth's fear and deep frustration build.

"This just might turn out to be to easy my dear. Hmm we shall see now won't we." The serpent creature then said as Elizabeth made her way back to her room, while David and Stalking Crow journeyed through the low lit cave.

"Man when you said deep you wasn't kidding. How far down do we have to go?"

"Not far David Tall Tree we're almost there."

"Oh okay so it's not that deep."

"No the cave isn't," Stalking Crow replied as they came to a large opening."

"But you said we were going to one of the deepest places."

"No," Stalking Crow replied and said as they approached a large, laye, d out circle of stone, "I said one of the deepest places in this laye, r of the universe. Not one of the deepest places on this planet. If we we're going there," Stalking Crow then laughed and said, "you'd be in a diving suit."

"I don't get it."

"You will David Tall Tree, you will. Now let's enter the circle and have a seat on the ground."

"Yeah on the ground," David replied and said as they entered the circle and sat, "your gonna have to help me up though my new hip is really starting to feel stiff."

"Maybe." Stalking Crow said as he clapped his hands and chanted while David stared at him and a orange flame shot up through the center of the circle and then swiftly hit the rocky stalactite ceiling, before it quickly came back down and condensed itself into a bright, burning fire.

"Woe!" David then yelled while Stalking Crow stopped clapping and chanting, "that was hot. Are you trying to burn me up or what?"

"No David Tall Tree," Stalking Crow replied and said with a laugh as he gazed into the fire, "I'm not trying to burn you up."

"You could have fooled me. Do me a favor."

"What's that?"

"Next time you plan on starting a fire, will you warn me first?"

"Sure but I'm not gonna be striking another fire, well not anytime soon."

"Good." David replied and said as he wiped some sweat from his forehead, "I'd like to keep my face for a while."

"Oh your gonna have your face for along time."

"I sure hope so," David mumbled while Stalking Crow reached into a pouch and pulled out a hand full of sweet herbal sage."

"What's that?"

"Medecine." Stalking Crow replied as he threw the sage into the fire, which caused the inside of the stone circle to fill with a sweet summer aroma, while the fire's flames turned from a bright orange hue to one of a deep, dark, blue. "Now David Tall Tree, stare into the center of the fire and tell me what you see."

"Why?"

"Because like I told you before, in order for you to complete your journey you must first come to terms with your past."

"I am at terms with it."

"You may think you are, but we know and he knows your not and in order for you to fulfill what has been written you have to be at peace first. Now look into the flames and find peace." Stalking Crow then said as the cave went dark while he disappeared and left David to meditate and stare into the center of the fire.

"If you insist." David replied with a mumble before he looked into the fire and abruptly found himself standing in a kitchen, "I don't wanna do this." David then sobbed as he looked around and found himself looking up at his mother through the eyes of a small innocent child, "Mommy."

"Yes David Tall Tree?"

"What doin?"

"I'm getting ready to start our din, din. What you doin?"

"I watching mommy I wanna help you."

"You do hu? Hm okay then, how about you help mommy by going into the other room and playing."

"Why?"

"Because," David's mother replied and said as she knelt down to David's level, "when mommy's cooking the kitchen is no place for little boys."

"Why?"

"Because there's a lot of things that could hurt you. Now go play and I'll call you when everythings done. Okay?"

"Okay." David replied as his mother stood back up and heard a knock on the door while he ran into the other room.

Hmm I wonder who that could be, David's mother then thought as she stepped to a window and whispered while she looked out into the yard, "a military car, what are they doing here? They haven't contacted me since David's father was killed. I wonder what their up to. Hmm I better find out, E Do DA knows if I don't answer they'll probably kick the door in."

Stepping to the door after she looked in on David,. David's mother slowly opened it and said, "yes as her eyes filled with the sight of two mysteriously well dressed military men, "can I help you?"

"Mrs. Leviticus?" one of the men then asked while the other one stood in silence.

"Its Ms my husband is deceased."

"Oh I'm sorry, I wasn't aware."

"Hm the military unaware of something. Now why doesn't that surprise me?"

"Excuse me?"

"Nothing. So what do you want?"

"Well ma'm."

"My names Debra."

"Ok Debra. We're here under article 362 via the president of the newly formed republic to take you in and process you for relocation."

"Relocation?"

"Yes ma'm, I mean Debra. You see your land is now global government property and you have to be processed before we can move you."

"Move me, what if I don't wanna be processed or moved?"

"Please don't make this difficult, just peacefully come with us and I promise you the process will be painless and you'll be in your new home with in a week."

"But I like the one I have."

"I understand that Debra, but I have my orders. Now are you gonna come peacefully or do we have to take you by force?"

"By force, you're gonna force me?"

"I don't want to but if you leave me no choice I'll have to."

"You have a choice!" David's mother then replied with anger as she quickly slammed the door.

"Very well," the military man grunted and said as he began to kick the door in, while Debra ran to David, "have it your way you fucking cunt!"

"David Tall Tree go to your secret lair and hide on mommy, don't come out until I say so. Okay?"

"Ok" David replied as the loud sound coming from the thumping of the man's foot that kept slamming the hard wood of the door so violently, that is scared David's innocent spirit so feverishly, that it caused his little childhood heart to beat abnormally fast as he tearfully stood up and frantically ran to an end table, where he swiftly crawled inside. "good boy." Debra then said as she, while the two men busted through the door, ran to another room and franticly fumbled through a closet, "Come on where is it? Where is it? It's not here. We're did I put that stupid gun?" Debra then said as she turned and ran back to the other room while the two men tore through the house and quickly cornered her.

"Now common Debra," one of the men then said while David stared through a crack in the end table, "lets make this easy."

"Why don't you make it easy and get the O TLE out of here and take your stinken Wa Che back to the pit it came from?"

"Oh we will but like I said," the military man replied while the other man quickly grabbed Debra by the neck and slammed his knee into her abdomen as he forced her kicking and screaming body against the hard wall, "you're going with us. Now hold still."

Pulling a small pen shaped neuron clicker from his pocket while Debra tried to break free from her captures strong hold, the man then quickly zapped her in the temple with the clicker which, as the other man slowly let go of her, caused her to go unconscious and fall to the floor, "Now Ms Leviticus it's time to go."

Putting the clicker back into his pocket while the other man picked Debra's limp feminine body up and quickly carried it out to the car.

The military man then looked around the house and left, while David sat inside of the dark end table and tearfully shook with childish fear as his big dark eyes peered through the crack and saw the emptiness of a room that now held the unsettling energy of a unruly, human scene that his large spirit and innocent mind should have never fell witness to.

Mommy where are you?

I'm right here, David's mother's voice said as it reached from her unconscious mind to his.

Where? I tant see you?

I'm in your heart, where I'll always be David Tall Tree.

I don't undertand.

I know you don't sweetheart and I know you're scared, the voice then said as David peered through the crack again and he saw the serpent creature sneak through the shadows of the empty room, *but right now and forever mommy needs you to be strong.*

I tant mommy, I tant. I want you to tum home, I scared.

Mommy can't come home right now. But I promise I'll see you again. Now, Debra's voice then said as the creature stopped moving when it herd David's heavy breathing, *leave your lair before the creature finds you and run, run out of the house as fast as you can. Keep moving and don't look back.*

I tant.

Yes you can! Debra's voice demanded while the serpent creature snarled as it slowly crept along the wall and made its way to David's hiding place, *now run David, run*! Debra's voice repeated as the creature drew closer to the end table while David cried.

"I tant, I to scared I want mommy!"

Yes you can David Tall Tree! *Now go*! *Go before it's to late.*

"No!"

Do it young man! *Do it Now*! Debra's voice then sternly commanded as the serpent creature yelled,

"Boo!" while it stepped out of the wall and opened the end table's door's with the wave of a hand, "I found you, now come see santa kid and tell him what you want."

"No! I want mommy!"

"Your mommy's not coming, now come and see me."

"No!"

Run David, run now!

"Come to santa kid."

Run!

"Mommy!"

Run David, do it. Do it now young man!

"Come see santa kid."

"No! I don't want santa," David then loudly cried as he like a fast moving spider finally heeded his mother's call and scrambled out of the end table, jumped to his feet and yelled as he swiftly ran out of the room and quickly found his way to an open door, where he, with his little feet pattering against the ground kept running while the creature appeared on the porch behind him and watched as David then disappeared into a field of newly grown wheat. "I want my mommy, I want my mommy, I need to find my mommy!" David then screamed as he slowed down and stumbled around in lost child hood fear while he cried and came to the edge of the field, where he in his confusion, tripped over his own feet and fell face first into a muddy road side ditch, "mommy! Where's my mommy? I tant find her. Where am her? I tant make it." David then cried as he rolled around through the wet mud and tried to sit up, while a young man who'ed been driving down the road, mysteriously appeared over him and said as he pulled David's muddy little, crying body from the ditch,

"Don't worry kid your gonna make it. I've got a feeling about you. Now shh," the man then said as he carried little David to his truck, while big David found himself sitting inside of the stone circle again, "your gonna be just fine."

"I wasn't fine as a matter of fact I never was."

"No you wasn't," Stalking Crow said as the cave slowly lit back up while he reappeared and David wiped away his tears, "and your still not."

"No I'm not! How could I be? And why did you make me relive that? You said I was supposed to find peace! There was no peace in that!"

"Yes David, yes there was. You just have to search yourself and figure out what it was before we can move on."

"Move on!" David yelled, "maybe I don't wanna move on! Why did that have to happen? Why!" David then screamed in fury as he looked up, "why couldn't I have had a normal life? You said I would see you again and I never did! Why didn't you come back? You left me all alone."

"No David, I never left you, I've always been here, now look at me."

"Mom is that you?"

"Yes David," the image of his mother replied as David looked up again and she appeared to float inside of the fire's smoke, "now search yourself. You know why I never physically came back."

"No."

"Yes David." the image said as it disappeared while David screamed,

"They killed her! Why did they have to kill her? Why does anyone kill?" David then said as he tearfully lowered his head and mumbled while Stalking Crow stood up and stepped to his side, "its not fare. Scott said it's all written. Well I don't like how it's written."

"Some of it is David Tall Tree."

"What do you mean?"

"Well a choice changes the outcome. If your species didn't make the choices it's made then you wouldn't be here searching for peace."

"No I would be where I wanted to be and I would still have my mother."

"Well like she said you do have her and you will see her again."

"How?"

"Once you reach the end of your path, you'll move onto the next laye, r of the universe where she probably resides."

"You mean heaven?"

"No David there's no heaven. Or hell at that matter. Just laye, rs."

"I don't understand."

"You will when your path ends."

"How long is that gonna be?"

"Oh probably a long time. The planet you are taking your family to has two stars, one of them gives off a certain kind of radiation that will sustain your human forms for centuries."

"Why can't we just die right now, you know get it over with and move to the next laye, r."

"Because it's not the way your path was written when the whole universe began."

"Well okay what if I make the choice not to complete it in the way it was written."

"Well just like a lot of your people," Stalking Crow replied while he knelt down and picked up a handful of dirt and said as he blew it out of his hand, "your energy will blow out of existence."

"I was always told that energy couldn't be created or destroyed, I was told that it just transfers from one form to another. So how could my energy just blow out of existence."

"Would you like me to show David Tall Tree how?"

"No that's Okay," David said as he stood up and leaned on his cane, "so why is it so important, I mean why do the three of you care where my energy goes?"

"Us three?"

"Yeah, you, Scott and the great combined singularity."

"Because your energy, my energy and all of the energy in the universe binds the laye, r's together and each time a piece of that energy is lost it brings us closer to the full implosion of the great laye, r. That's why the creature interferes."

"I get it now, I think. The negative anomaly is the creature. He doesn't care about life or death. He only cares about changing ones path so the energy will be lost. He actually wants to destroy the universe but he can't because something keeps getting in his way. What is it? Its choice those of us who choose to stay on the right path are the ones holding it all in place and like the formula said if he makes his way into other so called intelligent species, the results could be disastrous. But won't the loss of all the life on this planet cause a great loss of energy? No it won't. How? Because the numbers on the positive side are higher then the negative ones. Right?"

"Maybe. It sounds like you've found peace."

"More like acceptance."

"Peace, acceptance. What's the difference?"

"I've always thought there was a big difference."

"There is but in order to be at peace you have to accept what has happened."

"Hmm maybe," David replied and asked as the fire died down. "why does the creature only exists amidst humans? I mean from what I've gathered there's other intelligent life. Right? Why doesn't it exists among them? And please don't tell me because that's the way it's written."

"I wasn't going to."

"Good, because I'm really getting tired of hearing it."

"The creature only exists amongst humans because it only has a taste for your elithrical aura."

"You mean it only knows what it's been fed?"

"Yes and until humans come into contact with other intelligent beings within this laye, r of the universe your taste is all it will know. But once it gets a taste of a different species other then yourselves, well you saw the math."

"Yeah I did, but what happens besides my energy blowing out of existence if I choose not to go."

"Well the creature will go dormant until humans are reformed and the whole thing starts all over again."

"How is that possible?"

"You saw the numbers David. This laye, r of the universe is constantly breaking down and reforming. After earth's gone and if you choose the wrong choice another planet will form around another star and humans will begin again."

"That's only if I make the wrong choice. Right?"

"Maybe, now realize this if you choose the wrong choice not only will it all start again sometime. But you and your family will also blow from existence. You'll never see them or your self reach the next laye, r where you'll more then likely along with your children see your mother again. Now are you at peace with that idea?"

"No but I am at peace with ending all of it and along with my family seeing my mother again."

"Good."

"No not good."

"Why David Tall Tree, what's wrong now?"

"Well the raging question of why is it so important for humans to meet another intelligent species in this laye, r of the universe and why hasn't it already happened, keeps cycling through my mind?"

"Because with or without the serpent creature moving amongst you, your species is too immature. Plus it's not the right time."

"So why is it so important?"

"It's not."

"You and Scott made it sound like it is."

"No, you just took it that way. Plus its inevitable that it will happen and the."

"Yeah I know," David said as he interrupted Stalking Crow, "The anomaly has to be erased first and I'm the man for the job."

"Right." Stalking Crow replied and asked while the fire went out, "now are you at peace with that?"

"Yeah I'm at peace with it."

"Good," Stalking Crow then replied and said as he stood up and stepped to the now smoldering fire, "we can move forward now."

"Where are we going?"

"Your going to the fourth planet."

"Mars I'm going to Mars, why? I mean how? For what?"

"The crystal energy source you need to power your ship is there and you must get it."

"Really?"

"Yep. Now give me your cane."

"Alright." David replied in curiosity while he stepped to Stalking Crow and asked as he handed him his cane, "were you human once?"

"Once along time ago, yes I was human."

"Well what happened and what are you now?"

"Oh David Tall Tree that's a whole nother story and a long one at that. I'd love to share it with you but right now we have a lot to do."

"Maybe in another time or place you'll be able to?"

"Yes I hope so," Stalking Crow replied and said, "now stand back."

Raising the cane into the air while David stepped back, Stalking Crow then swiftly slammed the bottom of it into the hard rocky ground and yelled Ha Knee as each rock on the circumference of the circle began to glow with blue electrical energy.

"Now watch this David Tall Tree." Stalking Crow yelled as David looked around and the loud sound of enormous electrical energy that was building around them cause David to put his hands to his ears,

"Huh! What?"

"I said, now watch this!" Stalking Crow yelled again.

Jerking the cane from the ground and then swinging it in a counter clockwise motion while the electrical energy began to furiously swirl around the stone circle, Stalking Crow as the electrical energy then moved under their feet and charged its way into the smoldering fire yelled, "Wo cha Nee," while he slammed the end of the cane into the charged center of the circle, where as the cane slammed down, the electrical energy swarmed together and formed a tall cylinder of bright, green light, that while everything went dead silent, stretched to the top of the cave and burrowed through the dark matter of space time as it reached across the solar system and stopped in the center of another stone circle that laye, d deep within the ancient red ruins of the fourth planet called Mars.

"Wow! This is gonna take me to my Destination?"

"Yes." Stalking Crow replied and said while David Stood and stared at the cylinder of green light, "now come the charge doesn't last long."

"Alright, but what do I have to do?"

"Just step through the light."

"That's it?" David asked as he stepped towards the light.

"Yep now come."

"Um why do I have to take a ship to the other side of the universe, I mean couldn't I just use this method to make the trip?"

"Yeah," Stalking Crow replied and said, "you could but there's not enough power here."

"There's always a catch isn't there?"

"Sometimes." Stalking Crow replied while David stood and stared at the light again and asked,

"Okay after I step through, what then? What am I looking for, is this crystal energy source in plane sight or something?"

"No it's inside of a small carbin based container."

"Well what does the container look like?"

"It looks like what you would call a football."

"The container is shaped like a football?"

"Yes David Tall Tree now go."

"One more question. Why do I have to get it? Why couldn't you have gotten it and just brought it to me?"

"Because this is your journey not mine."

"Alright well how did you know where the crystal was?"

"You ask too many questions David Tall Tree, now go before the light shuts down."

"Yeah good idea." David replied as he watched the light momentarily flicker out and come back on, "okay here it goes."

Stepping into the cylinder of green light while Stalking Crow stood still and patiently watched, David then stepped out of the light and thought as he found himself standing inside of a cold and very low lit tomb.

This is amazing I can't believe I'm standing in a cave beneath Mars poisonous surface. How is this possible? David then thought as he looked around and saw ancient human statues through his misty exhaled breath, *and how am I able to breath*? *This is so strange. Man this stuff has to be millions of years old.*

Stepping further away from the light, David then slowly walked around the inside of the circle and gazed at old artifacts as he searched for the football shaped crystal container, while Stalking Crow's strong warrior spirit firmly stood still and watched through the light as David kept moving and his eyes kept searching, *okay where are you*? *Where could you*? "Ah he we go." David then mumbled as his eyes spotted a black carbon, football sized and shaped container that sat perfectly perched atop of a tall, square pedestal made of silver and gold, "now

I just hope I can reach it."

Stepping to the pedestal while the light slowly flickered again, David reached for the container then painfully jumped while Stalking Crow Yelled,

"Hurry David, the light's gonna close down."

"I'm trying!" David yelled as he thought, *This isn't gonna work, I can't jump again.* "I know." David then mumbled as he stepped to the back of the pedestal, "I'll just knock this thig over. Oh maybe I won't." David then said as he pressed his hands to the stand and tried to push, *oh boy think David. Oh here we go*, David then thought as the light flickered off and on while he looked around and just happened to spot a large rock lying between his feet, *this will work.*

Quickly bending down and grabbing the rock, David carefully stood up straight and tossed the rock at the container while Stalking Crow yelled, "Hurry! Hurry David Tall Tree!"

"I am!" David yelled back as the container fell from the pedestal to the ground, "Give me a second, it's cold in here and I can't move that fast!"

"You better!" Stalking Crow yelled as the light flickered faster.

"Yeah, yeah, yeah," David mumbled and said as he carefully scooped the container from the ground, "here I come and I'm not running for a touch down either."

Stepping close to the center of the stone circle while the light flickered on and off, David then stood for a moment and timed the light before he mumbled, "ok one, two, three, four, lets go."

Stepping into the center of the circle as the light kicked off, David then quickly found himself standing face to face with Stalking crow while the light kicked on and then finally off for the last time. "What's the matter? You look a little pale Stalking Crow, did I cut it to close for you?"

"Maybe," Stalking Crow replied and said with a smile while he stared David in the eye, "just a little."

"Just a little?"

"Yes just a little. Now David Tall Tree this part of your journey is over."

"Where am I going now?"

"Home," Stalking Crow replied and said as he handed David his cane, "you have a lot of work to do. Now go home."

"Well where are you going?" David asked as Stalking Crow turned and walked away.

"I'm going to go and take a nap. Remember to take your cane with you."

"Yeah I will but will you wait up and show me how to get out of here?"

"Why you don't remember?"

"No." David replied as Stalking Crow stopped and said while he turned around and pointed,

"The way out is right behind you. Now David Tall Tree turn around and look."

"No way."

"Yes way." Stalking Crow replied and said as David finally turned around and saw a white door form against the hard and rocky cave wall, "Now remember to take your cane."

"I will," David said as he turned back around and started to say before he noticed that Stalking Crow was gone, "but how? Oh never mind."

Shaking his head and turning around with his cane and container in hand, David then made his way to the door, where he stood and opened it. Stepping through the open door way and finding himself back in his house, David then closed the door behind him and said, "wow," as he reopened the door and shook his head while he stared out at his back yard, "how does he do that?"

PART XXXVIII

The Building of the Two Machines

Stepping away from his back door while Elizabeth laye, d and wondered where he was, David then walked through their house, and as Doctor John arrived at the military base in southern Nevada, David made his way out to their garage with the crystal's container in hand and thought, *what in the world am I gonna use to build a space ship? I told Scott I didn't have a single clue as what to do.*

Stepping to a work bench and setting the container down, David then, while Elizabeth tried to sleep to set her mind at ease, looked around the garage and mumbled as he gazed at all of the different tools he had collected during his career, "think David, think like the gifted architect you are. Gifted architect, I design and help build houses and small buildings not space ships. I have no idea how to," *Wait a minute*, David then thought as his mind paused in mid sentence, *what did Scott mean when he said you do now? Man think. What did he?* David then thought and paused again as he stepped to their large garage door and peaked out a small window, *he couldn't have. Or could have he?* "Maybe," David then mumbled as he stepped away from the window and walked over to a automated, home, monitoring system and said, "Helen. please open garage door."

"As you wish Mr. Leviticus. Do you need anything else?"

"No"

"Very well then, please stand clear while H.M.S. opens your garage door."

Standing and patiently waiting for the door to fully open while

Elizabeth finally fell asleep, David's mind raced with visual thoughts of magnificent engineering plans. But as the door fully opened and he stood staring out at Elizabeth's white sports car, his mind slowed down to one exact plan while he mumbled, "yep that's what Scott meant."

Stepping out of the garage and walking to the car, David then mumbled as he got into it, "this is gonna be easier then I thought." Firing the cars magnetic engine up while Doctor John stepped into a meeting, David then put the car in gear and slowly maneuvered it into the garage where he put the transmission in park and shut the engine down before he got out and heard.

"Mr. Leviticus."

"Yes Helen?"

"You have a message from Elizabeth, would you like to hear it?"

"I've been home for twenty minutes and your just now telling me I have a message. Are you stupid or what?"

"I'm sorry. H.M.S. doesn't understand that command. Please restate your phrase after my question. Mr. Leviticus would you like to hear Elizabeth's message?"

"Yes!" David replied and said as he shook his head, "what a worthless system."

"Very well then."

"David this is Elizabeth. Where are you? Why didn't you show up this morning? I'm starting to worry. Will you please call the hospital when you get this? Diane will you drive by my house and see if David's there? Mr goofy didn't show up today. Oh and please contact me if you don't find him or contact me if you do. Either way please let me know something, because you know as well as I do its not like him to be late. Thank you. Oh and David when I see you I'm gonna beat your butt."

"End of message. Would you like me to repeat it Mr. Leviticus?"

"No, but will you dial Billings Mercy Medical for me? Oh and shut the garage door please."

"Very well. Shutting garage door. Searching directory for Billings Mercy Medical. Mr. Leviticus?"

"Yes Helen?" David asked while he leaned against the car and watched the garage door close.

"East Billings or West Billings?"

"East."

"Very well. Dialing east Billings Mercy Medical one moment please."

Man it would have been easier if I dialed it myself, David thought while he waited for the H.M.S. to make its connection.

"Mr. Leviticus."

"Yes Helen?"

"I've established a connection. Would you like me to put it through to the audio amplifier?"

"Well Duh! I mean yes please!"

"Very well."

"Hello this is East Billings Mercy Medical. How may I help you?"

"Yeah hello. My name is David Leviticus and my wife's a patient at your facility, um I can't remember her room number but would you be able to tell me if she has a phone yet?

"What's your wife's name sir?"

"Oh it's Elizabeth, Elizabeth Leviticus."

"Okay hang on while I look and see."

"Okay thanks." *man she's gonna be upset*, David then thought while he looked around.

"Mr. Leviticus."

"Yes?"

"Your wife's audio phone is on. Would you like me to connect you to it?"

"Yes please and thank you."

"You're welcome. Now hold please."

Man I hope she's not gonna be to upset, David then thought as the line then rang through to Elizabeth's room.

"Hello."

"Hi Beth, you'll never guess who this is?"

"David, where have you been? What happened, you didn't get drunk last night did you?"

"Um yeah sort of, I guess."

"What do you mean you guess, did you or didn't you?"

"Yeah a little, I mean sort of. I think."

"You think, what do you mean you think?"

"Yeah I think I got drunk. Everything's a little fuzzy."

"David stop beating around the bush and tell me what happened. Did you wreck my car or something?"

"No Beth I didn't wreck your car. I did go to Mars though."

"Mars huh."

"Yeah and I also walked and talked with a great warrior."

"Ah ha ha ha ha, David you're so funny. You really must have tied one on, next thing you know your gonna tell me your going to build a ship and fly us to another planet."

"Well um," David slurred and then thought while he paused and stared blankly, *how did she know*?

"David are you there?"

"Yeah Beth I'm here."

"Well are you gonna tell me what happened or not?"

"Yeah I am but may I wait until I see you? Right now I have to go, there's something I have to do."

"I suppose yah brat."

"Brat. why am I a brat?"

"Because you just are. Now go and do what ever it is you have to do and then get your butt up here when your done."

"I will and I promise I'll explain everything. Okay?"

"Alright."

"I love you Beth and don't worry everything's gonna be fine."

"I love you too and remember what I said. You get your butt here when you're finished doing whatever it is you have to do."

"I will I promise. Okay?"

"Alright, I love you bye."

"Love you bye."

"Call ended. Mr. Leviticus Do you need anything else."

"No Helen I'm good."

"Very well then, H.M.S. will now switch to stand by mode."

"You Do that," David mumbled and said as Doctor John finished up with his meeting while Elizabeth tried to fall back to sleep, "I can't believe Beth didn't ask me what it was I had to do. Hmm her comment made it sound like she somehow already knew. I don't know whatever, anyways," David then mumbled as he stepped to the front of the car while construction of the energy fountain began, "it's time to work. Vehicle one, release and roll hood open. Security code edh, star, pound22."

"Very well please stand clear while vehicle control module unlatches and rolls vehicle one's hood open."

I still don't understand why all of these automated audio themes always have to say very well, David then thought as he stepped away from the car while the hood unlatched and slowly rolled back, *couldn't the designers have thought of something less bland like. Yeah sure if that's what you want. Or alright just hang on. Or g's, give me a minute. Yeah that would have been so much cooler*, David thought while the hood finished rolling back and he stepped to the cars engine compartment and asked allowed, "Don't you think? No, well I do. And I also think this is gonna be easier then I thought. Probably a little time consuming though, but here we go."

Leaning into the engine compartment while his thought's filled with the schematic that Scott had obviously implanted upon his neuro net, David unplugged the car's main power supply then unplugged 30 different color coded plugs. He then removed the vehicle's primary fiber optic wiring harness and carried it to a work bench, where he sat it down and said as he carefully laided it out, "this is almost gonna be to easy." *I think*, David then thought as he examined each plug and mumbled, "now which one sends direct power to the vehicle control module? Hmm something tells me that's the one I need. Ah and here it is and wouldn't you know it the plug says right on it, to V.C.M. Wow engineers finally did something that makes sense. That has to be a first. Wait a minute I'm an engineer. No David your an architect. Same difference now stop arguing with yourself, the people reading this story are gonna think your crazy. Yah think? Yeah I think, now common."

Reaching to an overhead cabinet while Elizabeth finally fell asleep, David opened it's door's and quickly found his pen shaped laser cutter which he used to cut the v.c.m. plug from the fiber optic cable, *hmm I bet I can use this to open that case the energy crystal is in*, David then thought as he looked at the laser cutter, *well lets find out but first where did I put it? Oh duh it's on the other bench*, David thought while he looked around the garage and then made his way to the other bench, *I must be losing it. Of course you are. No I'm not. Maybe*. "I don't know?" David then mumbled as he put the laser cutter in his shirt pocket before he grabbed the case and thought while he walked back to the other bench, *this thing feels thick I hope this cutter will do the job cause if it doesn't*, David then thought as he set one end of the container into a vertical claw clamp with one hand and pressed the automatic tightener switch with his other hand, *I don't know what will*. "Ah ha ha ha ha," David then laughed and said while he studied the container for a minute, "if the cutter doesn't work, maybe I could just beat you open with my cane. What do you think? Yeah, no, maybe, would you like that? I know I would but my shoulder sure wouldn't though. Anyways here it goes."

Pulling the cutter out of his shirt pocket and pointing the laser lens at the center circumference of the container, David then by pressing the butt end of the cutter with his thumb, fired the laser up while Elizabeth started to dream, and began to burn his way through the container's thick carbon casing.

"Oh Elizabeth wake up dear grandma's got something to show you."

"Na Nun is that you, where are you?"

"I'm right here sweet heart, now open your eye's and look at me."

"Why?"

"Because there's something I want to show you."

"I can't Na Nun., I can't see."

"Oh yes you can. Now come on sweet heart, look at me."

"Okay I'll try."

Slowly sitting up and wearily opening her eye's while she dreamt, Elizabeth as the blurry image of her grandmother came into focus and she appeared to be standing along the edge of her bed, smiled a wide, warm child like smile and said, "Na Nun, I must be dreaming. Is it really you? You look so young."

"Yes Sweet Heart it's me."

"But how, are you? Your."

"Shh, no time for questions little one, grandma has something she wants to show you. So come with me."

"What is it grandma?"

"It's a surprise, now come Elizabeth."

"Okay Na Nun."

Slowly pulling her blankets off as she swung her body out of bed, Elizabeth stood up and gently took her grandmother by the hand then quietly followed her to the bathroom and stepped inside, while the green fluorescent lights went out and the vertical changing mirror that hung on the back of the bathroom door slowly lit up and filled the room with bright glowing light as the door closed behind them.

Turning towards the glowing mirror, Elizabeth's grandmother then led Elizabeth into the light and stepped through the mirror then instantly emerged on the other side while Elizabeth followed and said as she looked around and found herself standing barefoot in a dimly lit snow filled forest, "now I know I'm dreaming, I should be freezing."

"Yes but your not," Elizabeth's grandmother replied as she turned to Elizabeth and smiled while she pointed to a winding path that led to the top of a high hill, "now come and let's go see your surprise."

"Okay Na Nun."

Following her grandmother to the path while David kept cutting away at the container, Elizabeth strolled through the ankle deep snow and thought as they began to make their way up the path, *wow this is so pretty I feel like I'm in a fairy tail.*

You are mommy, but it's his fairy tail. None of this is real and please don't believe him, he just wants to scare you.

Who wants to scare me little ones?

The blond man, he's a bad, bad man. He wants to keep you and daddy apart. Please don't let him.

I don't understand little ones. Why does the blond man want to keep mommy and daddy apart?

Because he's bad, the voices of the twins replied and said in

Elizabeth's mind while she and her grandmother approached the top of the hill, *please don't let him mommy don't let him do it. Don't let him split you and daddy up.*

I won't.

You promise?

Yes little ones, Elizabeth's mind passionately replied and said as they made it to the top of the hill and stopped at the end of the path, *I promise, now go to sleep little ones great grandma has a surprise for me.*

But that's not. The twins tried say as Elizabeth's grandmother turned to her and asked while she smiled and sinisterly with a blink of her right eye, caused the voices of the twins to quickly fade from Elizabeth's mind,

"Are you ready sweet heart?"

"Oh yeah I'm ready."

"Good now face the trees and close your eyes. Don't open them until I tell you to. Okay?"

"Okay Na nun." Elizabeth replied as she turned to the trees and closed her eye's while her grandmother waved her left hand at the back of her head and said as the trees slowly fell together,

"Now Elizabeth I want you to count to ten before you open your eyes, alright?"

"Alright Na nun."

"But not until I tell you."

"Okay." Elizabeth replied as her grandmother stepped back and said after she waved her hand again,

"Alright Sweet heart you may begin."

"Alright here it goes. One, two, three, four, five, six, seven, eight, nine, ten."

"Now open you eye's. Surprise!"

"No! Why this can't be!" Elizabeth then cried as her eye's popped open and she saw the painful image of a loud, flesh pounding session of deep, drilling sex between David and Diane form and quickly take place within the fallen trees tangled branches, "Why this can't be real?"

"Oh yeah," Elizabeth's grandmother replied and said as Elizabeth began to cry, "it's very real."

"No!."

"Oh yes. Why do you think he didn't show up this morning? It wasn't because he got drunk it was because he doesn't love you anymore and he was busy banging your best friend."

"That's not true." Elizabeth cried as she stumbled back words, "David loves me, he would never do this."

"Oh yes dear I'm sorry to say but yes he would and yes he did. Or should I say they did. Now come here sweet heart, let me dry those tears and make it all better."

"No," Elizabeth cried as she stumbled further back, "I can't. I'm."

"Lost." Elizabeth's grandmother said as she held out her hand, while Elizabeth staggered and stumbled around in emotional distress.

"No I'm scared, I don't know what to do I can't."

Run mommy run now, run before he gets us.

"Come to Na nun."

"No!" Elizabeth cried as she tripped and fell into the snow, "I can't."

"Come to Na nun, she'll make it all better."

Run mommy, the twins insisted in Elizabeth's mind as she tearfully staggered to her feet while the naked images of David and Diane began to hysterically laugh at her, *run*! *Run*!

"Come to Na nun."

"I don't, I can't find the way out." Elizabeth tried to say in emotional confusion as the voices over powered the laughter while she held her stomach and cried.

"*Please mommy yes you can.*"

"No she can't!" Elizabeth's grandmother replied to the twins voice and said as she transformed into the beautiful mystical figure of the serpent creature,

"She can't go anywhere, she belongs with me! Now come!"

"No, no, no, I don't want to!"

Yes you do Beth, *now go as fast as you can*, Elizabeth's alter ego also said in her mind as she began to franticly look for the path while the creature held out his mighty hand and said,

"There's no way out."

"Yes there is!" Elizabeth then cried as she looked down the hill and tearfully clenched her arm's around the back of her head before she threw herself over the edge and screamed as she uncontrollably, while a great white wolf came majestically charging through the woods, rolled down the snowy hill, hit the hard rocky bottom and tearfully passed out, as the wolf, like a horse jumping a hurdle in a human race came quickly running and leapt over Elizabeth's limp body, before it with the agility of a skilled acrobatic assassin, swiftly continued on and howled as it bound it's way up to the top of the hill. Where it, like a predator catching it's surprised prey, ferociously tackled the serpent creature and violently sank it's razor sharp teeth into his neck, which forcibly caused him to, while the laughing image of David and Diane dissolved back into the entangled abyss of the fallen trees, shatter and slam back into his bright white realm of soft, lustrous, satin.

Loudly howling out in victory, the wolf then did a quick about face and brisk fully ran back down to the bottom of the hill. Where it, like a wolf mother protecting her cubs, slowly circled and softly growled as it quickly found Elizabeth's warm body, unconsciously lying in the snow.

Moving in and gently nudging Elizabeth with it's soft, warm nose while it whimpered, the wolf then forcibly tried to wake her but had no luck. So it circled back around and sat at her right side and began to bark really loud. But this didn't wake her either. So the great, white wolf then looked around at the trees and sat eerily silent as the snow started to mysteriously move across the ground and slowly circle around its soft, white, body. Then with the force of a small and fast moving dust devil, the snow spun high into the air and quickly while the wolf looked up and howled, the snow then swirled back down and instantly with a flash of red sparkling light, it flung around the wolf like a fast moving comet and majestically transformed it into Stalking Crow.

Standing up straight while the snow dispersed into the air, Stalking Crow then stretched his arms over his head and said, "Ahh." As he leaned forward and cracked his back while he looked at Elizabeth, "that's better, now we can go."

Bending over and carefully picking Elizabeth up from the snow covered ground, Stalking Crow then swiftly carried her off through the woods and back to the glowing mirror, where he stepped into its bright light and transformed like a chameleon while he stepped through to the other side of the mirror and said as he instantly emerged in the bathroom as nurse Beard, "now Ms Elizabeth lets get you back in bed."

Opening the bathroom door with her mind while the mirror shut down and the florescent lights came back on, Nurse Beard then gently put Elizabeth down and swung her arm around her as she stood her on her feet and said, "Ms. Elizabeth you need to wake up girl, I can't get you into bed on my own."

"Huh?"

"Come on Ms. Elizabeth wake up."

"Huh, where am I, what happened?"

"You been sleep walking."

"I have?" Elizabeth warily asked while she slowly opened her eyes and said as she realized she still couldn't focus, "I had a terrible nightmare."

"Yes you did. Now common you need to get back to bed."

"Okay." Elizabeth softly replied and said while they began to walk out of the bathroom and make their way to her bed, "that dream seemed so real, I could feel everything. I could even see."

"I'm sure you'll see again."

"You think?"

"Oh yeah," Nurse Beard replied and said while they stepped to the side of the bed, "but when you do it's not gonna be a dream, it's gonna be for real."

"Thanks for the vote of confidence."

"Sometimes a vote of confidence is all you need. Now come on, in you go."

Carefully helping Elizabeth into bed and covering her up, Nurse Beard then put her right hand on Elizabeth's forehead and hummed a sweet sounding gospel song that slowly put Elizabeth into a deep sleep while David said as he finished cutting the container open, "man it's about time, that seemed like it took forever."

Shutting the laser off and tossing it into his shirt pocket, David then stared at the container for a moment and said, "I still can't believe this is happening. Why me? Yeah I know, because that's the way it's written." *Anyways let's do this*, David then thought as he pulled the top half of the container from the bottom half.

Tossing the top half to the work bench, David then loosened the clamp and pulled the football shaped crystal out of the bottom half and carried it to the other bench, where he sat it down while he stared at the car's fiber optic wiring harness. Then as the sun started to go down, David looked around the garage and began collecting steel coat hangers from various places, which he with the help of a few hand tools, formed into straight wires.

Laying each wire out on the work bench when he was done, David then vertically wrapped each one tightly around the crystal and created two razor sharp connection points at one end of the crystal and one at the other. He then grabbed the cars wiring harness and slowly forced one of the sharp contact points into the spliced end of the fiber optic cable, before he forced the spliced end of the v.c.m. cable into the other.

Picking the wiring harness and the crystal up together, David then stepped to the car and set the crystal inside of the magnetic engine compartment and carefully secured it into a tight space before he slowly plugged all 30 of the wiring harness's color coded plugs back in.

Securing the wiring harness to its fastener's, David then plugged the car's main power supply back in and said as he stepped back, "vehicle one. Roll hood shut and close latch. Security code edh star pound 22.

"Very well, please stand clear while v.c.m. rolls hood shut and closes latch."

Stepping around the car while the hood rolled shut, David got inside and tried to fire the car's magnetic engine up but his attempts kept failing, "okay what's wrong."

"Mr. Leviticus."

"Yes Vehicle one?"

"My systems have detected new hardware. Please up load a new operating system."

"A new operating system, how do I? I have no, woe yes I do," David then paused as his mind flashed him more instructions, "One moment vehicle one. I'll be right back."

"Very well."

Getting out of the car, David then stepped around it and made his way to a cabinet, where he opened its door's and said as he fumbled through it, "now what did I do with that thing? Ah here it is," David then mumbled as he found a hand held, automotive trouble code, diagnostic card, "hm I hope the battery is still good. Now how do I? oh I know."

Stepping back around the car, David then got inside again and unraveled the diagnostic card's two usb cords. He then plugged one end of the cord into the car's diagnostic usb port and turned the card on while he held the other usb plug to his right temple.

"Mr. Leviticus."

"Yes vehicle one?"

"To start upload, please turn the primary power systems to the run position."

"Oh yeah."

Setting the cord in his lap, David then flipped the car's main power switch to the run position.

"Very well, now you may commence with upload."

"Okay here it goes."

Picking the cord back up, David as he slowly pressed the usb plug back to his right temple, took a deep breath and passed out while the information that Scott had implanted upon his neuro net, slammed out of the chemical fiber's of his brain and passed through the cord like a loud static storm before all of it quickly collected inside of the diagnostic card's small circuits.

"Upload complete, please stand by while vehicle one down loads the new operating system and copies all files to carbon hard drive."

Falling further into unconsciousness while the car's computer slowly downloaded all of the information from the diagnostic card, David dropped the cord to his lap and slept through the night and unto the next morning, where he awoke at sunrise to the sound of the car's automated voice command, "down load complete Mr. Leviticus. Please shut down primary power systems and remove usb plug from diagnostic port."

"As you wish," David replied as he wearily sat up and said while he shut the primary power switch off, "man what a rush, that felt like something was trying to suck my brains out of my head. I hope I don't ever have to do that again."

Unplugging the diagnostic card from the usb port, David then got out of the car with card in hand and stumbled around the car in stiffness before he tossed the card to a work bench. Standing still for a moment he then tried to stretch the tight muscles of his healing hip and shoulder while he thought, okay now what?

"Mr. Leviticus."

"Yes vehicle one?"

"I am now ready to give you full operating instructions."

"On what?"

"On my new systems. Please step inside of the vehicle and remove primary filters from my ventilation system and replace them with the chemical element C followed by the atomic number six."

"You mean charcoal?"

"Yes that is correct."

"Where am I? Oh I have some."

Stepping to another cabinet, David then opened its doors and pulled out a small bag of charcoal, he then stepped around the car and tossed it to the passenger seat as he got back inside and said, "I can't believe I'm not hungry. Vehicle one do you plan on barbequing or something, because I'm not hungry yet?"

"I'm sorry, vehicle one does not understand your question. Please restate your phrase and ask again"

"Yeah, yeah, yeah, never mind," David laughed and said as he removed the panel that covered the car's ventilation filters, "I can see the new programming hasn't changed this thing a bit."

Setting the panel to the side, David then pulled the filters from their slots and tossed them to the garage floor. He then rolled the bag of charcoal open and put a handful of the black carbon coals into the empty slots and said, "there you go," as he snapped the panel back in place, "all set."

"Very well. Please stand by and wait for instructions while vehicle one reconfigures ventilation system and implements C,o2 scrubber."

"C,o2 scrubber?" David mumbled as he tossed the bag of charcoal to the garage floor, "good idea."

"Mr. Levisticus."

"Yes?"

"Configuration complete. Please remain in the vehicle while my secondary systems brief you on my new operating system and please close the door, your draining my storage chips."

"Yeah okay," David snickered and then closed the door while the monitor on the center display console lit up and a different automated voice said,

"Hello Mr. Leviticus. This is the voice of vehicle one's secondary system. Please listen closely and watch the monitor while I instruct you on your secondary controls. Are you ready?"

"Yes."

"Very well then, this vehicle will now run in two modes. Primary mode and secondary mode. In primary mode you will have all functions of the vehicle perform as normal."

"Such as?" David asked while he watched a schematic form on the monitor.

"Such as regular driving conditions. You will still be able to drive it as you normally would."

"Oh okay, primary mode. That makes sense. I think?"

"Now," the automated voice said as the schematic on the monitor changed, "in secondary mode the new hardware you have installed will use the electrons that are produced from the spinning magnets within vehicle one's engine to create a high energy, static ion field around the car's outer iridium shell."

"How?" David asked as the monitor changed to another schematic.

"By sending high energy particles through vehicle one's main ground wire, which are then transferred through vehicle one's outer molecular compounds."

"Really." David asked, "and the crystal does this by simply transferring the energy?"

"Yes that is correct."

"Alright, well how do I control the field?"

"Okay Mr. Leviticus the field through the electric steering monitoring system is simply controlled by turning the wheel left or right and acceleration is controlled by vehicle one's acceleration pedal. The harder you press the faster the magnets spin, thus producing more ions which are then expelled through the back of the static bubble, which also produces a quantum, inertial dampening field within the perimeter of vehicle one's cabin."

"Okay so Beth and I won't have our gut's splatter all over the place."

"That is correct."

"How about vertical thrust and decent?"

"Vertical thrust, while you press the accelerator with your foot is simply controlled by pressing and holding the plus sign on the cruise control button until your desired elevation is reached. Which will be numerically displaye, d on the center monitor when used. Decent is performed by holding the minus sign on your cruise control button.

"Okay what about direction and stopping, I'd hate to run into an asteroid or something."

"Forward direction and reverse direction plus slowing and stopping vehicle one are controlled the same way as they are in primary mode. Also vehicle one by moving the telescopic steering option in or out with the press of the forward and back button will also at your command diagonally rotate on a 180* vertical axis."

"Okay that sounds easy enough. Do I have to achieve a certain velocity to escape the pull of earth's gravity?"

Yes and in order to break away you must reach the speed of 6.96 m/s which is approximately 34 times the speed of sound."

"But that's only to leave the surface right?"

"False vehicle one's engine will produce enough kinetic energy for you to achieve that speed at any elevation within the earth's atmosphere, which will also be displaye, d on the center monitor."

"What elevation do I have to reach before I can maneuver out to the kuiper belt?"

"Approximately 100 miles from the outer edge of earth's atmosphere.

"Sounds simple."

"Mr. Leviticus do you have anymore questions?"

"Yes. How do I switch from primary mode to secondary mode?"

"Simply state which mode you would like vehicle one to perform in, anything else?"

"No thank you."

"Very well then. Vehicle one is now switching back to primary systems while it shuts down."

"Well I guess it's time to go and pack some things together."

Opening the car door at the same time Doctor John looked up at the almost complete energy fountain, David then got out and shut the door behind him. He then stood and stretched while Doctor John looked around at the workers in the hanger and mumbled to himself, "I think it's time to take a long walk."

PART XXXIX

The Day It All Came To An End

Walking around the house before he started to pack, David stared at the many pictures that he and Elizabeth had acquired together and thought for a moment, *I can't believe it's all gonna end. Maybe I should just stay here and end with everything as well*, "What do you think?" David then said allowed as he stopped and stared at a picture of Big Jim, "should I stay or should I go, what would you do if you were me? Yeah I know you'd probably go. wouldn't yah? Or you'd probably say, David what's wrong which you man? Stop whining and get your pussy, white ass moving before I put my big black foot in it. Yeah that's what you'd say. Hmm your probably saying that right now. Man I just don't know. I do know this though, if what Stalking Crow said about staying on your path in order to make it to the next laye, r of existence is true, then if you and your wife were on your right path's. Well then my friend you should see each other real soon, I hope. Hey if you can would you send me a post card or something, you know to tell me what it's like there?" Pausing for a moment David then said while he pulled the picture from the wall, "Yeah I bet you would if you could my well missed friend."

Slowly wondering around the house with the picture of Big Jim in his hand, David then collected a couple of their wedding photo's and a few of Elizabeth's grandmother. David then slowly made his way into the bedroom where he laye, d the pictures out onto their bed and blankly stared at them while he procrastinated and thought about not leaving. Then as the sun began to go down David had visions of a new life with his family and finally made up his mind while he snapped out of the vision and mumbled, “yep I’m going.”

Making his way out of the bedroom, David then made his way around the house and fumbled through closets and cabinets while he mindfully gathered, clothing, toiletries, pillows, blankets and a few of Elizabeth’s family heir looms together, which he piled on top of their bed as he placed it all with the pictures that he planned on taking with them.

David then gathered a couple of travel bags together while Doctor John walked down a dark, desert hwy, and strategically packed as the night crept by.

Boy its hot, Doctor John thought as he walked, *I thought the desert was supposed to be cold at night. Most of them are but I guess this one isn't. Maybe I should try and hitch a ride, that's if somebody drives bye. Hm there's no telling when that could be, especially at this time of night. I'll just have to sweat it out until someone does. Where you gonna go? I have no idea, probably a. Woe*! Doctor John’s mind then paused and said as a dark vehicle with dim head lights silently rolled up from behind him and mysteriously pulled along his side before it stopped, *where did that come from*?

Standing still while the passenger window rolled down, Doctor John then, as a female voice asked, “you need a ride?” tried to curiously see inside of the dark car before he replied,

“Yeah sure.” and thought as he stepped to the door while it slowly opened, *that voice sounds familiar*.

Getting inside, Doctor John then found himself to be mystically sitting in the car’s warm passenger seat as a seven year old boy while the door closed and the interior lights came on.

“Hi Johnny boy.”

“Mom,” John then asked as he looked up at the lady in the passenger seat while she smiled a warm smile, “is it really you?”

“Yes John it’s really me. Now hang on.”

“Where are we going?”

"We're going to a new place."

"Why." John asked as his mother began to drive down the dark road while the lights went out.

"Because your path here has ended and it's time to continue onto the next one."

"Are you gonna be there with me?"

"Always John." John's mother replied and said as she put her hand on his head, "I'm always gonna be with you."

"Forever."

"Yes forever." John's mother then warmly replied while David slowly finished packing and said as John and his mother drove off and dissolved into the warm night air,

"Well I think that's it."

Grabbing the packed travel bags together, David then made his way out of the room and through the house while he stiffly carried the packed items out to the garage, where he put everything into the trunk of the car while he thought, *I feel like I'm forgetting something.*

Closing the trunk David then stood and mumbled while he scanned the garage, "what did I forget?" *Man I don't know. Oh forget it. "Helen"*

"Yes Mr. Leviticus?"

"Please open the garage door."

"Very well, please stand clear while hms opens the garage door."

Standing in place while the door opened, David scanned the garage again and said, "what am I forgetting?"

"Mr. Leviticus."

"Yes?"

"Your forgetting your cane."

"Huh! How do you," David Started to to ask before the hms interrupted him in mid sentence while it said,

"Get your cane and have a safe trip. Oh and remember not to look back. Hms will now shut all power to the home down.

"That was just to weird. Nah in light of everything that has recently happened it really wasn't."

Making his way back into the house, David then went through the rooms and found his cane laying on the bed in the bedroom. He then grabbed it and mumbled as he made his way out of the room, "there I hope everyone's happy now."

Stepping back into the garage, David then made his way to the driver side of the car where he opened the door and tossed his cane into the back seat while he got in and shut the door. Firing the car's magnetic engine up, he then slowly backed the car out of the garage and said as he stopped in the middle of the drive way while he stared at his old beater of a car that sat along side of the garage all cold and lonely looking, "well old friend this is it. It's been nice knowing you, I wish I could have taken you. But you know how these things go. Um so maybe I'll see you again? No. Okay good luck then."

Backing the rest of the way out of the drive way after he stared at the house and car one more time, David then took off forward and calmly drove to the hospital while the sun began to rise.

Arriving at the hospital 15minutes later while construction of the energy fountain was finally completed, David then parked the car and grabbed his cane as he opened the door up and got out.

Closing the door down, David then made his way across the parking lot and into the hospital where he casually made is way up to Elizabeth's floor. Stepping out of an elevator, David then walked down a long hall and made his way past a Nurse's station as he stepped into Elizabeth's room while he stared at her soft, sleeping, body.

Silently creeping up to her bed side, David then stood over her and softly rubbed her warm cheek with his left hand while he said, "Beth, wake up baby girl we have to go. Common sweet heart," David then said as Elizabeth stirred, "you have to wake up."

"David is that you?"

"Yeah Beth it's me now common we have to go."

"Go where?"

"I'll explain when we get there, now common."

"David I can't, I'm to weak."

"Yes you can, now common, I'll help you."

"David did you screw around on me?"

"No," David calmly replied and asked as he pulled Elizabeth's blankets off, "why would you ask such a thing? You know better."

"Because I had a dream that you did." Elizabeth wearily replied as she opened her eye's and blankly stared at the blurry image of David while he leaned over and kissed her on the lip's.

"Yeah and I can tell you that something like that would only take place in a dream."

"Are you sure?"

"Yes Beth," David replied as he kissed her again, "I'm positive"

"Well where were you." Elizabeth then asked as David leaned back and walked around the room while he fetched her house coat and slippers together.

"Beth I don't have time to explain right now. But I promise when we reach our destination I'll tell you everything."

"David I'm to tired to go anywhere."

"Well you can sleep on the way," David said as he put her slippers onto her feet, "now common."

Carefully helping Elizabeth up out of bed and to her feet, David then slipped her house coat onto her shoulders and slowly helped her put her arms into the sleeves while she softly asked, "does the chip look sexy?"

"What chip?"

"The one that's attached to my head you ofe."

Stepping back and looking at the silver robotic chip that was attached to Elizabeth's head at her appointment, David then said, "you know what? I didn't even notice it."

"Yeah and you probably forgot about it too."

"No, yeah. I mean sort of."

"Well does it look sexy?"

"Beth your being silly." David replied as he stepped away and fetched her wheelchair.

"I'm waiting for an answer Mr."

"Yes Beth it looks sexy."

"Good I'm glad you think so." Elizabeth replied as David rolled the wheelchair to her.

Helping Elizabeth into the wheelchair, David then made sure she had her feet up while she asked, "do you have your cane Mr?"

"Yes mother I sure do." David replied and said as he grabbed it from the side of the bed, "it's right here."

"Good."

"Now lets go."

Stepping back to the wheelchair while he laid his cane in Elizabeth's lap, David then casually rolled her out of the room and down the hall, where they passed the Nurses station as they made their way to an elevator while Elizabeth drifted in and out of sleep.

Rolling Elizabeth into the elevator as the doors opened, David then spun her around while the doors closed behind them and quietly road the elevator to the main floor, "David."

"Yeah Beth?"

"What's wrong? Something doesn't seem right, things feel awfully eerie. Are you okay?"

"Yeah I'm fine."

"Are you sure? Because I get the feeling your not."

"Really Beth, I'm okay." David replied as the elevator doors opened.

"Alright, if you say so." Elizabeth wearily said while David rolled her out of the elevator as she then drifted in and out of sleep again.

Casually making his way down the hall and into the main lobby while he rolled Elizabeth along, David then thought as he rolled her out through the main doors, *I still feel like I'm forgetting something. What is it*? David's mind then asked as he began to roll Elizabeth across the parking lot, *I wish I could remember. It must not be anything important*, "Oh forget it." David then mumbled as he rolled Elizabeth up to the passenger side of her car while she opened her eye's and softly said as she stared at its blurry white, outline,

"Well that rules that out."

"Rules what out?" David asked as he stepped around the wheelchair and then lifted the car door open.

"You know it rules out you wrecking my car."

"What are you talking about?"

"Oh nothing." Elizabeth softly replied as David grabbed his cane from her lap and said,

"Oh. Yeah, yeah, yeah, you thought I wrecked your car didn't yah?"

"Well Duh." Elizabeth replied as David laughed and said while he tossed the cane to the back seat,

"Well as you can see I didn't."

"I don't see anything but a big white blur that looks like it could be my car. How do I know it's mine?"

"Now your being silly." David replied as he helped Elizabeth to her feet and onto the car's passenger seat, where he strapped her harness on while he kissed her face and said as she fell asleep again, "I love you Beth and I really hope you get well enough for the four of us to be together and stay together when this is all over."

"She will David Tall Tree," Stalking Crow replied while he stood and watched them from a hidden distance, "she will and the four of you are gonna be together for a long, long time. Now WA che David Tall Tree." Stalking Crow then said as he dissolved into the air, "WA che and have and have a safe trip."

Shutting the passenger door down, David then made his way around to the driver side and blurted out, "Food!" as he got in and closed the down, "I forgot food. Hmm I'm not hungry but that doesn't mean I won't be and I know Beth's certainly gonna be. Hmm should I go back home and pack some?" *Nah,* David then thought as he looked at Elizabeth's soft, sleeping face, *I highly doubt that what ever it was that decided to send us to the other side of the universe would be sending us to a place that didn't have anything for us eat. Or maybe it would have. What do you think? Yes. Maybe. Nah no way. Okay let's go then.*

Firing the car's magnetic engine up, David then said as it began to snow, "vehicle one."

"Yes Mr. Leviticus?"

"Please switch all systems to secondary mode."

"Very well please stand by while vehicle one switches all primary systems to secondary mode."

Staring out the window while the car's computer switched to secondary mode, David listened to the electrical hum of the engine and thought as a static blue energy field quickly passed through the car's iridium shell and formed a six inch ion shield around the outside perimeter of the now glowing ship, *I wonder which way which way I have to go*? *It would have been nice if they would have told me*.

"Mr. Leviticus."

"Yes?"

"Vehicle one is now in secondary mode. Do you need anything else?"

"No, wait I mean only if you know which way I'm supposed to go?"

"I'm sorry vehicle."

"Yeah, yeah, yeah, doesn't understand that command. Please restate phrase. Never mind yah stupid computer."

"Very well. Vehicle one's secondary systems are now standing by."

Pausing and staring through the glowing shield while president Conley went on the world wide broadcast frequency and announced the new energy fountain, David as people all over the globe gathered around view screens and audio devises to see and hear the president's speech, thought again, *why didn't they give me directions am I supposed to use my instincts or something*? *Man what a*. David's mind then paused in mid thought, "what am I." David then tried to mumble while he watched passer Byers point at the glowing ship, "I better get out of here, this thing is starting to draw attention."

Pressing his thumb to the plus sign on the cruise control button while he mashed the accelerator with his right foot, David said, "Later!" As the ship quickly lifted from the ground with out a sound while the passer byers stood in aw and watched it swiftly ascend into the clouds.

Quickly reaching the altitude of 18,000 feet, David then removed his thumb from the cruise control button and hovered above the clouds while he thought again, *which way besides up do I have to go*? *Man why didn't they*, "Oh wait." David then said as a detailed map of the solar system flashed through the chemical neurons of his mind, "now I know. Hmm it's about time, nothing like waiting until the last minute. Scott!"

Pushing his thumb to the plus sign on the cruise control while the ship's automated voice said,

"Cabin pressure is now 14.7 psi. please enjoy the ride," David then mashed the accelerator again and like fast moving lighting the ship with a large blast of positively charged ions searing from is underneath, vertically blasted upwards and quickly broke away from earth's gravity as it with outstanding speed ascended out of the atmosphere and into space.

Quickly reaching the 100 mile out mark, while the energy fountain's primary systems came on line, David removed his thumb from the cruise control button and slammed the ship's engine into a forward direction while he mashed the accelerator to the floor. Then with the tilt and turn of the steering wheel, David instantly put the ship into a vertical 160° clock wise diagonal climb and flung it around to the dark side of the planet, where he swiftly as the energy fountain's primary ignition was fired, pulled out of a dive while he set the ship onto a horizontal course to the kuiper belt.

Reaching the od speed of 266,666,666.6 mph while the energy fountain collected planet Earth's em field together, David with his sleeping wife by his side, reached the edge of the kuiper belt within 15 minutes time. Then as David began to make his way through the icy Kuiper belt the energy fountain condensed the em field into a focused beam of highly charged atomic particles. Then while the people of earth watched in aw, the beam blasted through the bottom of the crystal and immediately with the loud sound of electrical energy, it shot out of the top like a fast moving laser and traveled into space, where it directly slammed into the sun's core with such a force that it immediately caused the star's hydrogen fuel to forcibly bind together and swiftly form a high density mass of heavy atomic particles that quickly imploded as the once mighty star violently erupted while it collapsed in on itself.

Forming a dark spinning vortex of highly heated energy while David sped out of the kuiper belt and headed to the now dissolving Helios pause, the black hole instantly vaporized Mercury, Venus, Earth and Mars as it began to tidally stretch the solar system to pieces.

Quickly reaching the now dissolved Helios pause, David then

instinctively turned the ship into a 400,000 mile u turn and raced past a speeding comet as he flew straight back to the black hole. Picking up more and more momentum as they sped towards the dark swirling mass, the ship along with David and Elizabeth slitley stretched as the black hole's gravity increased their speed to 89,000mps.

Instinctively putting the ship into a steep diagonal climb as they drew towards the black hole's accretion disk, David then pounded the accelerator and matched the black holes gravitational pull with the speed of his ship. David then aimend the ship at the black hole's dark center and sped down its glowing tunnel as they blasted through the middle of space times mighty event horizon.

Slamming through the tunnel like a speeding freight train and quickly emerging on the other side of the universe, David then swiftly flew the ship straight through and out of the spiraling fountain of highly focused pulsar energy that spewed out from the end of the tunnel's torn spatial circumference.

Quickly reaching inner stellar space at the outstanding speed of light to the third power, David then gradually slowed the ship down while he focused his sights on two very distant stars and said as he sped back up, "I sure hope this is the right way."

PART XL

The Final Battle

13 hours later on a lifeless planet that revolved around two stars, one of a large burning yellow hue and the other of a smaller cool burning blue, the glowing ship that David had flown so easily across the universe suffered major systems failure and came crashing in.

Slamming into the ground with the loud sound of crushing alloys and violently skidding around like a out of control snow sled, the car as its engine and energy crystal were tossed out, quickly broke apart while it brutally slid around and finally slowed down.

"Woe man, that was intense!" David blurted as the car finally stopped sliding, "I hope I never have to do that again."

Catching his breath David then removed his seat harness while he looked at Elizabeth and said, "well Beth we made it we're here. Common baby girl wake up we're here. Beth." David then said as he stared at her face in worry, "are you? No she couldn't be."

Leaning over and putting his ear to Elizabeth's chest, David then said, "oh okay, good she's still breathing. Okay then while you sleep I'm gonna go and take a look around."

Carefully climbing out of the wrecked car, while the serpent creature laye, d sleeping in his bright white realm of soft lustrous satin and dreamt of his next move, David then stood and stretched for a moment and said as he looked around at the deserted, rocky scenery, "there's nothing here. I hope this is the right planet. Or better yet," David then said as he began to walk, "the right star system."

Making his way across the rough and rocky terrain, David then slowly made his way to the edge of a cliff that laid 60 yards away from the crash sight and thought while he gazed out a barren waist land that lied beneath an eerie brown sky, *ok now I'm really starting to worry. Either I crashed in the wrong spot or like I said, this is the wrong system*, "Boy I hope not." David then mumbled as he turned and began to make his way back to the car, "cause if I did crash in the wrong place, hmm well we're screwed."

Arriving at the smashed car while the serpent creature woke, David then stepped to the mangled up passenger side and carefully pulled the door off then slid it aside while he said, "Beth wake up baby girl I've got some explaining to do. Common," David then said as he leaned into the car and softly rubbed Elizabeth's cheek, "wake up sweet heart, I think your crazy husband landed us in the wrong place. Now common wake up so I can explain everything. Beth." David then said as he stared at her with worry some emotion, "you have to wake up we have a lot to do."

Leaning further into the car while his heart began to sink fast, David then put his ear to Elizabeth's chest and began to cry while he mumbled, "why's her heart not beating? She was fine when we got here. No way she can't be dead. Common Beth." David then cried as he wrapped his arms around her limp, lifeless body while he kissed her face, "you have to wake up, we have to build a new home for the four of us. Beth common baby girl please wake up. Man I can't believe this. I was told everything was gonna be just fine. Why is this happening?" David then screamed, "what did I do and why are you doing this? If I knew they were gonna die I would have just staye, d on earth. I can't believe this," David then cried as he fell to his knees while he still held Elizabeth tight, "What am I gonna do without you?"

"Feed her the fruit David and they'll be fine."

What? Who was that. David's mind whispered while he cried.

"Feed her the fruit David and they'll be fine."

"Huh!" David then blurted as he abruptly stopped crying while he looked around and asked, "who's there?"

"Feed her the fruit and you'll have everything you want."

"Who are you, what do you want?"

"I want you to be happy. Now common." the voice said as a blossoming apple tree slowly grew up from the ground while David looked around and quickly spotted it in the distance, "give her the fruit and you'll all be one happy family."

"No!" David yelled while his body filled with struggling emotion, "I can't."

"Yes you can, now common it's obvious someone lied to you, you shouldn't have trusted them. So trust me, feed her the fruit and It will make everything better."

"No I can't this isn't real." David mumbled while he struggled.

"Oh yes this is as real as it gets. Now common feed her the fruit."

Struggling with his emotions while the voice kept taunting him, David feverously looked around and growled out with deep contentment, "they lied to me! Maybe that would be the only way to save Beth and the twins! Feed her the fruit and I'll have what I want."

"Yes David feed her the fruit and you'll have everything."

"I will!" David tearfully cried as he started to stand up, "I have to save Beth." David then said as he stumbled to his feet, "the fruit's the only way."

"Yes David it's the only way."

"No I can't. I don't know what to do."

"Yes you do. Now Common."

Spotting his cane as he stumbled around the car's wreckage in confusion and the voice kept saying "Feed her, feed her now." David stood and stared at it while his mind heard more voices,

Don't forget your cane David.

Don't forget your cane.

"Feed her the fruit David."

David Tall Tree, you have to destroy the anomaly.

"Feed her David!" The main voice then loudly said as David leaned over and grabbed the cane, "feed her now!"

Slowly standing up straight while all of the rage pored from his body and traveled into the cane through his hands, David then held it over his head as it began to glow, and howled while bright electrical light healed his wounds, as it with the loud sound of clapping thunder, spewed out from his body and circled around him while it magnificently transformed the wooden cane into a bright and shiny sword of glimmering steel.

Lowering the sword while his eye's flipped into ones of pure white, David then with sword in hand, charged towards the tree while the serpent creature slithered out from it's branches and quickly transformed into its beautiful human form.

Leaping into the air as David charged towards him, the creature then drew its mighty sword and ferociously swung it at David while he lept and swung his as well. Meeting in mid air as their swords slammed together with the loud sound of blasting steel, the two warriors of now even strength tumbled and danced across the sky like lighting as they ferociously fell into a loud and powerful sword fight that spun them around and around, until David with the cross of his sword, brutally slammed into the creature's chest with the speed of a powerful rocket and drove it screeching to the ground while he tore its head off with his bare hands, which caused the creature and his bright white realm of soft lustrous satin to instantly shatter and implode into the dark fabric of the universe as they hit the ground with the force of a exploding bomb.

Quickly scrambling to his feet while the dust settled, David's eyes rolled back to their normal deep coal black color as he dropped the sword and watched the blossoming apple tree quickly wither away. Wiping himself off, David then watched the sword dissolve away and abruptly stumbled backwards while the energy crystal that was tossed into a deep chasm when the ship crashed, erupted with a hard pulse and shook the ground as it sent all of its genetically coded energy that was stored in it when it was formed deep with in the core of Mars, crashing through the crust of the planet, where the energy began to terraform the desolate land scape into a earthly green paradise as it passed to the air and soil.

Stumbling in place while grass and trees began to quickly grow every ware, David looked around and said as the sky turned blue, while the solar systems stars cast a bright warm hue, "I can't believe this. This is so amazing, I have to get back to Beth."

Turning and quickly making his way through a rapidly growing forest, while lakes, oceans and land began to fill with the sound of life, David dodged many different animal species as they bound up from the canyons and caves while he swiftly ran back to the car, where Elizabeth lie coughing as he arrived and said with a heart warming smile, "Beth your alive."

"Yeah, why," Elizabeth replied and asked as she opened her eyes and focused them on David, "did I die or something?"

"Oh wow, you can see too!"

"Oh yeah David I can see, now get in here and kiss me."

Leaning into the car and feverously kissing Elizabeth, David then put his arms around her and squeezed her tight while he passionately said, "I thought I lost you three. Please don't ever do that again."

"I won't." Elizabeth replied while the mechanical chip fell from her head, "I won't, well at least I don't think I won't."

"You promise?"

"Yeah I promise." Elizabeth replied as David passionately kissed her warm lips again and then rubbed her stomach.

"How are my girls?"

"There fine David. They'er asleep though, so shh don't wake em."

"Okay I'll try. Are you hungry?"

"Naw. I'm a litte thirsty though."

"Alright I'll go and fetch you some water."

Stepping away from the car while Elizabeth said, "okay but before you go and get me something to drink are you gonna tell me where we are?"

"Yeah Beth I'll tell you all about it when I get back."

"You better Mr."

"I promise." David replied with a smile. "I promise."

"Then what happened Grandpa?"

"Well David Tall Tree made his way to a clear running stream and gazed out across the land and watched a large ship descend out of the clouds and swiftly land on the new world called Eden."

"And then."

"And then it was time for Walking Tall to walk his grandson Stalking Crow home."

"Aw that's no fun."

"Ah ha ha ha ha ha, come on little one it's getting late and your mother is probably starting to worry."

"Okay." young Stalking Crow replied and asked as they stood up, "am I gonna do all of those neat thing's papa?"

"Maybe young Stalking Crow," Walking tall replied while the serpent watched them from a dark and hidden tree, "Maybe."

LaVergne, TN USA
04 January 2011
210771LV00002B/35/P

9 781451 284560